Praise for *Savage Hunger*

"Dark, sultry, and primal romance… The chemistry is blazing hot and will leave readers breathless."

—*Fresh Fiction*

"Has moments of humor, of tenderness and pure hot loving… Leaves a reader hungering for more of this awesome and exciting new world."

—*Long and Short Reviews*, 5 Stars

"Well-written paranormal romance featuring a couple that sizzles right off the page."

—*RT Book Reviews*, 4 Stars

"The strength of Spear's writing lies in her ability to keep the reader emotionally in tune with the characters… Spear's lush descriptions of the Amazon… will leave readers hungry for more time in paradise."

—*Booklist*

"A sizzling page turner. Terry Spear is wickedly talented."

—*Night Owl Reviews* Reviewer
Top Pick, 5 Stars

"Terry Spear makes fantasy come to life through the magical pages of her book. She packs action, romance, and paranormal shifters into one great read."

—*BookLoons*

"A sexy, action-packed paranormal romance that is sure to captivate you from the very beginning."

—*Romance Junkies*

JAGUAR FEVER

TERRY SPEAR

sourcebooks
casablanca

Published by Sourcebooks Casablanca, an imprint of Sourcebooks, Inc.
P.O. Box 4410, Naperville, Illinois 60567-4410
(630) 961-3900
FAX: (630) 961-2168
www.sourcebooks.com

Printed and bound in Canada
WC 10 9 8 7 6 5 4 3 2 1

In memory of Mary Bunch and my condolences to her loving family.

And thanks to Sarah Woddy for sharing her family's story. My condolences again to the family for a life cut so short. I was very touched by Sarah and her aunt's story.

Chapter 1 ✓

"DAVID, IF YOU'RE GOING TO BE MY PARTNER IN THIS, pay attention." Wade Patterson glared at his twin brother as they sipped beers in the noisy Houston club—a shifters' club where humans, who didn't know any better, mingled with jaguar shifters.

South American jungle music rocked the building, and colorful lights roamed over the silk ferns and plastic banana plants. Vines cascaded from the ceiling and along walls painted with jungle scenes. Leopard-print vinyl covered all the seats. Tiny lights simulating stars dotted the black ceiling. On stages above the dance floor, a couple of scantily clad women in leopard-print thongs and feathers dangling over their nipples danced around vine-painted poles. A man wearing a leopard-print loincloth was dancing nearby on another pole.

"I *am* looking for the guys who could be involved in this, okay? Just because a stray cat catches my attention…" David shrugged. "Don't tell me your eye doesn't wander to take in every cute brunette in this place."

Wade hated that David could see right through him. "For your information, I'm not *just* looking at the brunettes."

Every blonde who looked even remotely similar to Maya Anderson made Wade take an extra look. He told himself that it was because the Andersons were the only shifters in the vicinity that he knew and they might end up there tonight. The rest of the sea of people dancing or drinking were unfamiliar to him. David gave him a skeptical look.

Wade took another swig of beer. "Drop it."

David nodded, then smiled at a pretty redheaded human. She smiled back but joined a dark-haired guy at another table. The man glowered at David as if he were ready to expose claws and teeth.

"Humans," David said, slightly amused.

"The last human male you dealt with over a woman shot you." Wade reminded David often because he'd come so close to losing his brother that day. He didn't ever want to deal with those kinds of emotions again. Shifters had fast-healing properties, but they could bleed out too fast, and then they were as dead as any human might be, suffering from the same trauma.

"Don't remind me," David said, finishing his beer.

Rebels in their youth, the two of them had done everything and anything they wanted to do after their mother died. Their dad had been so broken up that he'd forgotten he had two sons to raise.

Martin Sullivan, the director of a special elite force for jaguar shifters—the Golden Claw JAG, or Golden Claws for short—had been their salvation.

"I still don't know why Martin called us in. We just finished that Peruvian extraction and we're long overdue for a break." David folded his arms across his chest, his gaze straying to a brunette this time.

"Sorry, David," Wade said, and he meant it. Wade suspected it was his own fault that Martin was sending them on another mission so soon after their last one. Wade's previous vacation had turned into a fight with a drug dealer, and as if that wasn't bad enough, he'd lost the woman he had wanted to get to know better to Connor Anderson. Connor had turned her into a jaguar shifter, too, which still galled Wade. Especially since Connor had been traveling with a beautiful shifter named Maya Anderson. Wade assumed they were mates. But if Connor already had a mate, why did he have to get between Wade and Kathleen McKnight? Wade could do nothing about it, but losing Kathleen had definitely put his tail in a twist.

"Martin needs agents who are familiar with the territory. Since you and I have both been to Belize several times to run wild in the jungle as jaguars and were there just six months ago, he figures we're right for the job." Wade shrugged. "Besides, we've dealt with the trafficking of exotic animals before."

David studied him. Wade hardly ever apologized to his younger twin brother.

"You want to let me in on the secret?" David asked.

Wade shook his head. He wasn't about to mention that Martin was worried about him after his vacation in the Amazon had turned into a battle to keep the Andersons safe. "Watch for anything suspicious. Listen to the conversations around us. Martin said that this is usually the night they come to make arrangements to hunt the jaguars, but…" He frowned as his brother's gaze drifted to a newcomer, knowing David was only halfheartedly listening to him. Not that he wouldn't do his job, but he acted as though he really needed a break.

"Holy hell, now *she's* a cat," David purred.

Wade turned to see who he was drooling over this time. Holy hell was right. She was a *wild* cat: Maya

Anderson in the flesh. Wade looked beyond her, expecting Kathleen and Connor Anderson to be with her, but she was by herself. What was she doing here alone?

Meeting someone, obviously, Wade chastised himself.

David left his seat before Wade had a chance to tell him who the curvaceous blonde was. *Trouble*. That's all she could be. She didn't have a clue who Wade and his brother worked for, and she'd never seen Wade in human form. But she'd recognize his scent if she got close enough. They hadn't met in the Amazon, but he'd been close enough to be of help to her in a bad moment there.

His brother smiled broadly at Maya and motioned to the table where Wade sat, leaning back with his arms folded across his chest. Wade was wondering why in the hell he'd agreed to be his brother's partner on this operation. Besides wanting to keep David safe—which meant Wade needed to stop this now. Connor Anderson would kill David if he knew he was encroaching.

Wade recalled when he'd seen her swimming with Kathleen and Connor in the Amazon River. Diving with the pink dolphins, Maya had worn only a sexy black lace bra and panties. He wished he'd been swimming with her in human form and not having to watch their backs, hidden as a jaguar in a tree, unbeknownst to them.

Connor had been kissing Kat in the river nearby, holding her tight, possessively. Wade had had mixed emotions about that. He wasn't sure why Kat had given Connor the time of day when he already had a wife. He couldn't understand why Maya would go along with it, either. He'd felt bad for her when she stood wistfully watching Kat and Connor.

When Maya waded out of the river and onto the bank,

Wade's jaguar jaws had hung open. Hot damn, she'd been hot then—just like she was now.

He just couldn't understand why Maya would share her man with another woman. Unless that's how they liked it. He realized that he'd never seen Maya and Connor hugging each other, no molten looks of desire cast between them, or anything else that would lead him to believe they were mated. Almost like family... like brother and sister. Hell, maybe their relationship wasn't what he'd thought it was after all. That had him thinking of different possibilities.

Maya's blond hair was pulled up into a twist, showing off her naked neck and making her look sexy as hell as straggles of curls framed her face. She wore sparkly high heels and a blue T-shirt minidress that accentuated her long legs. The dress had a casual sexiness, unlike the revealing short-hemmed dresses and plunging necklines many of the other women at the club wore. Maya was just as arousing. Maybe more so because he damned well would like to see more of what he could only glimpse, given the way the dress clung to her curves. Her body was toned and tanned, and she moved like a cat—sleek, sure-footed, and dangerous.

Wade was suddenly very hot and *very* thirsty.

If any male shifter approached her and gave her a hard time, the shifter would be flat on his back, facing one angry jaguar—*him*.

As always, David was the charmer, his hair flopping over his forehead, his skin bronzed, his blue eyes smiling as he led the female shifter to their table.

They couldn't involve a shifter civilian while they were undercover, so why was David breaking the rule?

"This is…" David didn't manage to say anything further as Wade stood up to his full six-foot height, towering over Maya by half a foot, and looked down into her golden eyes, which were wide with surprise.

Once she breathed in his scent, she'd know he'd been the cat helping them out five months ago, and most likely she realized he was the same one who'd been seeking to meet up with Kathleen.

"Wade Patterson," he said, hand outstretched.

She stood there staring at him, her pink lips parted in silent astonishment.

"We've met," he said, not liking how concerned she looked to see him there.

David cleared his throat and crossed his arms. "Figures the two of you already knew each other. I'd kind of gotten that impression when she thought I was someone else—*you*—but she waited for me to identify who I was first. I'm always late to the party. Where'd the two of you meet?"

"The Amazon," Maya said, finally breaking her gaze with Wade.

David's jaw grew slack. "Anderson," he said too loudly. His worried gaze shifted from Maya to Wade. He almost looked apologetic that he'd brought her over to the table.

Wade could tell his brother had finally made the connection. Kathleen, Connor, and Maya.

She still hadn't taken Wade's hand, and he finally dropped the offer. Turning to David, she asked, "Would you like to dance?"

Wade understood the slight. He had gone after Kathleen, and Maya hadn't liked it.

"Hot damn, yeah." But then David looked at Wade as if he remembered how upset his brother had been over the issue of the Andersons and sought his approval in his usual affable way.

Annoyed that his brother wanted to dance with Maya, but also concerned for him, Wade went for nonchalant. "She's got a husband."

David's face fell as if the she-cat had dazzled him to such an extent that he'd forgotten about *that* part of the equation.

Maya smiled so brilliantly that her expression was as stunning as the colored lights flitting across the room. "Come on. I'm safe," she said and tugged at David's hand, with a flitting cat-who-ate-the-cream smile cast in Wade's direction.

Wade didn't think she was safe in the least—not if Connor got involved.

Exhaling heavily, Wade sat back down. He watched as Maya led David to the dance floor, trying not to wish *he* was the one with her instead.

Unable to look away, Wade knew he should be searching for the men involved with the exotic-animal smuggling ring. Two women approached Wade, and he spared them a glance.

"Can we sit here with you? The tables are all taken."

He grunted a yes. The table was big enough for six, and since the women were both humans, they could help with his cover.

The redhead and the brunette thanked him and took seats next to him. They attempted to engage him in conversation, but Wade was too busy worrying that Connor might show up at the club any minute and try to kill David.

—···—

"So… you're Connor's…?" David let the question fall away.

Maya smiled at him as they moved together across the dance floor. "Sister."

A hint of a smile crossed his lips.

David was so sweet. His hair was a darker brown than his twin brother's, but since it was damp, it might just look darker. He smelled of chlorine, so she assumed he'd been swimming in a pool recently. He'd been so eager to meet her, and she'd been startled to think he was Wade Patterson, but he didn't smell like the same jaguar shifter who had helped them in the Amazon. She'd said she was Maya, not bothering with her last name, and he'd given her just his first name also.

David expelled his breath in a combination of relief and laughter. "He thought… Wade, that is… believed you were Connor's wife and that Connor took Kathleen for a wife also—jaguar style."

Maya shook her head. "That's what we assumed."

"You did?" David asked.

She smiled. "Yeah. I wanted to meet him when we were in the jungle, but my brother wasn't keen on it."

When David had taken her to the table where Wade was sitting, she had recognized him immediately, courtesy of his photos on the social networking sites that Kat had shown her. Taking in a deep breath of his masculine scent, she had been assured he was the same jaguar that had risked his neck aiding them.

Still, Maya couldn't believe her good fortune that he was here. She was dying to talk with him and thank him. But she hadn't wanted to appear *too* eager to meet him—especially after his rather chilly reception—so she'd asked his brother to dance with her instead. Not to mention that David *had* greeted her first when she arrived at the club, and she felt she owed him a dance at least.

David glanced in his brother's direction. "You… wanted to meet my brother."

"Sure."

"So… why did you ask *me* to dance? Seemed to me you would have danced with him instead." David didn't sound upset about it, more resigned than anything.

"I wanted to talk to you. I do want to thank him for all that he did for us in the Amazon. My brother didn't want Wade to get close to Kat. So… what are you both doing here? I thought Wade was supposed to be from Pensacola." She frowned a little, beginning to get suspicious.

"We have a job to do in Houston."

Maya raised her brows, waiting for an explanation, but he didn't give one. She asked point-blank, "Does Wade still want to get together with Kat?"

He'd better not even think of it. Not only would Connor turn into one feral cat, but so would Maya. Kat had dropped all correspondence with Wade—mostly because Connor didn't want Wade thinking he had a chance at getting to know Kat better. Some men didn't know when to leave well enough alone.

She glanced back at Wade. He was sexy, in great shape, and had dark brown hair and the most beautiful blue-green eyes she'd ever seen. In his photos, he had smiled in a way that said he liked to smile, liked to have fun when he wasn't fighting bad guys. Putting his best face forward for Kat might have been nothing but a ploy, but Maya thought he was being honest. Maybe because she wanted him to be.

"You think Wade is still interested in Kathleen McKnight? He isn't. Wade knew he lost that battle," David said. "Besides, I got the impression he was kind of intrigued with another cat."

"Oh." Well, of course she should have figured Wade was interested in another jaguar shifter. Why wouldn't he be? She could just imagine she-cats wanting to rub against him up close and personal.

"Yeah," David said, sounding like it was just his luck. "He didn't like that Connor was paying so much attention to Kat and leaving you to your own devices."

"*Me?*" She frowned at David, wondering just how much Wade had seen.

"In fact, he was pretty incensed."

"Because my brother was paying so much attention to Kat when Wade wanted to."

David shook his head. "No, but I'd better not say anything else."

She could have kicked him. Now he sounded like *her* brother. "What?"

"Well… I shouldn't really say, but… when you were swimming in the Amazon River, he wanted to swim with you."

She *knew* Wade had been watching them. "You mean with Kat."

"Nope. With you. That's what he said. So what are *you* doing here?" David asked. "Wade said you and Connor had a garden nursery a couple hours out of Houston."

For a moment, she was so flabbergasted to learn that Wade had wanted to swim with her and not Kat that she forgot what she was doing there. Refocusing, she cleared her throat. "I'm meeting a couple of cousins I just learned of."

She was so excited about getting to see them that when David had approached her at first, she'd thought maybe *he* was one of her cousins.

"Female cousins?" David asked, sounding hopeful.

"Male. Two of them at least. They have a sister, but she's not coming this time."

"I see." David's voice reflected disappointment. "Do you come here often?"

She shook her head. "My cousins told me about this place. I've never been here before." She didn't want to let on how naive she was. She and her brother hadn't ever found other shifters in their travels. Jaguars were elusive by nature, and the shifter variety even more so by necessity. Maya was certain Connor would have had a fit if he knew she had come here by herself.

Maya had expected a dark, smoky room full of loud music, drugs, and drinking in the Jungle Cat Fever Club, and had been thinking that when her cousins arrived, she'd convince them to go someplace else. Instead, the air was clear. Alcoholic beverages were readily being consumed, and the music had a beat to match the jungle theme, but it wasn't overpowering. The place looked normal to her. If her cousins hadn't told her it was a shifter club, she would never have known.

The club was decorated like a theme park version of the rainforest. Audio clips of macaws screeching or squawking, gibbons singing, howler monkeys calling out, and elephants trumpeting—*elephants?*—were played over the piped-in jungle music. Fake giant ferns, hanging vines, palms, and fig trees added to the jungle ambience.

When she first arrived at the club, Maya had observed three men watching her from a wrought-iron balcony above. As soon as she had parked the car, Maya felt all eyes on her as she left the vehicle, the newcomer to the scene, and entered the club. She'd hoped her cousins were already there. She didn't do club scenes, and she hadn't felt all that comfortable being here by herself.

She glanced again at Wade. He was watching her, a scowl on his face, his gaze latching onto hers. She didn't think right at this moment that he would have been interested in swimming with her anywhere.

He was wearing jeans and a sky-colored, soft chambray shirt—the long sleeves haphazardly rolled up his muscular arms, the buttons only closed to halfway up his chest, as if he hadn't bothered to finish dressing or he wanted to give viewers a peek at his bronzed skin.

In comparison, David had shaggy, darker brown hair, and his eyes were greener than Wade's. He wore a white polo shirt that stretched over his muscles, black dress pants, and loafers—a mix of casual and dressy as if he couldn't decide which way to go. He had just as beautiful a smile as Wade did.

Not that Wade was smiling right now. He looked like he was about to use his clenched fists to pummel someone, his gaze hard on Maya. Maybe because he thought she was married to Connor, and he worried she was going to get his brother into trouble.

Maya also noted the buxom women who had joined

Wade at the table, their provocative dresses cut so low that she could almost see their navels. The women practically slobbered all over Wade, though his attention was clearly focused on Maya and David.

"Come on," she said to David. "Let's put your brother out of his misery."

The three men who had spied her from the balcony outside had entered the building and taken the stairs to the dance floor, all of them watching her dance with David. A tall and muscular redhead wore blue jeans and a T-shirt, his amber eyes raking her up and down. She immediately didn't care for him. He smiled at her like they were already best friends.

He spoke to a man with long blond hair that reminded her of a lion's mane. Lion Mane held her gaze. She wished *she* had such gorgeous hair, but she had to admit his body was nice, too, under a muscle shirt and tight-fitting jeans.

The last of the men was dark skinned with black curly hair, wearing nice black slacks and a white shirt, the collar open, making her think he had just gotten off work at some professional job. When he caught her eye, he gave her a nice show of white teeth.

Lion Mane and the redhead drew close to the dance floor, watching her as if getting ready to pounce on her.

When the song ended, Lion Mane motioned to a small table. "We have a table here for the pretty lady."

His two friends stood on either side of him, all motioning to the four chairs. The men all smelled like cat shifters. The inference was that David could get lost.

She opened her mouth to say "No thanks," but David beat her to it. "We've got a table over here." He pulled her along quickly. "The problem with someone like you coming to a club like this is that other shifters want a bite."

She frowned up at him, not getting his meaning.

"They instinctively know you're different."

"Different, how?" She was a cat. They were cats. She couldn't detect any difference in them.

"You're a jungle cat."

"Jungle cat?" Weren't they all?

They reached the table before she could ask anything further. Wade was already standing, pulling the chair out next to him, his feral gaze fixed on her. Maya hesitated to sit beside him. He seemed so primal. So dangerous.

"She's Connor's *sister*," David quickly said.

"Sister." Wade studied her. His mouth quirked up fractionally as if he was seeing her as someone different and intriguing now.

"I'm not *Kat*." She hated sounding annoyed. She loved Kat as a sister and was thrilled she had fallen in love with Connor. But she didn't want some guy who had been interested in Kat thinking that Maya was just like her.

"*No*," he said, drawing out the word, "you're *not* Kat."

She frowned. Then she was irritated at herself for caring when it shouldn't have mattered.

The three male cats watched Maya as if they were calculating how much of a risk it would be to approach her when she had two male bodyguards. She didn't think she would have all that much trouble around other shifters. Until she saw Wade in the Amazon, she had never witnessed another jaguar shifter, except for her mother and brother. She'd been more than interested in Wade.

Who wouldn't have been when the jaguar had risked his life for them, and he hadn't even known them?

Wade and David were still waiting for her to take the seat between them. She hadn't expected other cats to be so territorial with her. She shook her head and took the seat Wade offered her.

The brothers traded relieved looks. The other cats looked like their pumped-up egos had instantly been deflated.

As if the brunette sitting on the other side of Wade was afraid she might lose out, she stretched out her hand to him. "I'm Candy, and you are?"

Too hot for you to handle, Maya wanted to say. David grinned at his brother.

"Wade." He gave her a brief handshake and glanced at Maya, as if he were worried about what she'd think.

Candy frowned at him. "We all just give club names in here. Like the guy over there, the redhead who's watching *her*"—she poked a finger in Maya's direction—"that's Red, though he's asked me out before and told me his real name is Bill Bettinger. The blond dude, the one that's also salivating over your friend here, is Blondie."

"Lion Mane." Maya hadn't meant to say anything, but that's the nickname she thought suited him.

"Lion Mane?" Candy stuck her tiny nose up in the air. "He goes by Blondie."

Maya wanted to call Lion Mane over to the table and prove to Candy that he would come no matter what she called him—or didn't call him. The way he was eyeing her, she was certain a crook of her finger would bring him to her.

Wade shook his head at Maya, just slightly, telling her not to do it. He seemed to know what she had in mind.

David was studying her just as closely, waiting for whatever would happen next. Wade appeared settled and complacent, but a jaguar would change his posture into combat mode in the blink of an eye if necessary.

Maya had no plans to stir up a lot of trouble, though it was tempting.

Candy eyed Maya. "So what's your club name?"

"Wildcat," David answered for her, smirking.

Chapter 2

WILDCAT? MAYA WAS OPENING HER MOUTH TO protest—she did not make up aliases for any reason—when Candy replied, "*Really*. I wouldn't have thought you'd be a wild *any*thing."

Maya snapped her jaw shut and glared at Candy.

Wade said, "You have *no* idea."

He said it in such a deep, sexy way that Maya stared at him, trying to discern his meaning. He wasn't smiling. He was looking straight at her with those jungle-cat eyes that said he *meant* what he said.

He was still watching her as if he knew just what was going on in her head. The music was beating away, but it had faded into the background. She vaguely heard the women ask David what his name was.

Lion Mane finally got up the nerve to move closer to their table.

"What do you mean by that?" Maya asked Wade, ignoring the blond guy.

Everyone at the table stopped introductions to hear what Wade had to say.

He smiled in a feral way and took Maya's hand. "Let's dance."

Candy took Wade's cue and grabbed David's hand. "Come on. Wanna dance?"

David grimaced, as though he'd prefer doing anything else, but he got up and took the woman to the dance floor.

"What are you doing here in Houston?" Maya asked in Wade's ear as he danced her across the floor to the slower-paced beat. His brother might not want her to learn the truth, but she had to know.

"David and I have a job to do."

"And it has nothing to do with seeing Kat?"

He frowned. "I thought Kat was one of us when I first contacted her. You know how it is. It's difficult to find more of our kind. I thought that when she posted on her networking sites about jaguars, she was throwing out a lifeline, looking for someone special to be in her life."

"I can understand that," Maya said sincerely. "Until Kat arrived, Connor and I had never met any shifters. I've certainly wanted to meet others of our kind." She took a deep breath. "I wanted to thank you for helping us in the Amazon."

"I thought you were Connor's mate."

She smiled up at Wade. "I know. David told me."

Wade smiled a little.

She sighed. "You know, Kat and I wanted to thank you when we were there. It might have been nice if we could have all stuck together. Of course, it would have been even better if we could have just enjoyed the time being big cats—fishing, swimming, lazing in the trees—like we'd planned and not had to deal with those assholes."

"Hmm," Wade said, his expression unreadable.

"Well, I'm sorry we messed up your vacation plans."

"It all worked out." Wade narrowed his eyes a little. "Why are you here alone? As protective as your brother is, I wouldn't have thought he would like you coming here by yourself."

She shrugged. "He doesn't know."

"So you sneaked out to come to a shifters' club?"

"*No*," she said in an elongated, irritated fashion, not liking that he sounded annoyed with her for slipping out of the house without her brother's approval. She didn't need her brother's say-so, even though Connor might think differently. "He's gone on a vacation with Kat. I'm to join them. I heard from my cousins, and they wanted to meet here."

He didn't say anything more and just danced with her, which she loved. She hadn't danced in ages, and never with a big cat.

Maya and Wade had started a respectable distance from each other as they moved to the music, but somehow they'd quit dancing apart. Their bodies were sliding against each other, rubbing like cats would, scent-marking, claiming each other. Her arms were wrapped around his neck, his arms around her waist.

"You feel good," he murmured, nuzzling her face with his cheek. If they'd been cats, their whiskers would have been touching, sensing each other.

He felt good. Hot and sexy and hard—very hard—as he showed her just how good she was making him feel.

"You smell good," he whispered, his husky voice breathy against her ear, making her shiver with expectation.

He smelled good. Like one turned-on, spicy-scented, musky male big cat.

"You taste good," he finished, licking her earlobe, then moving his sensuous mouth over hers with barely a kiss, just a sweet caress of lips.

Maya cupped his head and held him in place as if he might release her. She wanted to see how good *he* tasted.

She pressed her lips against his mouth and slipped her tongue between his lips. He growled low as if he hadn't anticipated her to go that far. She'd never been with a cat shifter before, only humans. His hot kiss made her forget where she was, that they were surrounded by a lot of shifters, that his brother was watching—*everything*.

With Wade rubbing against her as they continued to move to the beat, and his hands secured around her back, she felt sinfully sexy.

And aroused. Her blood heated with the press of his body against hers. She wanted to do more as the jungle drums pounded through the floor and filled the air around her. Her heart pumped just as loudly, the rush of blood thrumming in her ears.

She wanted to unbutton more of his soft chambray shirt, to skim her hands across his chest, to flick her fingernails against his pebbled nipples. She craved running her hand over the rock-hard erection she was gently rubbing against her thigh as they continued to move to the rhythm of the music.

Growling, she kissed him more fiercely, penetrating his mouth again with her tongue, making him groan as he tongued her back, his hands remaining at her waist. Infuriatingly, she wanted him to cup her buttocks, to touch and kiss her breasts, but she knew she couldn't. Not here. She shouldn't have wanted it. But she did.

A male voice beside them broke through her lust-filled thoughts. "Your cousins are here, but they were afraid to break things up between you and Wade so they sent me."

David grinned at her and then at his brother.

Feeling flushed and needy, Maya refused to appear

embarrassed in front of Wade and his brother or
her cousins.

David observed her for a moment before he said to
Wade, "Remember, we've got a room if you want to
use it."

Okay, so she might feel like she wanted to get a room
and finish the moves with Wade in privacy, but she
didn't appreciate Wade's brother saying so.

Maya instantly pulled away from Wade. "My cousins, where are they?"

Wade looked like he was ready to slug his brother.
He slipped his arm possessively around Maya's waist.

"At our table. I saw these two new cats looking
around as if they were searching for someone, then
heard one of them ask about a Maya Anderson. They
saw you dancing with Wade and wanted to know who
you were."

"Wildcat," Maya said, casting David an annoyed look.

"Hell, yeah." David grinned. "Candy had nothing
on you, and she's been stewing with her girlfriend ever
since you hit the floor with Wade." He glanced at Wade.
"I don't remember *you* ever having dance moves like
that. Must have been Maya who inspired you."

"She's *inspirational* all right." Wade tightened his
hold a little on Maya, as though he wanted to make sure
the other cats in the place knew she was with him, although she wasn't. Not exactly.

"Maya's cousins' faces fell when they learned she
was their relation," David said smugly.

Amused, Maya smiled. As they returned to their table,
Wade asked Maya, "What would you like to drink?"

"A Singapore sling."

She hadn't been out with a man in eons, and she was having fun. She thought all she'd be doing was getting the garden nursery ready before her flight to Belize tomorrow. She'd never expected to hear from cousins she didn't know she had, or visit a shifter club she didn't know existed, or meet up with Wade and his brother there.

A well-built man a couple of inches shorter than Wade and his brother and her cousins, wearing denims and a black T-shirt, approached the table. His gaze took in the men seated there, but his light brown eyes quickly fastened on Candy. Maya assumed he knew her and was a bit bothered by the other men sitting with her.

Maya took in a deep breath, like every shifter at the table did, trying to smell his scent. Jaguar shifter. Not purely human.

They could differentiate a human from a jaguar shifter if they got a good whiff. The big-cat scent was enough to clue them in. The only other way to know was if they saw them actually shift.

"Candy," he said, raking his hand through ash-blond hair and drawing close as every male shifter at the table fixated on him. He turned his broad back on them, looking a little as though it bothered him to see the attention he was gathering. "We got a date later?"

Candy smiled, cleared her throat, and said softly, though the cats could still hear what was being said, "Yeah, George, later."

"Did you want to dance?"

"Um, we're getting together later. All right?"

He squeezed her hand, then turned and gave the men at the table a hard look. Candy appeared to be hedging her bets, looking to add to her stable of boyfriends in case one of these guys appeared to be interested in her and she grew tired of poor George. "I'll see you later, George," Candy reiterated.

George leaned down and kissed her lips, taking his time about it.

"What was that for?" she asked, red faced.

Showing off, claiming her, Maya thought.

"Just to let you know how much I'll be thinking about you." Then George gave the other men at the table a growly look and headed for the bar.

Poor guy. Maya felt sorry for him and hoped he'd dump Candy for someone else.

Wade ordered beers for David, himself, and her cousins, and a sling for Maya, while Maya introduced herself to her cousins, Everett and Huntley. Candy and the other woman, Cherry, were still nursing margaritas.

Everett was taller than Huntley by a couple inches, with grass-green eyes and blond hair sweeping his shoulders like Lion Mane's. He was dressed in black leather pants and a black muscle shirt. Huntley, dressed in blue jeans and a navy T-shirt, was staring hard at Wade, his eyes a bluer green than his brother's.

"Have we met somewhere before?" Huntley asked Wade. There was a seriousness to the question that made Maya sit a little taller.

"The Service," Wade answered.

Huntley's mouth dropped for a fraction of a moment, then he snapped it shut and nodded.

Everett shook his head. "Small world. Thought you lived in Pensacola."

Wade lifted his beer mug off the table. "I do. I'm just here with my brother, now visiting Maya."

Her cousins knew Wade? Maya wanted to learn more, but the two human women were listening in, delighted more hunky guys chose to sit at their table.

"The service," Candy said, grinning, looking from one to another, as if trying to decide which of the men was the yummiest. "How cool. Which branch of the service? My dad was a Marine."

Huntley looked over at her as if he'd just realized she was sitting there. "Special unit. Classified."

Her eyes grew big. "All of you?"

No one responded.

Maya had been about to ask her cousins what they did for a living, but now she didn't need to. The idea that they were in some secret service unit intrigued her.

Everyone's drinks arrived, and Wade paid for the first round.

"I wish you could meet Connor and his wife," Maya said to her cousins. "I'm joining them in Belize tomorrow."

"Belize," Wade said, his eyes widening. "You didn't say that's where you were going."

David choked on his beer. Everett and Huntley frowned at her.

"I didn't realize you had a need to know." When no one said anything, she asked, "*Okay,* is there something wrong with going to Belize?"

"Yeah, it's really not safe for you," Wade said. "Can you cancel?"

"No. I'm flying out tomorrow afternoon. We're staying all next week." She waited for Wade to tell her what the trouble was.

"Where are you staying?" Wade asked, his cell in hand.

"The Treetop Cottage Jungle Resort."

Wade punched it into his phone and shook his head.

She folded her arms beneath her breasts. "Okay, so want to tell me what's wrong?" She was starting to feel antsy. Her brother and Kat were down there.

Everett and Huntley exchanged looks, then Everett said to Candy, "Want to dance?"

"Sure. I thought you'd never ask."

Huntley took the other lady to the dance floor and Wade moved Maya's chair closer to his, then spoke in a low voice for her hearing only as David watched them. "We're with a special unit, tracking exotic animal hunters down—jaguar hunters specifically."

"You think they're in Belize?"

"We've had word that the buyer meets with hunters here, then the men—or possibly women, though I'd lay odds they are men—head for the regions where jaguars live. To our knowledge, they plan to hunt in Belize this time."

Belize was a big place. Tons of unexplored territory—places in the jungle where no man had ever set foot. She and her brother and Kat would be fine. She took a deep breath. "Okay, look, it's illegal to hunt jaguars in Belize, but we both know hunters do kill them. It's a risk we're willing to take. We've always done so. Drug runners can be a danger, too. It's the same with them. If we worried about this all the time, we'd never return to our native jungle habitat."

He was wearing a worried frown.

She tilted her head to the side. "Are you going there?"

"Yeah. David and I."

"You're going after these guys." She didn't ask him.

She knew from the feral look in his eyes that he wasn't planning on just talking to the hunters who used the club as a rendezvous point. "Is… is this just a job?" She didn't think so. He was so tense that he looked like he was ready to snap.

"Yeah, it's a job."

But it seemed personal. Or maybe she was just projecting.

The dance music ended, and Everett and Huntley hurried the women back to their chairs.

"Um," Everett said, glancing at the human women, who were all ears. "Did you come to some decision?"

He seemed to be asking both Maya and Wade.

"They've got a job to do in Belize," Maya said, waving her hand at David and Wade. "And I've got a vacation coming up."

Everett turned his attention to Wade. "Can we have a word with you? In *private*?"

Maya ground her teeth. She suspected the "word" had something to do with her and her family.

"Can it wait until we leave?" Wade glanced at the shifters just waiting for an opening to ask Maya to dance.

Right now, with four male jaguars sitting with Maya, none of the other three shifters dared approach. She might as well have been with Connor for all the freedom she had.

"In fact, we could leave now," Wade said.

"No, I don't want to leave this instant." She'd never been around other shifters before, and she did want to dance. She wanted to discover if one of them might interest her more than Wade did. If she left now, would she ever have the nerve to come back?

"We need to talk *now*," Everett said to Wade. *In*

private. He didn't have to tack on the words; the message was clear.

David cleared his throat. "I'll watch over her."

Candy snorted. "She's a *wild* thing. Why does anyone need to watch over her?"

Maya smiled and gave her a thumbs-up.

Maya's cousins stared at Candy like she was nuts. Her cheeks reddened a bit.

Wade gave David a warning look as though he'd just better take care of Maya, and then he stepped outside with her cousins.

Time to dance, and when the guys returned, she wanted to make plans for her cousins to meet Connor and Kat at a later date. She wasn't sure how her brother would react, but she was thrilled to have found more family.

As soon as Wade left with her cousins, the jaguar piranhas moved in.

Maya was going to demonstrate to David she'd be fine, show Candy she had the blond guy's nickname down pat, and dance with another shifter to prove to herself she could do it—and nothing bad would come of it.

"I'm dancing with Lion Mane," she said to David, then held her hand out to Lion Mane.

He hurried to take her to the dance floor, though the redhead gave him a manly shove, telling him "Way to go," and no doubt wishing Maya had invited him to dance instead.

She cast a look over her shoulder at Candy and mouthed, "I told you so."

Eyes narrowed, Candy gave a little shrug like she didn't care.

David didn't come after Maya, which she appreci-
ated. Instead, he pulled Cherry, the other lady seated
at their table, onto the dance floor. He moved her
nearer to Lion Mane and Maya as if he was going to
protect her that way. She really liked Wade's brother.
He was sweet and not half as controlling as Wade.
Looks could be deceiving, though. If she'd been someone David was interested in dating? Might have been
a whole different story.

When Lion Mane pulled her close, she let him, figuring it was only one dance and then she'd take a new
dance partner.

He had some wild moves, twirling her and pressing
her intimately against his very hard body, their blond
hair colliding as he dipped her and swung her around.

"Beautiful," he purred and tried to kiss her. When
she turned her head away from his mouth, he said, "You
gave me a nickname."

The implication was that she wanted him to kiss her
like she had kissed Wade—and probably go much further. "Yes, because the name suited you."

His hands slid up her waist, his thumbs brushing
underneath her breasts like she wished Wade had done,
but she didn't care for this guy's intimacy. "Because you
want me," Lion Mane said.

No, she didn't want him. She just wanted to dance
with other shifters.

She tried to appease him somewhat. "I love your hair."

He smiled. "Run your hands through it, beautiful cat."

"Thank you, no. I'll just enjoy looking at it."

Lion Mane twisted his head a little and looked at her,
his expression one of disbelief. He knew she wanted to

touch his hair. Probably all the women loved to. "The man you danced with earlier does not want to see you with others of our kind."

She didn't respond to his comment. He was fishing about her relationship to Wade. As far as she was concerned, she and Wade didn't have one yet.

"He is not the one for you. He's too controlling. You need your freedom." The music ended and Lion Mane kept her close. So much for his sentiments about her needing her freedom.

She tried to back off, but David was coming to her rescue. The redhead, Bill Bettinger, was headed their way, too.

Another man, one she hadn't noticed before, reached her first. Even though he was human, he was well over six feet tall and towered over Lion Mane and the others. The intimidating blond-bearded human quickly took charge of the situation. Wearing camouflage, he seemed out of place despite the club's jungle theme. His vivid blue eyes studied her the way a hunter would its prey. Not that he appeared to be a bad man, but he *did* look like a hunter minus the rifle. Hunters were bad news for big cats like her.

The male cats closing in on her looked like they'd love to shift and take care of the interfering human.

"You seem extremely popular here," the human said, as he began to dance with her. "Come often?"

"First time."

He raised a brow. He wasn't holding her too close. He was gentlemanly, in fact, and she liked that.

She had a feeling, though, that he had some other purpose in dancing with her.

He cleared his throat. "I saw your picture on the website."

"Website?" she said, trying to figure out the connection. "You must be mistaken." Only her jaguar picture was on their garden nursery website, not any of her in human form. How would he have recognized her?

"You're Maya Anderson, part owner of the Anderson Garden Nursery?"

"Yes," she said, hesitating. "How do you know that? Which photo are you talking about?" They had dozens of pictures on their website showcasing the pottery barn, the greenhouse, and the sections that featured the variety of plants they offered.

"I was particularly interested in the greenhouse," he said.

That still didn't answer how he would know her by some photo. "Are you considering building one?"

He shook his head. Blue eyes narrowed, he studied her. "*Where's* the jaguar?"

Astonished at the question, she stared at him open-mouthed, took a misstep, and only managed not to trip because he hurried to steady her.

"What jaguar?" she asked, using her most annoyed voice, which wasn't difficult.

The mention of the jaguar made her heart begin to pound. With Kat's help, she'd revamped their nursery website to include a picture of her—in her jaguar coat surrounded by glossy-leafed tropical plants—inside the greenhouse. She'd also added some special links that talked about the plight of the jaguars. She'd posed for one picture as a ferocious cat, but Kat had also caught her snoozing on a bench, legs and tail just hanging off, eyes closed—one happy, sleepy cat—and snapped a picture of her.

Maya had objected to putting *that* picture on the site, but both Kat and Connor had insisted, though Connor hadn't liked featuring jaguars on their webpage in the first place, worried it would draw undue attention.

The human didn't say anything further about the jaguar on her site, just continued to dance with her as if he was giving her time to come up with a good alibi.

The man finally smiled at her, then said, "The picture of the jaguar on your website."

"Oh," she said as if it finally came to her. "The jaguar in the greenhouse. What about it?"

"Where did you get the cat?" He continued to dance with her slowly, not tightening his grip on her as if wanting to shake the truth out of her or ensure she didn't run away, but just as gentlemanly as before.

She should have jerked away from him, but she couldn't. She had to know where this was leading. "I don't understand what you're asking."

"The *jaguar*," he said. "Where… is… the… jaguar?"

"Photoshopped," she blurted. What else could she say? They'd borrowed a cat from somewhere?

Telling the truth was so much easier. Not believable. But easier. Telling a lie? It just snowballed into something totally unmanageable.

His smile said he knew she'd lied. "I verified that the picture was authentic. Real greenhouse. Real cat in greenhouse. Not Photoshopped." He waited a heartbeat for her response. When she didn't offer him any explanation, he pulled a card from his pocket and handed it to her.

Henry Lee Thompson, Agent for the Preservation of Wildlife, Portland, Oregon.

A picture of a gray wolf's head was featured in one corner.

She frowned and looked up at Thompson. "Portland, Oregon? What are you doing way out here?"

"I'm a zoologist for the Oregon Zoo. One of our jaguars was stolen. I was asked to look into it."

"Do you often have problems with people stealing predators from the zoo?" she asked, trying to sound flippant, like she couldn't believe anyone would be that stupid.

"Only the wolves," he said.

Her eyes widened. "Wolves?"

His jaw tightened. "Yeah, but I'm here because of a missing jaguar."

She couldn't wrap her mind around the idea that someone was stealing wolves and jaguars from a zoo. Finally, she focused again on the real issue at hand, the only one that should concern her—that he thought *she'd* stolen the big cat. "Oh, and you naturally assumed my Photoshopped cat was your jaguar."

"The cat was real. The setting was real, Miss Anderson. The jaguar looks just like ours."

Her lips parted, then she frowned again. "So you're telling me all spotted cats look alike? If you knew anything about them, you'd know the rosettes are uniquely patterned. That's how scientists can tell them apart." She almost said *us* apart because she was so angry.

Most humans would think jaguars all looked alike. Even though she and Connor were twins, they had differences in their jaguar appearance other than the shape of their rosettes. Her cheeks and chest had more white than his did, for one thing.

"Search the garden nursery if you want. You'll find plenty of plants. Maybe a kitty cat or two. They're kind of wild, but they catch mice, and we've found them curled up in the catnip and basil before. We don't have any big cats there."

"Big cats?" he asked, sounding suspicious. "I was asking about only one."

She felt her cheeks warm. Maybe Connor had been right, though she hated to admit it. Maybe trying to catch a jaguar shifter's attention on social networking sites was going to cause more trouble than it was worth.

"So where's the cat in the photo?" Thompson asked again.

Thompson was like a wolf, she decided. Just like the picture on his business card. All people had an animal type. Some were snakes, some sharks, some butterflies; others cats, doe-eyed deer, or bull terriers. Thompson was a lone wolf, and right now he wasn't letting go of his potential prey.

The truth, then. "It was me," she said, cocking her head. "I confess. I was having a bad hair day so I shifted, and one of the other jaguar shifters in the family snapped the photo. We all sat around looking at it afterward over glasses of ice-cold milk—cats like milk, you know—and decided it would be great for the website since jaguars love the jungle. The jaguar gave the greenhouse a wilder appearance and would catch a viewer's attention. We'd make more sales that way, don't you see?"

He nodded agreeably, a lifted brow saying he didn't believe a word she said.

She smiled. "I like you, Thompson. I *love* jaguars. I

wish I could help you find your jaguar and return her to the zoo."

"I believe you. So where did you get the cat for your website photo?"

Chapter 3

"MAKE IT BRIEF," WADE SAID, AS HE MOVED OUTSIDE the club with Everett and Huntley. He knew Maya would dance with the other shifters, as much of a free spirit as she was. He didn't like it, even though he knew he had no claim on her. He didn't like that she was more vulnerable without her brother—or him—to watch over her.

He walked with her cousins into an alley between the buildings for privacy. "David can't hold them all off for long."

Everett folded his arms and scowled at Wade. "I thought you were going to talk her out of going to Belize, Patterson. Until the hunters are dead, our kind aren't safe down there."

"I can't. She was right. Anytime we go south of the border, we're at risk."

Huntley growled, "Okay, so she said you're going there. Are you planning to protect her?"

"I can't stay with her. I have my orders. If I can take the hunters down, that'll be the end of the problem."

"So your orders were to go to Belize," Everett said. "Not to stay here and dance with our cousin."

Wade tried to keep his temper. He understood her cousins were concerned for her safety. "We had word that the buyer was meeting here with the hunters commissioned to locate and smuggle a cat out of Belize. We had no idea that Maya would be here, or that her brother and sister-in-law and she were going to be in Belize."

"All right," Huntley said. "We've got a job here, but if we can finish it and get there in time to help out, where would we meet you?"

"Our source there said the hunters are headed to the area between the Macal and Mopan rivers in one of the rainforest preserves in Central Belize. We'll check on the resort where Maya and her family are staying once we get in. No flights are available until tomorrow."

Everett glanced back at the club. "I take it you don't know who the buyer is. We could at least take him down."

"No. That's why we're here. To learn what we can about the deal going down before we target the men who are going after a big cat. We've been here for three hours already. Haven't seen anyone who appeared to be making a deal with hunters."

"One or more of the shifters here are sure to follow her back to her place," Huntley said. "At least three damn male shifters in the club are interested in her. Hell, if she wasn't my cousin, I would be, too."

"What are your plans with her?" Everett asked, as if he was playing the role of her brother while Connor was away.

Wade would have told him to take a flying leap, which for jaguars was an easy task, but because he might work with these men on an assignment in the future, and because he was interested in dating Maya and these men were family, he said, "I want to get to know her better. I was able to help protect her, Connor, and his wife in the Amazon jungle in an ugly situation five months ago. I only have her best interests at heart."

Everett studied him for a moment, then nodded. "Yeah, and you're one of us." He sounded as though he approved.

"Our mission is in Brazil tomorrow or we'd go with her to see to her safety," Huntley said.

"I understand," Wade said.

Something crashed inside the club, and shouts could be heard over the music. A brawl, Wade thought, just what they all needed now—not.

Maya and David could be in the middle of it.

Wade and her cousins hurried back to the club. As soon as they got inside, they saw several humans heading for the exit as one male cat slammed another into a table, knocking it over and shattering the glasses on the terra-cotta tile floor.

"Hell," Wade said, hoping Maya was safe and trying to make it through the fighting cats to reach her and his brother.

Maya wasn't sure what happened next. One minute she was finishing a dance with Thompson and skirting around the issue of the jaguar on her website. The next minute, Lion Mane, the man with the curly hair, and three other male cats got into a fight just as the music ended.

Thompson used his body as a shield to move her away from the conflict as David came rushing to her rescue.

As a jaguar, she could let the men know with a roar and a bite just how much their fighting over nothing irritated her, but as a human, the best way to handle it? Leave.

Her heart was thundering as she, David, and

Thompson headed for the door. Her cat shifter and
human bodyguards were protecting her from the fighting
when she saw Wade and her cousins barreling through
the brawlers to get to her.

She was glad to see they weren't involved in the
clash. She hoped they'd all make it out without injury
or being arrested and avoid most of the skirmish.

Thompson had one hand on her arm as he shielded
her from the blows and punches and crashing furniture
as some of the cats used chairs to make their point with
less damage to their knuckles. Glancing down at her,
he said, "I haven't seen a brawl like this in years." He
shook his head, but he was smiling.

Men.

David had hold of her other arm and was moving
as fast as possible with her. She was wearing high
heels, not running shoes, so she knew she was slowing them down.

David was using his free arm as a battering ram to
shove fighters out of their way when he was struck in
the head by a flying bottle.

"David," she said, worried, concerned, and trying to
stop to take a look at the cut on his forehead.

"I'm all right," he growled, sounding like he would
have made the bottle-tossing brute pay if he hadn't been
watching out for her. He wasn't stopping as he hurried
her to the exit.

Maya had wanted to meet shifters, but not like this.
Why couldn't she just make eye contact with someone
who seemed nice, get together, dance, have a little conversation, and move on—or not. If the man really appealed.

The problem was… *Wade* really appealed.

She couldn't see Wade or her cousins for all the fighting in front of them. Then suddenly, as if a wrecking ball had swung into them, the fighters scattered. Wade and her cousins were headed straight for her, looking like a force to be reckoned with. She wondered if that had something to do with the *Service* they were in.

His hard, black gaze only on her, Wade seemed concerned that she was all right. She barely paid any attention to her cousins clearing the way on either side of him like a bulldozer force of jaguars. Then Wade turned his attention to his brother, his eyes widening a little, then narrowing. His jaw tightened and he socked the next man he threw a punch at so hard that the man went flying into two others who were fighting.

Wade turned his scowl on Thompson as if to say: Relinquish the woman now, human.

Thompson gave an almost imperceptible smile. He handed Maya over to Wade but continued to help her cousins and the Patterson brothers kick chairs and debris and knock scrapping men out of the way as they escorted her out of the club.

"What the hell happened to you?" Wade asked his brother. He was ready to bash out the lights of the guy who'd hurt David.

"It's just a scratch," David said.

It was *not* just a scratch! Maya slipped on broken glass, nearly taking a spill. Wade swept her up in his arms, and she gave a little gasp of surprise.

He looked ferocious as he took a deep breath, inhaling her scent, and growled. "You danced with that blond guy."

She couldn't believe it. No one had ever acted jealous about her dancing with someone else before. "I wanted a closer look at his hair, to see if maybe his shampoo was what gave it so much pizzazz."

Wade scowled down at her.

She sighed. "He wasn't half as sexy as you..." She knew as soon as she said the words and his eyes widened that she'd made a mistake. "If you must know, I didn't kiss him." She heard the low, rumbly growl in Wade's throat before he spoke again.

"He tried to *kiss* you?"

"I didn't let him." She shrugged. "I wasn't interested."

"You sure know how to add excitement to a club night." He didn't sound irritated this time, but she had the distinct feeling that if she said she wanted to return tomorrow, he'd say *no way in hell*.

As he carried her out to an unfamiliar car, she squirmed to get loose. "I have my own car here."

Wade set her on her feet.

Her cousins were acting as bodyguards, hovering over her, when Huntley said, "We really need to talk and tell you what we do. David needs looking after. Maybe we could go to your place, if you don't object?"

"You're afraid someone from the club might follow me home?" She could see they were from their concerned expressions. "Okay."

"If you don't mind, I'll drive your car home for you," Huntley said. "Someone needs to take care of David's gash."

She suspected they wanted her to ride with David and Wade so she would have protection. What did they think? That someone would run her off the road and try to kidnap her? But she didn't mind having some protection, once she thought about it. Having the company would be nice, too. She'd believed having a couple of days away from her brother and Kat would be nice, but in reality, she'd been lonely. And she would love to get to know her cousins better.

Wade and his brother, too.

She nodded. Her cousins left to get their car and hers.

"Do either of you have anything to stop David's bleeding?" she asked the Pattersons.

Wade looked down at her dress as if considering that *she* might be wearing something else she could use. She raised her brows, and he gave her the wickedest grin. Her minidress didn't have an ounce of extra hem that she could rip off—like the damsels did in the movies.

Wade began to unbutton his shirt. She stared at his fingers moving from one button to the next, waiting to see him open his shirt.

As soon as he tugged his shirt off, she took her fill of his chest—bronzed, nipples puckered, muscles ribbed, and stroke-able, and she promptly forgot why he'd removed his shirt in the first place.

"Bandage for my head," David said, his tone damned amused as Wade gave her a smug smile and David mirrored his brother's expression.

"Uh, yeah." Trying to ignore the way her skin felt flushed with embarrassment, not to mention interest, she took the soft and heated shirt that smelled of Wade, cat, man, and delicious. She wanted to get a closer feel and press it against her nose to take a deeper whiff of its unbidden scent as David got into the backseat of the car. But Wade was watching her. She quickly dismissed that notion.

That was the problem with their wild side as jaguar

shifters. Their heightened senses amplified *intriguing* smells... and bad.

Once she joined David in the backseat, she pressed the shirt against his forehead. Wade closed the door for her, then climbed into the driver's seat.

David glanced at his brother. "I should have known that before I could remove *my* shirt, you'd bare your chest to the lady."

Wade chuckled.

She loved the teasing between the brothers.

"I haven't been in a good catfight in years." Wade glanced in the rearview mirror at Maya. "But the prize this time was definitely worth fighting for."

She snorted and he chuckled, as if he knew what she was thinking.

"Not a prize," she said.

"For some, no," he answered. "They don't know what they'd get with a woman like you."

She frowned. "What do you mean by that?"

"Maya, if some of the city cats had seen you in action in the Amazon, they'd know you were one hellcat. I mean that in a good way. But some would be afraid to mince words with you. As to another matter, all of us are leaving on flights tomorrow. Your cousins are going to Brazil. David and I are going to Belize. Would you mind if someone stayed with you tonight and took you to the airport in the morning?"

"Me," David said. "I volunteer to stay and watch over Maya."

She let out her breath on a sigh. "*You're* injured."

"How about if we both stay with you, Maya?" Wade asked.

She didn't think he was really asking. No way did he want to leave her alone with his brother. Little did he know that he had no worries there. If she wanted anyone to stay and watch her back, it would be Wade. But she had *no* intention of feeding into his ego.

She studied Wade. "Don't like your hotel accommodations?"

"They're fine. It's you that I'm worried about," Wade said.

And this time she heard something different in his voice. Real concern. After he had helped them in the Amazon, she'd assumed he was the kind of guy who would go out on a limb for those in need. But she really didn't think she needed any jaguar shifter to protect her. She had canines and claws enough for the job if anyone hassled her.

"I… don't think it's really necessary," she said, wanting to see how hard he was going to try to get her to concede.

"You know what happened last time," Wade said.

"We were in the jungle. And the men were after Kat."

Wade glanced in the rearview mirror. "Yeah. And she had you and your brother to protect her. But that hadn't been enough. You, on the other hand, are alone."

She still didn't think anyone was going to follow them home from the club.

"Maybe your cousins could stay also, if they want to. It's a long drive back to Houston from your place," Wade said.

She shook her head. How had she gone from planning a night alone before she left on her trip to having a houseful of male guests? She did rather like the idea. She could get to know her cousins a little better. And having them there would make her feel less self-conscious about having two males staying with her who were not related and who she didn't know very well.

"Slumber party," she said. "Okay. I can fix us something to eat after I bandage up David. What happened to you exactly? All I saw was the bottle hitting and you ducking too late."

"The guy wielding it was that redheaded guy."

She stiffened. She hadn't liked Bill Bettinger from the beginning.

"He didn't like that my brother was protecting my interests," Wade added.

She harrumphed. "If only he knew the real situation. We've only just met. Now that I know that there are others of our kind nearby, I can make some more shifter friends."

David winced as she applied more pressure to his wound.

"Here I thought we were nearly old friends, me watching your back in the Amazon…" Wade reminded her.

"Just my back," she said.

He cast a wicked smile over the backseat that said otherwise.

"So what's going on in Belize, and how do you know my cousins?" she asked.

Wade turned onto another road. "The reason I know your cousins is that we belong to the Service."

She considered David's jagged wound and was relieved to see his healing genetics were beginning to take hold. The bleeding had nearly stopped. "You mean you work for one of the branches of the military, like Candy said?"

"Not exactly. We've done a number of extractions over the years, but we're not part of the government."

"Extractions of what?"

"People. Shifters like ourselves who get into trouble. City cats who aren't prepared to face the dangers in the jungle. The Service is more like our own special government, a body that was started years ago to police jaguar shifters and attempt to protect our jaguar cousins who don't shape-shift. We're in service to the organization, so cryptically we're in the Service."

"Jaguar police force," she said. No wonder Wade had been so good at tracking Kat and her brother when they were in the rainforest—he was a first-class act.

Then what about Wade was true? Maya frowned. "You aren't a respectable businessman in Pensacola, Florida—a computer programmer during the day and a game-design hobbyist at night?"

He shook his head.

"Your cover?"

"I would have told Kat eventually, but not in an email. We were supposed to hook up."

"But you really do live in Pensacola?"

"Yes."

"You had pictures of yourself on Facebook, Twitter, and a number of other networking sites. That's how I recognized you. So that was all you."

"Yeah."

She asked David, "What do you do for a living? Are you with this agency, too?"

"Yeah. But it's not called the Agency."

"Four main branches exist," Wade explained. "The Enforcers, who police shifters, ensuring everyone abides by some rules. The Guardians, who protect our people, secrets, and real jaguars. The Avengers, who take out the trash. They go after the hard-core criminals that we have no hope of rehabilitating. Then there's the Special Forces unit that David and I belong to. Your cousins, also. I saw them on a mission in South America. Another extraction."

"How come Connor and I never knew about any of this?"

"Your parents—"

"Mother," Maya corrected. Except for donating the sperm, her father hadn't taken part in their lives.

"Your mother, then, must have kept you isolated from our kind and stuck to the old ways. My father was like that, too. Not until David and I began raising hell on our own did we learn about the Service."

"What about your mom?"

He shook his head. "She died when my brother and I were sixteen. A man involved in the exotic-animals markets trade killed her. She'd fought him tooth and claw, attempting to free herself. We guessed he thought she wasn't worth the battle and terminated her."

"I'm so sorry, Wade."

"Yeah, well, Dad was in his own world then. Without his heavy hand, David and I cut loose. We got into trouble and learned all about the Service. We were lucky that one of the Enforcers thought we were salvageable."

She shook her head. "I can't imagine you did anything that bad."

"Don't tell her all the stuff we did, and I won't, either," David said.

She smiled, intending to learn what she could later. "So you guys are…?"

"Part of a Special Forces unit called the Golden Claw JAG Elite Force. We do a little of everything."

She thought the organization sounded like an admirable cause and important for their kind.

"It sounded too dangerous for me to join. But… we weren't given much of a choice." David was smiling when he said it.

She shook her head and wondered how often Wade and his brother had faced danger on their jobs. And off their jobs. She and her brother had certainly encountered trouble from time to time while visiting the rainforest over the years.

"What about the man who murdered your mother? Did they ever catch him?"

"No." Wade glanced out the window, and she suspected that wasn't the end of it.

"Are you searching for him?"

Wade's gaze swung around to meet hers. His eyes were dark and feral—a hunter's eyes. "Yeah."

She swallowed hard. No wonder Wade was in the business he was in. "Every time you look for a hunter, do you suspect it might be the man who murdered your mother?"

"Yeah. But he might have given up hunting after that. We're still looking for him."

She bit her lip. "But if she was killed as a jaguar, she would have turned into a human. Wouldn't he have reported it?"

"You'd think so."

Realization dawning, she gaped at him. "You think he knows? About our kind?"

"Yeah, like he's one of us."

That sent a chill racing up her spine. "Why would he have hunted her?"

"We don't know. Speculation? To give her to some-one who wanted a female jaguar shifter."

"Slave trade—only not in humans."

"That's what we believe, but we haven't been able to uncover such a market. So we really don't know. Unless he's just human, was scared out of his wits to see her shift, and took off. What could he say? 'I killed a jaguar that turned into a human?' And all he has left to show for it is a murdered woman. So yeah, we're still looking."

"I'm so sorry," she said again. "What about Belize? What's going on there exactly?"

"A team of hunters has gone down to Belize to cap-ture a jaguar, and they're staying at another resort only a few miles from yours."

Maya stared at Wade, then slumped against the car seat. "You hadn't told me that. I've got to get word to Connor and Kat as soon as I can. They'll have been run-ning in the jungle as jaguars from the time they arrived."

"We have another problem." David leaned back against the car seat, looking wiped out.

Wade looked at Maya as if she was the source of it. "What's the problem?" Wade asked.

"The human, Thompson, looks to be real trouble," David said.

Chapter 4

THOMPSON. OH, HIM. MAYA HAD NEARLY FORGOTTEN about the zoo man who had questioned her about the jaguar on her web page. She pulled Wade's shirt away from the gash on David's head and was not happy to see that the bleeding hadn't completely stopped.

"The one who helped Maya out of the dance club," David said, explaining to Wade who he meant. "He was asking her about the jaguar on her website."

"What jaguar?" Wade asked, frowning.

She clenched and unclenched her teeth. "I told him the jaguar was Photoshopped, but he believes the cat in the photo was stolen from his zoo in Portland, Oregon. I put the picture up only a couple of days after the jaguar was taken."

Wade glanced back at Maya. "I take it the jaguar was you."

She smiled at him.

"He didn't believe the jaguar was Photoshopped," David added. "*And* she told him *she* was the jaguar and was from a family of jaguar shifters."

"Yeah, like any human would believe me," she said, giving David her fiercest look.

Wade wished that Maya's sweet body was pressed up against him in the backseat, instead of his brother. Not that he wanted the head laceration to go with it.

His whole outlook on Maya had changed the moment

he learned she was single and Connor's sister, not his wife. Dancing with her at the club had stirred a male response Wade couldn't deny. It wasn't just lust, either. They had a history, even if it hadn't been up close and personal. Now it was. And he wanted more of it. His jealousy over Lion Mane dancing with Maya confirmed his own feeling that he felt something deeper for her.

He'd never acted like that about a woman. He hadn't felt possessive toward the shifter woman he'd intended to marry five years ago. She'd still wanted to see others when he finally sought to make a commitment or end the dating game. That had been the end of their relationship.

Now he was fascinated with a shifter who wanted the same thing, he realized grimly. Having his head examined seemed like a good idea. But he had never backed down from a challenge, and right now, Maya was one woman he wanted to get to know much better.

Wildcat. Yeah, that's exactly what she was. He smiled back at her, recalling the way she had stared at his naked chest—intrigued, forgetting why he had removed his shirt in the first place. Hell, he was ready to dance with her again and feel her pressed against his body, kissing her sweet mouth and showing her just how much he wanted to get to know her better, every silky, mouthwatering inch of her.

When they arrived home, Maya was helping David out of the car as her cousins pulled behind them in the parking lot. Where had David been that he'd heard so much of what she'd said to Thompson? Probably dancing nearby. Jaguar hearing could really be a nuisance sometimes when a shifter was listening in. Her brother was testament to that.

David looked pale and was a little unsteady on his feet, though he was trying to show how tough he was. She was attempting to hold him up, but his weight was too much for her.

Wade quickly took charge of his brother, giving them both an out. "Can you get the door for us, Maya?"

She gave David the shirt to hold to his forehead, then opened the front door. As she walked inside, she turned on the lights for them. "Put him on the couch if you would. In the first bedroom on the right, if he prefers a bed."

"The sofa's fine," David said.

Wade's gaze caught Maya's. She couldn't read his expression. Concern his brother's injury might garner too much of her sympathy maybe? He looked a little unsettled.

"Did you want Wade to sew you up?" she asked David.

David shook his head, then winced and moaned a little. She stroked his arm, and Wade said, "Boy, have you pulled the wool over her eyes."

Giving Wade a smile, she said, "Next time someone cracks you in the skull with a bottle, I'll take care of you."

"Maybe we should have dumped you at a hospital tonight, and you could have had a pretty nurse look after you," Wade said to David.

Maya laughed. So Wade *was* worried that she was paying too much attention to his brother.

"I'll get some bandages and a wet cloth to wash off the blood. We probably don't have bandages that are very big," Maya said and headed for the bathroom.

"Anything will do." David leaned back against the couch cushions.

She returned and caught Wade shaking his head at his brother, while David grinned up at him. When they saw her, they both instantly looked red faced.

Wade stalked across the living room and peered out the picture window. "Your cousins must be checking the grounds for any unwanted visitors. I'm sure if anyone thought of bothering you tonight, they won't now."

"Not with four bodyguards." Maya set the wet cloth, a towel, and bandages on the coffee table.

She took Wade's bloodied shirt from David and set it nearby. "Sorry about your shirt, Wade. I especially liked it."

Her gaze shifted to his abs. She would offer him one of Connor's shirts, but her brother definitely wouldn't approve. Besides, she liked looking at Wade's hard muscles when he wasn't watching her.

She was starting to wipe away the blood off David's forehead when he closed his eyes and clenched his teeth. "Can you get some pain medicine from my kitchen, Wade? It's the first one on the right," Maya asked as she finished washing the blood off David's cheek. "And a glass of water."

Wade returned with water and the medicine.

After David had taken it, she began applying bandages.

Wade grinned and David frowned as he looked at the box. "Kids' bandages? Sea turtles? Porcupines? Butterflies?"

"Store was all out of the regular kind. I'd give you a choice, but I'm afraid I've got to use too many of them, so you're going to get an assortment."

Wade chuckled. "Looks like a new fashion statement."

David cast his brother an annoyed look.

She placed the bandages horizontally over the long gash.

David closed his eyes, looking tired and like the pain-killer hadn't kicked in yet.

The front door opened, and her cousins each carried a bag into the house.

"Hell, I forgot our bags are at the hotel room," David said. "You've got to go back into Houston to get them and check out of the room."

"Tomorrow," Wade said. "Before we go to the air-port, we'll drop by the hotel and get our stuff. No sense in making a four-hour round-trip back to Houston."

Everett let out a bark of laughter when he saw David and his bandage collage. Maya frowned at him. "Just think if it had been you."

Huntley was grinning. "Remind me not to get injured when I'm visiting your place, Maya. Either that or I'll have to remember to bring my own first-aid kit."

Maya kissed the uninjured side of David's forehead, making everyone quit smiling as if she'd put them in their place. "At least he's man enough not to let it bother him."

David offered them all a smug smile. But Wade was grinning the biggest, arms folded across his chest.

Everett headed for the kitchen. "Got anything to drink?"

"Who's taking first watch?" Huntley asked.

Maya felt like she had joined the Service on a mis-sion, watching for the bad guys, but instead of being in the jungle when it happened, she was at home—the first time she'd had to worry about such a thing out here.

"Jaguars?" she asked.

"What else?" Wade responded. "I'll take first watch in about half an hour."

Chapter 5

HIS BROTHER LOOKED TORN BETWEEN WANTING TO help patrol the area with the other male cats and wanting to stay inside with Maya. But Wade knew that with the way David's head had to be splitting and the bandages arranged diagonally over his brow, shifting was out of the question.

Before Wade could shift and take first watch, Maya said, "As for the sleeping arrangements tonight, without Connor and Kat's permission, I can't allow anyone to stay in their bed. We don't have a spare bedroom. But Connor and I both have separate offices. I also have a queen-sized bed if a couple of you want to share it. I can take the couch."

"No worries, Maya," Everett said. "My brother and I will sleep as jaguars on your living room floor."

"Works for me," Wade said. "I'll do the same."

Wade knew his brother hated that he couldn't be just one of the guys. "I don't think the bandages will stick to fur," David said.

The guys chuckled.

She smiled. "No. You should leave them on until at least tomorrow. You can sleep in my bed if you want."

David smiled so broadly that Wade was ready to sock him. The thought of sleeping in her bed conjured up all kinds of notions. All he could think of was being in the bed with Maya and finishing the moves they'd started on the dance floor. Shifters could have consensual sex with one another and not be mated for life, so it would be just another way to see if they were compatible and if the relationship could blossom into something more serious.

Since she'd wanted so badly to mix with others of their kind, he was fairly sure she didn't want anything long lasting with him. Not yet. Which meant he had to give her some space. That was something he was having a difficult time doing. Maybe when he returned to Florida…

He shook his head. When he returned home, he'd be thinking of every moment he'd already spent with her. And want to come right back to her—mainly to ensure some other shifter didn't think she was available.

What was wrong with him? She *was* available.

Everyone watched David to see his response. Would he take her up on her offer?

"You can sleep in my bed *alone*," she clarified and quirked a brow as if inviting a response.

"I'll take the couch."

Wade breathed a sigh of relief. He didn't want to act all caveman and say David couldn't, but he didn't want his brother in her bed, smelling her scent on the sheets and leaving his own in her room.

For the three-and-a-half-hour flight from Houston to Belize City, Wade had every intention of making adjustments in the seating arrangements. "About the flight tomorrow… David and I have seats together in the middle of the plane. He can swap with you."

She gave Wade a knowing smile. "What if David prefers sitting beside you?"

"What if David prefers that Wade switch seats with

you, and you sit beside David?" David said, grinning at her.

"What if my seat is first class?" she asked.

"I'll switch with you," David said.

Maya smiled. "Ah, now there's the truth of the matter."

"If push comes to shove, Wade's going to win this battle," David said.

"So you're going to be a gentleman and concede."

"Exactly."

"My seat isn't first class." She took Wade's hand and squeezed.

Both her cousins laughed.

She smiled at Wade but then asked about the Pattersons' reason for being at the club. "So you were at the club to see someone involved in the jaguar smuggling?"

"Yeah, we were," Wade said.

"How do you know where to go in Belize if you missed any intel you might have gotten at the club?"

"We had been at the club some hours before you arrived and were just looking for visual confirmation," Wade said, glad he'd been able to take care of her when the situation got out of hand. "We know the location where the men have gone."

"You said it was close to where we're staying. Where exactly?"

"Four and a half miles from your cottages, due southwest," Wade said.

She shook her head. "There's so much uncharted territory that I still think we'll be fine as long as we shift far from the treetop villas. Or even if we stick close to them. These men wouldn't be after a jaguar frequenting a human-populated area, would they?"

"Most likely not," Wade said. He thought again about Thompson, the man from the zoo, and wondered about the pictures on Maya's site.

He pulled out his phone and searched for her website. He couldn't believe she'd told the human she was a jaguar shifter and that her whole family were shifters, too. Not that he thought Thompson would believe her story—who would?—but still, Wade couldn't fathom her saying that.

When he located the web page, he realized she was watching him. "Here, let me. You want to see me in my fur coat, right?" she said, flipping to the page he was looking for.

He studied her jaguar form—golden fur and white cheeks and breast—as she looked at him with that cat's predatory gleam. He felt like he was seeing a flashback of her in the jungle when he looked at the picture of her crouched among the tropical plants—orchids, hibiscus, even a banana tree—in the high-ceilinged glass house with verdigris corners on its cathedral-style windows. In another photo that had him smiling, she was sleeping on a bench, looking like the photo session had worn her out.

Would others of his kind be affected in the same way if they saw her jaguar form and knew what she was? Hell, yeah. She was like a feral call to their past. But even so, they couldn't tell that she was a shifter from just the photo.

Everett and Huntley crowded around to get a look.

Wade studied her feral gaze. "Hell, all he has to do is compare rosettes with a picture of his own jaguar, and he'll know the truth."

"That's what I told him. I asked him if people

normally steal dangerous animals from his zoo. I was surprised when he said only the wolves."

Wade and her cousins raised their brows.

"Long story, Thompson told me. He hoped the same thing wasn't going to happen to their big cats now." Maya took a deep breath. "I saw something in Thompson's expression. He looked really... sad. Like the animal really meant something to him. In that instant, I wanted to offer help in trying to locate the jaguar, which is crazy. I haven't had any success until now in finding my own kind. I wouldn't have a clue how to search for it."

"We'll get in touch with our sister, Tammy," Huntley said. "She's an Enforcer."

Maya frowned. "Isn't it a Guardian's duty to protect the jaguars?"

"It would be, except that an Enforcer also goes after the people who commit crimes against jaguars. Once she locates the cat, if she's able to, a Guardian will see that the animal is returned to the zoo," Huntley said.

"Good. I hope she can find the jaguar—and soon," Maya said.

Wade hoped so, too. Maya didn't need the trouble.

"I don't understand why the cats acted so badly at the club," Maya said, annoyed.

Wade saw the smile Huntley gave her. "You're wild, Maya."

She frowned.

"That's how the city cats refer to your kind."

"My kind? Sounds derogatory."

"Actually, most admire your kind. Most of us in the Service have adapted to being both so we can take care of situations in either our wilder environment or the other. There's something to be said about the advantages of being both kinds of cat. Most city cats think the jungle cats are hot. Wild cats are rarer. Not as many shifters visit the jungle. They wouldn't have a clue how to survive there. That makes you a mystery. Once you met other shifters at the club, you'd have a multitude of offers."

"Of marriage?" Maya asked, wide-eyed.

Wade shook his head, thinking how very sheltered she must have been living with Connor and not mingling with city jaguars.

"Some men would be eager to touch the predator in you," Wade added. "Some won't be sure what to expect when they meet your kind."

Wade could see that the untamed side of her nature was infinitely curious, and that she had been dying to see the club for herself.

"I see. Kind of."

Wade took in her heavenly, sexy smell. He sighed, wishing they could take this to the bedroom.

Everett shook his head and paced like a caged cat. As wired as he was, he would be the next one out the back door to go on a hunt. They should be hoping none of the shifters at the club would come to Maya's place, but the expression on Everett's face said he was looking for a fight just to prove to anyone else that no one would be bothering Maya further.

"I'm off to check the grounds." Wade went to the guest bathroom, removed his clothes, then willed himself to become a big cat predator, his muscles stretching, his skin turning into a fur coat, his teeth growing to savage lengths. He stalked into the living room as a jaguar.

His coat was a distinctive golden color like other jaguars, but he had more white on his belly and under his chin than David did. His brother's fur was much more tan. All the cat shifters were considering Wade's jaguar appearance. They liked to get a visual so if they saw him again, even if they couldn't catch a whiff of him, they'd know he was friend, not foe.

David looked wishful that he could go.

They loved prowling in their jaguar halves, stretching their legs, moving unconfined.

Wade was just as eager to prove to anyone who had a death wish that Maya was to be left alone. With a low growl, saying he was on his way, he ran to the door where Everett quickly opened it for him.

Moving along the garden path, Wade stretched his jaguar muscles, searching the dark and looking for signs of anything moving.

Though he was trying to concentrate on smells and sounds and subtle movement, he couldn't help thinking about Maya.

He'd been so busy working missions for the Service that he hadn't seriously looked for any female jaguar in eons. Not until he'd thought Kat was one. Both he and David had been burned in past relationships. Most of the time, neither of the brothers discussed their jobs with the women they hooked up with. Most women didn't like their secretiveness. In the few instances when they had explained the work they did, the women had rejected both David and Wade.

Wade took another deep breath of the hot, muggy air.

Scanning the gardens from the planters of herbs to the trees and from the shrubs to the flowering plants, he smelled basil and mint and other herbs. He observed the watering hole featuring fountains and ponds, saw koi swimming around in one of the ponds, and smelled the fish in the hot, humid breeze. Whirligigs spun around as the leaves of trees fluttered. His roaming gaze stopped when he spied the greenhouse, its glass walls framed in sage-green wrought iron. It was an intriguing focal point beyond the trees in the south half of the nursery.

He paused at the glass door and peered in, searching for any sign of movement among the plants. He spotted a tub filled with Amazon water lilies and a tall banana plant, which he recognized from the website photos. He could envision Maya there now. Smiling, he shook his head.

Seeing movement to his left, he jerked his head around and saw the striped tail of a house-sized cat as it scurried away, disappearing under the low-hanging branches of a pine tree.

Wade took another deep breath, smelled the cat, and continued his walk, hoping the only kind of critter he'd find here tonight was of the small variety. He really didn't want to believe that anyone from the club would give her trouble here.

Chapter 6

CONNOR WAS CERTAIN THAT KAT WOULD WANT TO run as a jaguar as soon as he got her settled in their treetop cottage in the rainforest in Belize. But the trip and being five months pregnant with twins had worn her out. She smiled at him, then peeled out of her clothes, dropping them on a chair decorated in jungle-print pillows, and promptly slipped between the covers of the king-size bed.

Forget running in their spotted coats for now. He quickly yanked off his clothes, pulled out his cell phone and set it on the bedside table, and joined her. They snuggled, her eyes drifting closed, but he couldn't help worrying about having left Maya by herself.

Connor sighed. Maya had wanted to give them a little time alone together, even though they had arranged for separate treetop cottages and he would have his private time with Kat anyway. But Maya was arriving tomorrow night, after the flight and bus trip earlier in the afternoon. It wouldn't be long before she was safely here with them.

He couldn't imagine that anything could have gone wrong with Maya being alone for only a day and a night. Yet, they hadn't been apart much in all the time they were growing up, and he couldn't help worrying about her.

He reached for his phone and opened it—not enough

of a signal—and then sat it back down on the table. He glanced at his watch. *Again*.

Damn. Next time, Maya was coming with them.

———⚬———

Thompson had parked in the forest and stayed hidden among the trees surrounding the Anderson house and garden nursery. He waited for at least an hour before he finally made his way closer to the house.

He'd watched as Maya's cousins followed the car she was riding in, so he knew she had a full house—the two visiting brothers and her two cousins, he'd learned from Candy while trying to discover who all the men were who seemed so protective of Maya.

If she wasn't involved in the theft of his cat, he did not plan to give her trouble. If she was? He would file charges against her. *Guaranteed*.

Hunkered down among the ferns and shrubs, he watched and waited.

As soon as the lights went out in the house and everyone had gone to sleep for the night, Thompson planned to take a look around the gardens to see if they had any kind of structure that would house a big cat. He'd looked for evidence earlier in the day while Maya had been busy with customers. He'd confirmed that the greenhouse was the same one that the cat had been photographed in, and he'd found evidence of cat hairs on the tile floor. Then he'd followed her to the club and thought how appropriately it was named: the Jungle Cat Fever Club, a place where the sellers of illegal cats could gather and no one would be the wiser.

Now he was watching the front of the house, wishing

he had his hunting buddy, Joe, with him so that Joe could watch the back door when he heard it open and shut.

Thompson moved as quietly as he could, keeping to the forest until he could see the back side of the house. He saw a small clearing of land back there—a slate patio and a grassy area. Except for the light slipping through one of the windows of the house and a couple of softly glowing iron lanterns hanging on posts, the area was cloaked in darkness. He saw no one, suspecting that whoever had opened the back door had stayed on the patio. The gardens were too dark to explore without using a flashlight.

He heard no footfalls, either. Men and a woman were talking and laughing inside, so Thompson figured Maya was still in the house.

Trying to get comfortable, Thompson settled down next to a tree, using it for a backrest and wishing everyone would go to sleep so he could investigate the property, then retire to his hotel room for the rest of the night. This was the part he hated about the hunt. The waiting.

He was stiff, hot, hungry, and getting drowsy after two hours of being hunkered down among the shrubs and trees, his thoughts drifting to his wife and adopted kids. He loved what he did—protecting wildlife from human predators—but sometimes he thought he should let someone younger do the job and stay home more with his family.

The back door opened, and he was immediately wide awake. The remaining lights suddenly shut off inside the house, but the pale golden glow from the lanterns outside cast a soft light. He held very still, waiting. The back door was still open, but no one was coming out.

In his peripheral vision, he saw movement and couldn't help but turn his head. He quickly stifled a cry of distress. *A jaguar*. A large *male* jaguar! The big cat sniffed the ground at the entryway to the garden path, then loped toward the back door.

Thompson's jaw went slack. He wanted to yell, to warn Maya that a jaguar had run into the house—which he couldn't believe—when another male, more golden in color, ran outside through the same door.

Two. Holy crap. *Two* male jaguars. Cold sweat dripped from his pores.

No one inside was screaming for dear life, which he couldn't understand. The back door shut with a clunk, and the jaguar stood outside the house, sniffing the ground and the air, and then taking off down the garden path.

Thompson was having heart palpitations, while thanking God that he was downwind of the jaguar so the big cat didn't notice him. Thompson couldn't get his breathing under control. Trying to consider a plausible explanation, all he could think of was Maya saying she was the cat in the photo, that her family of jaguar shifters had taken her picture, then they all had milk to drink, that Wade's brother had called her Wildcat... and that all added up to? One damned, big jaguar-smuggling ring.

Now the jaguars were loose in the house and in the garden. When he thought humans were in control of the jaguars, that had been different. If the jaguars had escaped their pen and were running loose, that was a much more terrifying prospect.

Thompson was in a hell of a fix. He had no way to get to his truck and his rifle with the tranquilizer darts without the jaguar possibly seeing his movement or hearing him.

Then the cat growled in a low, angry tone. The jaguar must have smelled Thompson or heard his out-of-control heartbeat or seen him move.

Thompson waited, knowing that running would trigger the jaguar to chase him. He was very tempted to run. Jaguars didn't often attack humans, but Thompson knew never to tempt fate when dealing with predators. No matter what, they *weren't* supposed to be running loose in a nursery garden so close to Houston, Texas!

The cat growled again, then again, but the sound was different—lower, angrier.

Thompson stared at the area of the gardens where the growling was coming from.

Two jaguars running free in the gardens? He was a dead man.

David had fallen asleep on the couch, resting against the pillows. Sitting in one of the velour recliners, Maya had nearly drifted off when she heard big cats' angry cries in the garden.

She was sure that Everett had run into one of the men from the club who was also wearing his jaguar coat. Wade had been sitting in another recliner, but he'd already headed for the door, stripping off his clothes. Even though she was concerned for Everett, she couldn't draw her eyes away from Wade as he shucked his jeans—no boxers—hot, hot, very firm ass and legs and back. Before she could close her gaping mouth and look away, he shifted.

Everett roared. Huntley was yanking off his clothes to shift. David jerked awake and sat up too quickly, swayed a little, and groaned.

"Does your head still hurt?" she asked, taking hold of his muscular arm and knowing she couldn't deter him if he wanted to help the others.

He couldn't go out. Not the way he was feeling. He frowned at her.

"Enough of them are going after him. Stay with me. What if he is just a diversionary force and someone else tries to come in the front way?"

David didn't object, but he stood slowly and walked toward the kitchen, which had a view of the backyard and gardens. He peered out the window.

Wade was waiting at the back door, Huntley beside him, wearing a beautiful black jaguar coat with barely visible rosettes. He was clawing at the door to get out. When she opened it, Huntley rushed out to protect his brother. In his golden jaguar coat, Wade peered out, breathing in the air, testing it, and attempting to smell any sign of what was happening outside.

"Did you want to go, Wade?" Maya asked. "Or stay here with us?"

David snorted. "Wade's not leaving you for a second."

"I can shift and I don't have any qualms about fighting a male cat if he comes into the house," Maya said. Not that a female against a male would be an even match. But David could shift if he had to.

"He's not leaving you behind," David said, sure of his statement.

It didn't take long for one of the cats to cry out near the pottery barn. Another responded, then a third.

Her heart thundering, Maya strained to watch for any sign of the cats but she couldn't see anything because of the vegetation and stone wall surrounding the gardens.

A few minutes later, Everett poked his spotted orange head through the rose-covered arbor, as if telling her he was all right. Everything was fine now. Since he was still on guard duty, he turned, waving his long spotted tail in his wake, and went back to prowling. Huntley ran through the arbor and straight to the house to tell them what had happened. Once he was inside, Maya took a relieved breath and closed the back door.

Huntley walked behind the couch to where he'd dropped his clothes and grabbed his boxers with his teeth, then headed for the bathroom. Wade shifted and grabbed his jeans. She turned her attention from how well-hung he was to his face. He winked, then headed into her bedroom to change. Not that he'd want to use the bathroom when Huntley was in there, but once he left his scent in her room, all she would think about whenever she was in there was how he had looked.

Naked, ripped, hot.

Her eyes were fixated on his backside as he entered her room, but he didn't shut the door.

Seconds later, Huntley left the bathroom wearing his boxers and running his hands through his hair. "Hell, that was that Bettinger guy. He sure has balls. Even *I* am reluctant to fight Everett when he's angry."

"Bettinger?" Maya groaned. "Connor isn't going to be happy." She pulled a quilt from an oak chest near the fireplace while David resettled on the couch.

"I doubt he's going to want to return here and get

another whipping," Huntley said, going into the kitchen. He paused. "Is it okay for me to get some milk?"

"Only if you drink it out of a glass and not out of the jug," Maya warned.

He chuckled and continued to the kitchen. "Everett must have told on me. I live alone and it's my jug of milk."

Wade rejoined the party and reclined on the chair again, his claimed territory for the night. She was a little surprised he wasn't sleeping in his jaguar form like he'd said he would.

As she moved past Wade's chair, he snagged her hand, startling her. "Go to bed. David will be fine. I'll keep an eye on him." He pulled Maya down for a good-night kiss.

She thought he meant to give her a light peck on the mouth and send her off to bed, but unexpectedly, he pulled her on top of him, their mouths fusing. Tongues licked and stroked, lips pressed and rubbed, both of them just as eager to kiss. His fingers combed through her hair as she held his face gently in her hands. Wickedly, he spread his legs so she fell between his thighs and felt his erection, thick and hard and ready for her. She ground slightly against him, wanting to feel him stir against her body. He did with a surrendering groan.

That will teach him not to play with a female jaguar. She licked his lips and said, "Good night, sleep tight, don't let the jaguars bite."

"Only this one," he said, stroking her arm as she got off him.

She smiled again and kissed his forehead. David was watching them, green eyes wide.

She'd forgotten he was there, close enough to see all. She turned and found Huntley smiling at her, glass of milk in hand. He shook his head. "I suppose you don't want to give me a good-night kiss like that, too."

"You're my *cousin*," she said, crossing the floor. She gave him a quick peck on the cheek and headed into her bedroom.

David cleared his throat, as if he wanted her to come back and kiss him, too.

She chuckled and closed her door, hoping that no one else would visit the property tonight and cause more trouble. If there were more catfights, they'd never get any sleep.

Chapter 7

SWEAT DRIPPING INTO HIS EYES, THOMPSON WAS frozen to the ground, his heart pounding as if he'd been running a marathon.

He listened for any sign of the cats. One had returned to the house, and even *more* of a shock to him, Maya had been standing in the doorway with another. Three had been fighting in the garden before that. The other that had encroached on these jaguars' territories had to be an outsider. Where the hell had he come from? Not one he saw was female.

He had half a notion to walk straight up to the back door, knock on it, and ask Maya about the female jaguar again. Then what? Would she turn the big males loose on him? For trespassing in the middle of the night in her backyard?

Instead of guard dogs, she had guard cats. It couldn't be possible.

He couldn't get his feet to move. For the first time since he could remember, he was truly terrified.

He sat down with his back to the tree, trying to stay awake, but drifting off, only to be awakened by the sound of the patio door opening. A jaguar loped out of the garden toward the house, ran inside, and another ran out. The door shut again with a soft *thunk*.

Thompson blinked. They actually *were* serving guard duty.

He was losing his mind.

He must have finally fallen asleep, because the next thing he heard was the sound of vehicles pulling out of the parking lot in front of the house, tires crunching on the gravel. Darkness still cloaked the early morning hour. Still hidden by the woods, he hurried around front, saw three cars take off, and waited.

When no one seemed likely to return anytime soon, he peered through the picture windows, expecting to see jaguars lying around on the couches and floor. The room was too dark, and he couldn't see anything.

He returned to the woods until it was light out, then made his way back to the house and peeked again through the window. There was no movement in the house, no cats lying on the floor or lounging on the couches.

He looked back in the direction that the cars had gone. Hell. Had they packed the cats up in the cars?

He shook his head. They couldn't have. He heard the rumbling of a pickup truck and tore into the woods for cover. From his hiding place among the shrubs, he saw two men and a woman get out of the truck. Customers?

Then as they began to water plants, he realized they had to be the hired help. Should he ask them about the jaguars?

He waited until the place was open for business, then drove his truck around to the entrance and parked.

What was he going to ask them? *Seen any really* big *kitty cats around lately?*

———⁓———

Wade thought David looked a hundred percent better after having slept on Maya's couch the night before. The gash on his head was just a white line against his tan forehead now, the colorful bandages gone. They'd shared lunch with Everett and Huntley, who afterward had gone to their own terminal to wait for their flight to Brazil. Now he, Maya, and David were waiting to take their flight to Belize.

Maya had acted anxious most of the day, wringing her hands, pacing, and not paying attention to conversations that had included her. Wade knew she was worried about the hunters and her brother and Kat.

He finally pulled her into a seat and wrapped his arm around her shoulder, trying to relax her. "So tell me, what is your favorite food?"

She looked up at him as if he was crazy, then gave him the warmest smile and nestled her head against his shoulder. "Ice cream. Coffee-flavored, covered in hot fudge topping."

"Sweet," he said, meaning she was, just like her choice of food.

"Yours?"

"Juicy red steak."

"Hmm, sounds yummy," she said.

David looked up from the romance novel he was reading. "Fried chicken."

Maya laughed. "Fried foods are not good for you."

"I run it off."

She glanced in the direction of the gate next to them where passengers were beginning to take their seats. Wade and David followed her gaze. A woman with hair as long, blond, and full as Lion Mane's was talking to another woman waiting for a different departure. Wade noted that every person with long, blond hair had caught Maya's eye.

But Lion Mane wouldn't be flying anywhere, he didn't think, and he couldn't get into the terminal without a plane ticket.

"Favorite color?" Wade prompted.

"That blue chambray shirt of yours."

He kissed her cheek. "Thanks for trying to get the blood out."

She looked at him with her beautiful golden eyes. "Sorry it didn't work."

David said, "Turquoise, like the Caribbean water."

Wade thought for a moment, then smiled. "Golden like your eyes, Maya."

David snorted. "I didn't know you had a romantic bone in your body."

Wade glanced at him. "Aren't you reading something?"

David grinned back at him. "It's hard to read when I'm more interested in…" He paused to take a look at another blond-haired woman.

Maya sighed. "Did you think it was Lion Mane?"

"Yeah," David said.

"You didn't happen to get his name when you danced with him, did you?" Wade asked.

"Of course not. Then he would have really thought I was interested in him, more than just his hair. Besides, after Bill Bettinger came to the nursery, we should be more concerned about looking for him showing up here."

"Everett tore into him good from what Huntley told us. I doubt you'll have any more trouble with Bettinger," Wade said. He hoped to have taken Maya's mind off her worries, at least for the moment. "What do you like to do that's fun?"

"Swimming."

That made him think of her wearing the black lace bra and panties again, swimming in the Amazon. Did she pack those this trip? He smiled.

"What?" Maya asked, observing his expression.

David looked at Wade.

Wade said, "The chase."

Maya purred, "I just bet you love that."

David shook his head.

They both watched him.

David closed his book. "I like to read, swim…" He grinned. "…and chase things."

"Wade said you were reading a romantic suspense story. Do you really like them?"

David smiled. "I'm learning what it takes to get the girl during a high-action adventure."

Maya chuckled and rolled her eyes.

Maya had tried to hide her nervousness about leaving for Belize, but she hadn't been able to. Now that hunters could be in the area, she was more than anxious to get there. She had to warn Connor and Kat about the hunters. She was certain her brother and Kat would have made a couple of treks into the jungle already, exploring and marking their territory—it was just instinctual.

Maya prayed that they were fine. She wished she could have reached them by phone, but that was one of the problems with going to remote places. Yet the remote places were just what they needed so they could shift and run in the wild.

She was grateful that Wade had tried to take her mind off her worries. She swore she'd seen Lion Mane and

Bill Bettinger at the airport earlier. The blond guy's hair had been pulled back in a ponytail, which had changed his appearance, but the redhead—well, she had to admit they'd been really far away.

Still... the way the blond had caught her eye and looked startled had caused a shiver to run up her spine. When she tried to get Wade and David to verify who she'd seen, neither had caught sight of them. She guessed her mind was playing tricks on her.

"About last night..." Wade began. His whole body posture was saying she was his—*his girlfriend*—his thigh touching hers, his head leaning close to hers, his arm slung over her shoulders with tenderness, even the way his eyes swallowed her up. That all made her resolve—*to date lots of other shifters before she settled on one*—melt at the edges.

"You were out of your head." Maya leaned back against her seat. "I understand."

His mouth quirked up a little, his darkened eyes smiling. "You don't really believe that, do you?"

No, she didn't. She wanted to run with Wade in the jungle, wanted to see more of him. Wanted more of his kisses. And just... more. From the dark gravelly tone of his voice, he sounded like he already knew that.

Yet, she was afraid of... making a mistake. Her mother had made one with their father. Would she also? Daughter like mother?

Maya rested her hand lightly on Wade's thigh. She hated that he had to run off and confront smugglers, even though his brother would be with him. She wished he could vacation with her.

"I want to see more of you, Maya. I'll be at the resort

if I can make it." Wade kissed her softly on the mouth. "Just get word to your family. David and I have to stop these men."

She wanted to see more of him, too, but she didn't want him to think she was desperate. Not now that she knew others of their kind existed close to where she lived.

"Connor could assist you in locating the hunters. He won't want to leave Kat alone, but once I'm there with her, he can help the two of you." She didn't want just Wade and David dealing with however many men were behind this operation.

"If we *can't* track them down, we'll ask Connor to join us."

She didn't believe Wade was being honest with her. She was certain he had no intention of asking Connor for his help. Macho guy thing.

"In the meantime, see the caves, take a boat ride, enjoy the jungle, but as humans. All right, Maya?"

She nodded.

Boarding call was announced and they all made their way to their seats on the plane, David taking hers. Maya was sitting beside the window, Wade in the middle, and a nice grandmotherly lady in the aisle seat.

Ever since Wade had told her about the possible danger to Connor and Kat, she'd been fighting the worry. Once she took her seat, she closed her eyes as the flight took off. She couldn't do anything until she reached the resort. At least the flight was fairly short. The bus ride was nearly as long, though. Connor and Kat would meet her once she arrived, so they wouldn't be running around as jaguars until *after* she got there. *Tonight*.

When they arrived in Belize City, they took a bus for the three-hour drive to the resort. What was supposed to be strictly a vacation could very well turn into a nightmare.

"We'll watch you get off and join your brother and Kat," Wade told her, squeezing her hand. "We'll be in touch if we stop these guys before your vacation ends. When we have word, we'll let you know."

"I wish you could stop and visit, but it's late and—"

"Connor won't like seeing us," Wade finished for her. "We need to get checked into our place."

When the bus came to a halt, he stood and gave her a hug and a kiss—not sweet in the least, but more of a promise he'd be seeing her again, soon. David gave her a brief kiss and a hug that was just as comforting.

Wade slugged him in the shoulder. "Enough."

David had the nerve to grin at him and released her.

"Are you going to be okay, Maya?" Wade asked.

"Yeah. Be careful, both of you." Maya hurried off the bus as the driver unloaded bags.

"She'll be fine," David said as they retook their seats.

"Yeah." Wade watched as Connor greeted Maya, then frowned at her and looked up at the bus. "Her brother smells us on her, and he looks pissed."

"You know she wants to see other shifters, don't you?" David asked, his voice sympathetic as the bus continued on its way.

Wade nodded. He wanted to say it didn't matter to him. That if it was important to her, he'd be happy for her.

"You're not going to let her if you can help it, are you?" David raised his brows, trying to look serious, but a smile was begging to appear. "I'm serious," David added.

Wade wanted to protect her from her brother, Connor, who would give her a hard time for having been with so many shifters. He knew she carried their body scents because she'd hugged them all soundly.

Wade looked out the window. "She lives in Texas with her brother and Kat. We live in Florida. Kind of hard to keep her from seeing anyone else."

"So? You know she really has a thing for you."

"Yeah, and that's why she danced with the blond guy."

"She's scared."

Wade frowned. "Of me?"

"Of getting too close, falling in love, and marrying a shifter who would take off like her father. Everett told me that's what her father did."

Wade ran his hand through his hair. "I wouldn't be like that. If I found the right woman…"

"I know that. She's interested in you. She kissed you like there was no tomorrow. She wants you. Hell, even that woman, Jeanie, that you thought you would marry, never kissed you like that."

Wade smiled.

"Or *danced* with you like that. You're not going to let Maya date a bunch of other shifters and make a mistake with one of them, are you?"

Wade shoved his hands in his pockets.

David folded his arms. "Okay, if you're not going to stop her from dating other shifters, I will."

"The hell you will."

David grinned and slapped Wade on the back. "That's what I wanted to hear."

Chapter 8

As soon as she got off the bus, Maya saw Connor. His brow was furrowed, but then he smiled a little. Where was Kat?

Trying not to anxiously drum up worst-case scenarios, Maya took a deep breath and hurried to give Connor a hug. "Where's Kat?"

"Sleeping. She was feeling tired and nauseated."

"Oh." Maya wanted to say "good," only because she was so grateful Kat was safe. But Connor wouldn't understand. She opened her mouth to tell him right away about the hunters, but as soon as she embraced her brother, his somberly pleasant expression soured. She realized he had to have smelled Wade and David on her... and two other male cats, her cousins, who had given her hugs before they left her for their terminal.

She and Connor were walking along a path that seemed to be taking them straight into the jungle until it opened up to reveal a group of treetop cottages half hidden by jungle vegetation.

"How come I smell four different male cats on you?" Connor asked, his tone accusing as he frowned at Maya. He motioned with his head to one of the cottages as they made their way along the treetop walkway. "That's our cottage."

"I'll tell you when I'm unpacking. I've got to warn

you and Kat that hunters are in the area. They're looking for jaguars."

"That's always a possibility." Connor did not sound the least bit concerned.

"It's a certainty."

As they continued on their way along the path, she noted that the lush tropical foliage hid each of the cottages from the others, giving them privacy. Maya loved the way the trees surrounded them, reminding her of the hut where they'd stayed in the Amazon.

"How do you know this?" Connor asked while she unlocked her door.

She carried her backpack in while he rolled her large suitcase into the room.

The five-hundred-square-foot cottage was spacious, featuring a living area and a raised bedroom with a king-size bed covered in a white duvet and jungle-print pillows partially hidden by mesh netting. She glanced at the floor-to-ceiling windows that wrapped around three sides of the cottage, offering a view of the bright green jungle. A couple of beige couches and chairs decorated in jungle-print pillows filled the living area, and a tree grew off center through the floor and the ceiling, giving the room its treetop feel. She adored the place.

"Wow." A wooden railing dividing the living room from the bedroom gave the cottage a more open feeling. She instantly thought of Wade with her in that bed. She shook her head at the notion, but she couldn't rid herself of the desire—just like Connor sharing his bed with Kat.

"Maya, what makes you so certain the hunters are here? You just got here. And why do I smell four different male cats on you?"

"Cousins," she said. She mentioned them first so that Connor wouldn't be too upset with her. "We've got family. Huntley and Everett Anderson. And Tammy, their sister, but I didn't get to meet her this time." She couldn't hide her enthusiasm as she grinned at Connor. Her expression quickly changed to concern when Connor folded his arms and looked at her with disbelief.

She sat on the edge of the bed. The mattress was soft and comfy, and again she was thinking of what it would feel like to have Wade naked in her bed.

Connor rested his butt against the dresser, still looking peeved.

"Do you remember Wade Patterson?"

Connor was already scowling, but now his expression turned feral.

She quickly said, "He's with a secret jaguar agency that polices our kind."

Connor's scowl turned to disbelief. "And you believe that crock of bull? Next you'll tell me he's part of some Special Forces group—that he's a SEAL or some damned nonsense. Do you know how many real SEALs there are and how many men claim they were one?"

She cast him an annoyed look and folded her arms. She should have known her brother would think Wade was making it all up. "No, listen. Our cousins, Everett and Huntley? They're also working for this organization."

"Maya…"

"It's true. We kept ourselves isolated from others just like our parents did. And probably their parents before them. We knew there had to be more of us. We've never met any shifters in our area, so all we see are humans.

The others are city jaguars, not... well, wild like us. They don't visit the jungle like we do. They had to make up a police force to keep shifters in line who don't follow the rules. Regular police wouldn't do because of the problem with jaguars shifting."

"We don't even know what these supposed rules are so that we can follow them," Connor said. "If what you're saying is true, why haven't these people come knocking on our door before?"

"We're law-abiding citizens. We don't do anything that would cause this police force to bother with us."

Connor narrowed his eyes. "So you hugged our two cousins, which is the reason for their scents on your skin. What about the other two?" He had to know one of the others was Wade Patterson, since he was the only other male cat she'd been talking about.

"Wade and his brother, David Patterson."

Connor shook his head and moved toward the one chair in the bedroom. "I think I'm going to have to sit down to hear the rest of this."

As she unpacked and noted all the niceties in the cottage, she explained everything—the brothers, the cousins—but not the brawl—and as much as she hated to admit that Connor might have been right about advertising their nursery by featuring a jaguar, she told him about the zoo man, Thompson.

Connor let out his breath in exasperation. "Don't tell me you want to see this Wade Patterson further."

Why wouldn't she? He'd been such a help to them before, took care of her at the club, and watched over her at the house. He was really sweet, if she didn't think of the moves he made on the dance floor or while kissing her on the couch. Then he was hot and sexy and all the more intriguing.

She shrugged. "He lives in Florida. But yeah, maybe."

She didn't believe she could be interested in a jaguar shifter who wouldn't visit or feel comfortable in the jungle.

What if she found a city jaguar who she thought she could acclimate to the jungle, and he hated it? Or was afraid of the rainforest? A man like that wouldn't appeal. So even though she had more of a choice now, the notion that some didn't visit the jungle limited her options.

"What about Kat?" Connor asked, his eyes narrowed.

"He's not interested in her."

Connor harrumphed.

Maya opened the door to the deck.

"The cottages are actually built on the side of a hill with walkways winding through the trees. The deck leads to stairs and another path to the main lodge where meals are served," Connor said.

"We're not catching dinner as jaguars?" She wasn't surprised, not with the layout of these cottages. Their hut in the Amazon was much more primitive, with no restaurant within walking distance.

Maya smiled. This was going to be a good trip. She hoped.

Connor fumed about his sister. He was fascinated with the idea that an enforcement agency was run by and for jaguar shifters. If he'd learned of such a force before he and his sister had started their successful garden nursery, he might have considered joining it himself. Then again, he'd always looked out for Maya, and he couldn't see spending long periods away from her.

Hell, he left her alone for two days, and she opened the house up to Wade Patterson, his brother, and two other male shifters. Sure they were cousins, but Connor hadn't met them first to ensure they were safe. On top of that, she'd started a fight in a shifter bar? Not to mention that a zoo official believed Maya had stolen a jaguar from the Oregon Zoo. He couldn't imagine what would have happened if he'd left her alone for a *whole* week! He wondered if she'd left anything out in telling him what had gone on. Like how intimate she'd been with this Wade Patterson.

Connor admitted that he had approved of her and Kat's idea of posting Maya's picture in her jaguar form in the greenhouse. They'd had quite a boost in garden sales. Now he was regretting that decision.

"I think you should find Wade and help him take down the hunters," Maya said, appearing worried as she exited the closet. "I'm here now. I'll take care of Kat."

"No," Connor said.

Maya gave him a cross look, just like she always did when he disagreed with her over an important issue.

"He's on a job. He's trained. He's getting paid for it. We're strictly here on vacation, and I'm staying with the two of you to keep you safe." Connor was not leaving Kat alone, even with Maya's protection, if hunters were close by.

"How's Kat feeling?" Maya asked, changing the subject.

He knew from the way she'd done so that she hadn't given up on the subject of helping Wade. She'd revisit it when she could. Maybe by soliciting Kat's help to back her up. He loved that the two women were the best of friends, but their friendship kept him on his toes because they often conspired against him.

"Kat's having a little morning sickness. Shifting seems to help settle her stomach. She can handle the pregnancy better as a cat. We don't go until it's dark out."

"You saw no sign of the hunters?"

"None. Thousands of acres of rainforest exist out there. Half of Belize is covered by dense jungle. A lot of it hasn't even been explored yet—by humans anyway. Because of Kat's condition, we've stuck close to the cottages. And hunters wouldn't suspect jaguars would hang around people. But if she's feeling better, we'll go farther out where we can't smell any signs of humans."

"You've marked your scent around the area," she said, knowing he would.

It was part of what they were. That primal, territorial aspect couldn't be tamed. Not when they were in the wild like this.

"Yeah, we have." He smiled. "Kat hasn't quite got the hang of it. She thinks if she scent-marks over where I've scent-marked, she's claiming *I'm* her territory, and any other females can keep their paws to themselves."

Maya chuckled. "I love Kat."

Even when they visited the forested area around the lake on their property, they left their stamp on the area. Humans didn't know jaguars existed in Texas, but the wildlife in the area certainly did. Not that the jaguars ate any of the critters around there, except for fishing in the lake, but the birds and snakes and squirrels and armadillos knew.

"I missed you both," Maya said.

Connor knew she was being honest, but he snorted anyway. "Sounds like you didn't have time. You were never alone."

She was opening her mouth to rebut his comment when Kat opened the door to the cottage and smiled, her dark hair pulled into a ponytail, her green eyes sparkling with excitement. "You're here!" She turned to Connor and scolded him. "You should have told me right away! Why didn't you wake me?"

He only gave her a half smile.

Dressed in a pale blue long-sleeved shirt, blue jeans, and hiking boots, Kat looked refreshed and ready to take a walk in the jungle.

Maya ran down the steps from the elevated bedroom to join her and gave her a big hug. "We have cousins!"

"And *Wade Patterson* is in the area," Connor said, as if the devil himself had just shown up in their neck of the rainforest. He couldn't help it. He was certain that as soon as Wade saw Kat, he'd make a move on his wife, and Connor would kill him.

Then both Maya and Kat would want to kill Connor.

Chapter 9

WADE HAD ALREADY DECIDED THAT AFTER THEY investigated the cabana where the two hunters were staying, he would check on Maya.

The smugglers had used a credit card at one of the resorts in the jungle town, and Wade's boss had informed him that the two men were named Mylar Cranston and Tierney Smith.

They had rap sheets with crimes ranging from carjacking and jewelry-store theft to attempted murder over the past twenty years, as well as drug deals in Central and South America, which was where they undoubtedly got their connections to chase down jaguars.

Nice guys. The latest message from his boss was that the men were armed and considered extremely dangerous. No surprise there.

Martin had reserved a cabana for Wade and David at the same resort. The thatched roofs gave the buildings a rounded appearance and fit in with the jungle theme. Each of the cabanas was backed up against the jungle, with trees screening one from another. Inside, the two bedrooms were of simple fare, three twin beds and a queen. A blue tile floor matched the floral bedspreads, and a blue tablecloth over a table seated between two rattan chairs was also covered in floral print. Hanging on one wall, a large print of a jaguar reclining in a tree made Wade smile. He could have posed for that picture himself.

"Looks like you," David remarked, glancing at the print.

"He's not as handsome."

David chuckled.

"Ready to take a look at their cabana?" Wade asked.

David dropped his bag in the other room and returned. "Ready if you are."

They made their way through the jungle behind the cabanas, silent and cautious, working around toward the back side of the rental unit where they would be hidden from view. Several keel-billed toucans were sitting in a tree watching them, their necks and chests covered in brilliant yellow feathers, the rest of their plumage black. Looking like the Fruit Loops toucan, they had large rainbow-colored beaks in bright green, orange, blue, and red that made them stand out. They were sociable creatures and the national bird of Belize. A couple of them were making a croaking sound while insects whirred and buzzed and clicked and chirped in the dense jungle foliage.

Brushing against the leaves of a tree, Wade felt his long cotton sleeves gather rain droplets collected on the broad surfaces. He could smell that it had recently rained here, making the atmosphere steamy and heavy with moisture.

They drew closer to the back side of the building and listened for sounds within the structure—trying to hear voices or showering or anything that would indicate someone was inside.

Wade heard nothing. "They're gone," he whispered to his brother. Peering through the window in the bathroom, he observed two shaving kits, toothbrushes, and toothpaste sitting on the bathroom counter.

He pried open the window, climbed in, and took a deep breath, smelling the scents of the men so he'd recognize them in the jungle. The pungent odor of the lemon-scented insect repellent the men had used still hung heavy in the air.

David slipped in through the window after Wade, observing everything for himself, two pairs of eyes being better than one.

Wade looked around the bathroom where muddied white towels lay scattered on the floor. The towels were no longer wet, and there were no droplets of water in the tub. Dirt had collected near the drain of the tub and dried. Toothpaste spittle was dried on the sink. The men hadn't been here for a couple of days. From the disarray, he figured they must have told the staff they didn't want maid service.

He moved into the room where the beds sat. The top sheets were rumpled on the queen bed as if it had been slept in. Discarded dirty briefs, socks, muddy jeans, and a T-shirt lay on the floor beside the bed. In the other bedroom, he found the queen comforter hanging half off the bed. Various articles of clothing smelling of sweat and heavily splattered with mud were scattered on the floor.

In the living area, he smelled the odor of two other men who had stood in the front entryway—a fainter scent as if they'd walked in and left right away. *Jaguar shifters*. They were two of the men he'd seen at the shifter club in Houston, he thought darkly.

Bill Bettinger, the one who'd struck David in the head with the bottle, and the other who had shoulder-length blond hair—the one Maya called Lion Mane and thought she'd seen at the airport. *Hell*. Their own kind was selling out non-shifter jaguars?

He growled low. *Bastards*.

David joined him, sniffed the air, and swore under his breath when he smelled the men's scents. "Do you think they're wild?"

"Might be, and they may be serving as the guides rather than hiring someone they didn't know."

When humans hunted jaguars, it was bad enough. He *couldn't* understand why his kind would harm the jaguars when they had a kinship to them and the jaguars' only predator was man. Then again, some would sell their own family if meant they'd get money for it.

Wade glanced around the living room. "If Bettinger and the other shifter return to the cabana, they'll know you and I have been here snooping around. They'd most likely assume we're with the Service. And we're after them. Since the smugglers are human, if they return here before we find them, *they* won't know we've been here."

"Hell," David said. "You're right."

"I hope the shifters won't revisit the cabana so we have a better chance at reporting the information to the boss and keeping our business here secret until we can learn who the buyer is. Too bad Internet service is only available at the main lodge and not in the cabanas. We'll have to let Martin know what we learn later."

David walked toward one of the bedrooms. "I'll search this one."

Wade opened each of the drawers in a couple of dressers in the other bedroom, finding them empty. A bag sat on the floor next to the dresser. Inside the bag, the man had left behind civilian clothes—jeans, T-shirts.

He must have planned to return and wear these when not in the jungle, or he would have taken them with him. Wade found the man's airline ticket itinerary, showing he had already been here two days.

"The hunters came early," Wade called out to his brother. "I wonder why Bettinger and the blond guy were at the club and not down here?"

He found no return flight information and assumed that was because they'd be here until they located the jaguar and took the cat out of the country via some means other than by plane. He noted a tag on the man's bags. Address and phone number. "Mylar Cranston's name is on the bag in here." Now he knew his scent from the other by name.

Mentally, Wade filed the information away.

"This one belongs to Tierney Smith, according to the luggage tag. They apparently aren't worried about anyone checking up on them," David said from the other room.

Wade searched underneath the mattresses for any-thing of importance that might have been tucked away. His hand touched something metal beneath the mattress, and he lifted it to see what he'd found. A wicked-looking dagger. Wade smelled blood on it, though the weapon had been wiped clean.

"Looks like I might have found a murder weapon," Wade said, grabbing a T-shirt from Mylar Cranston's bag. "He probably kept it under his mattress, being paranoid that someone might break in and attempt to kill him."

David joined him in the bedroom and studied the dag-ger. "Smells like old blood. Maybe a murder committed?"

"Yeah. It'll undoubtedly have Cranston's fingerprints

on it, and the T-shirt has some of his beard trimmings. We should send these to Martin first chance we get. Did you find anything in the other room?"

"No. It was clean."

"Let's take a run through the jungle and see where they headed."

David nodded. "Think Lion Mane and Bettinger will be with them?"

"Yeah. That means we'll be dealing with at least four of them."

David and Wade returned to their cabana and stripped. Wade opened the window in the bathroom, easy enough for them to get in and out of as cats, and with no lights in the jungle beyond. Perfect for a nighttime run.

He didn't know if the two men were using their cabana as their place of operation while looking for the cats, or if they had set up tents in the rainforest and searched for the elusive jaguar from there.

They wouldn't have to get a guide if Bettinger and Lion Mane knew their way around the jungle. They might have to pay a couple of men to help them carry the big cat to a waiting vehicle, then take off for Mexico and the States. Wade's mission for now was to try to locate them and then take it from there.

Two miles from the resort, in the thick of the jungle, he smelled Connor and Kat's scent. All he could think of was Maya and her safety, and his mission flew straight out the window.

David looked in the direction Wade did, and then Wade took off in the direction of her treetop cottage.

David bolted after him.

Chapter 10

EATING DINNER WAS NEXT ON THE AGENDA BECAUSE Maya and Kat said they were starving.

Connor almost felt left out when Maya and Kat linked arms and strolled ahead of him on the narrow walkway as they headed toward the main lodge. "Tell me what the club was like," Kat coaxed.

"Maya started a brawl," Connor said, "and the place will probably never be the same."

Kat glanced back at Connor. Maya rolled her eyes at him. He smiled.

Maya said, "We had drinks and…"

"Dancing?" Connor suddenly asked. "You danced with Wade Patterson?"

"And Thompson…"

"The guy from the zoo?" Connor asked, not believing this.

"Yeah, he was protecting me from the other shifters who wanted to dance with me."

"Where the hell was Wade when all of this was going on?" Even though Connor still wasn't sure about the man's intentions with regard to Maya or Kat, he thought Wade would have looked out for her welfare better than that. "Where were our cousins?"

"They wanted to talk to Wade about business—you know, as it pertained to their line of work."

Connor shook his head.

"The club sounds like fun," Kat said, a sparkle in her eye.

"You're not going," Connor said.

Kat frowned over her shoulder at him. "For your information, I believe I've been to one like that in Florida. I didn't know that's what it was, of course. But I loved the jungle theme and seeing the men and women dancing on stage in loincloths."

"You weren't a wild cat back then, Kathleen," he said. "It would be different now. Hell, as bad as Maya made the fight sound, can you imagine the two of you together, stirring things up? We'd be banned from ever entering the club again."

Kat smiled at Maya. Connor shook his head again. He wondered if that was the reason their mother had kept them away from others of their kind, ensuring they lived in a more natural environment.

When they walked into the dining room, they found they were the first to take their seats for the evening meal.

Each of them chose to begin with the chicken soup.

Kat happily chatted about all that she'd seen in the jungle, from the largest flying bird in the Americas—the jabiru stork—to a rare agami heron, tons of hummingbirds, neon-green parrots, macaws, and a snowy egret. She described several of the orchids they'd witnessed. Then she said, her eyes bright with excitement, "We saw an ocelot!"

"No jaguars, though?" Maya asked, a teasing light in her eyes.

Guests said hi to them as they took their seats around some of the tables. Connor and Kat always arrived early for dinner so they could go on their jungle treks at dusk, while the other guests spent their days in the jungle and stayed in their cottages at night.

"Did you hear the howler monkey?" one woman asked another at a different table. "It nearly gave me a seizure until I figured out what it was."

"What was Wade like?" Kat asked Maya.

Connor tried not to stiffen, but he didn't manage well—especially when Kat was asking about Wade.

"He's protective," Maya said.

Connor meant to keep his mouth shut, but he couldn't let that go. "Yeah, like he left you alone and a barroom brawl started over you."

Two of the men and a woman at another table looked in their direction. Maya's cheeks blossomed with color.

She tilted her chin up and said to Kat, "He came to my protection and even carried me out of there when I slipped on all the broken glass." She gave Connor an "I told you so" look.

All conversation at the other tables concerning what the guests had discovered on treks to a nearby cave and the jungle died as soon as the barroom brawl was mentioned. Connor *knew* Kat and Maya should have had this discussion in one of their cottages.

Then he began to consider the sleeping arrangements at their home, and before he could stop himself from saying something about it, he asked, "None of the men slept in our bedroom, did they?"

"Of course not," Maya said, sounding irritated. "We all slept in *my* bed."

He knew she was kidding because there was no way in hell all of them could have slept in her queen-size bed with her. Not that he would have believed she'd slept with her cousins or David. Wade? Connor wasn't certain about him.

Kat laughed. "As if four men could sleep in that bed of yours with you."

Maya sighed. "If you must know, our cousins slept on the floor in the living room. Wade took one of the recliners so he could watch David. Poor David had gotten hit in the head by a bottle, and it cut him. So he slept on the couch."

One of the male guests was smiling and shaking his head, and another was watching Connor and waggling his brows.

As dessert was served, Connor saw Maya suddenly look in the direction of the window as if something had caught her eye.

"What did you see?" he asked.

She shook her head. "Nothing." She dipped her fork into her banana rum crepe.

She looked pale and her heart was thumping hard.

"Maya?"

"I… I thought I saw something."

"Someone," he said, knowing her better than that.

"Okay, someone. After what Wade told me about the hunters, I'm just feeling a little jumpy."

"They wouldn't come to the lodge or the cottages looking for a jaguar," Connor assured her.

"One was spotted last night in the jungle below our deck," a woman at another table said, smiling. "The owner said several guests have seen it. Nothing to worry about, though." She poked her fork into her dessert and continued talking to her companions.

It couldn't have been Wade because he had arrived at

the same time as Maya, she knew. Hell. If it was a true
jaguar and word got out that it was frequenting the area,
that could bring the hunters down on top of them.

Chapter 11

IN THE MIDDLE OF THE NIGHT, WADE REACHED THE treetop cottages where Maya was staying. He and David hadn't needed a GPS to locate them. In their jaguar forms, they'd followed Kat and Connor's scents to the resort. Wade had smelled another jaguar in the area—a female, which didn't bode well if Bettinger and Lion Mane got wind of her and led the smugglers this way. He wanted to warn Maya and the others that Bettinger and Lion Mane were in on the jaguar-smuggling plans. As jaguar shifters, the men could scent another jaguar and tip off the smugglers who would take the big cat into custody.

While he suspected that Bettinger and Lion Mane wouldn't lead the smugglers to a shifter, Wade didn't like the fact that they could make a move on Maya if they learned she was here.

The cottages appeared to be suspended in the trees, a walkway connecting each to the next. Wade and his brother roamed through the trees below, listening for sounds of people up and about. Everyone appeared to be sleeping. No talking or laughing, just silence from the human population.

The jungle noises still cloaked Wade as he searched for the cottage that could be Maya's. He leaped into a tree next to a deck and smiled his jaguar smile as he smelled that Maya had been sitting in one of the rocking chairs a short while ago. There was no sign of Kat or Connor's scent on the deck, so he assumed this cottage had to be Maya's.

He glanced down at David, who motioned with his large spotted head in the direction he planned to go while Wade checked on Maya. David would leave him alone, but he knew his brother would stay close by until Wade left Maya. After that, they'd return together to search for the smugglers and their guides.

His paws muddy, Wade shifted, then turned on the shower on the deck. If she was asleep, she wouldn't hear him. After he cleaned up, he planned to check on her and tell her about Bettinger and the other men. A bottle of eco-friendly soap was sitting on a table nearby, so he poured some out into his hands and then started to soap himself down, the citrus scent pleasantly natural and sweet. He hoped she wasn't running through the jungle tonight, though he hadn't smelled her scent down below. Probably too busy dealing with her brother and explaining why she smelled of four male cats.

As soon as he had rinsed off, he saw a wide-eyed Maya staring through the glass door of her cottage, taking in every inch of him. He couldn't help his reaction. Her perusal of his body instantly made his other head stir to life. That, and what she was wearing.

A slinky, pink itty-bitty nightie barely covered her crotch. Instantly, the cool water drizzling over his body felt as though it sizzled against his suddenly hot skin. Her rigid nipples pressed against the silky fabric in response… to his arousal? He grinned at her, but she wasn't looking at his face.

He fought the urge to leave the shower, pull her close, lift that dreamy excuse for nightwear, and take her against the wooden table covered in towels nearby.

Oh… my… God. Maya couldn't help staring at Wade's gorgeous body. Bronzed. Muscles hard with vigorous workouts—the only way they could look *that* good. And he was hung. But that stunning part of his anatomy wasn't just hanging there… He was quickly becoming aroused.

What was he doing here? A shiver stole up her spine as she thought of Connor and what he'd do to Wade if her brother found him naked on her deck.

Wade's hands were rubbing soap all over that kissable, lickable skin, washing away the dirt on his feet and legs, then moving over every inch of the rest of his body. Her body heated so much that she felt that she was having a hot flash, although she was certain she was too young for one. She was standing inside the cottage, the air-conditioning on, so she shouldn't have been burning up. She continued to peer out the glass door at the incredible hunk, unable to do anything but stare.

Her gaze rose further up his body, only this time she realized she'd been seen, forgetting that she wasn't hidden from his perusal any more than he was from hers. He was grinning at her, appearing perfectly smug that he'd caught her appraising him so thoroughly. Her body's heat rose again.

She slid the door open and hurried outside, shutting the door behind her to keep the biting insects out. "What are you doing here?" she whispered, crossing the deck to the shower so that she wouldn't have to whisper so loud.

Even though Kat and Connor were probably asleep or
busy making love, and the jungle was so noisy, she still
feared her voice would carry and her brother might hear.

She glanced around, realizing that Wade must have
been a jaguar when he arrived because a pile of his
clothes wasn't on the deck anywhere.

"I had to see you," he said, his voice as hushed as hers.

"Connor will kill you if he finds you here naked on
my deck. Did you locate the smugglers?"

"Yes and no."

"Where's your brother?"

"Guard duty. Come here," he said, his blue-green
eyes dark with desire as he reached his hand out to her.

His mouth curved up as he noted the hesitation in her
expression, but the gleam in his eye said he wasn't going
to be thwarted, not when he had to know how much she
wanted to be with him.

She didn't know exactly what he had in mind. Surely,
he didn't want her to join him in the shower. She didn't
take another step in his direction. But like a jaguar that
moved without warning, he snagged her hand and pulled
her into the cool, soft spray and his hard, hot embrace.
She was still wearing her nightie! That was now wet and
plastered to her body, along with him.

Her fingers curled through his hair as his hands
molded to her bottom, pulling her tight against him, and
she instantly felt the stirring of his cock. They were kissing, the water sluicing down their faces and bodies, and
she'd never felt more sexy or alive.

She thought about his brother's comment at the club
that she and Wade could use the brothers' Houston
hotel room if they needed to, and she wanted to move

this inside—to the big king-size bed overlooking the living room.

"I want you," she said, against his mouth, knowing he wanted her just as badly. Jaguar shifters didn't mate for life. She could do this and still date others, but she had to let him know how she felt.

He stopped kissing her, looked down at her as if he was judging her sincerity, and pulled away from her a little. It was okay if he didn't want her tonight, she told herself. But she was already afraid he'd leave her alone, and she knew she'd hate it if he left. Yet she had to be honest with him.

He cast her a slow, predatory smile. "Whatever you want, Maya." He said the words with tenderness, though she suspected he hoped to change her mind.

"I want you," she repeated, running her hand down his slick naked back, all muscles and silky skin, "in bed with me. Nothing permanent."

He leaned over her and turned off the water, then looked at her nightie plastered to her skin and smiled. "You're beautiful." He tugged off the sopping wet garment and laid it over the table, then wrapped her in one of the towels stacked there. Naked, he lifted her in his arms and carried her to the door.

She didn't know why she was feeling so guilty that she was setting limits with Wade. Maybe because he seemed to want exclusivity, and she wasn't ready for it. Or maybe because deep down she was afraid he might be the one for her, and he would be turned off by her reluctance to commit to him—even for the short term. Or that she would lose her heart to him, and he, in turn, wouldn't be able to commit to her.

As they entered the cottage, the cold air blasted them so that their skin instantly wore goose bumps. Maya shivered and reminded herself that Wade had initially wanted to date Kat. So if he could become interested in Maya just as quickly, why not someone else, too?

"You're thinking too much, Maya," he said, carrying her up the steps to the bedroom before he took her into the adjoining bathroom. He set her down on the cool tile floor so she could towel-dry her hair while he snagged another towel and dried himself. He was watching her the whole time, as if he could read all the thoughts running through her mind.

She smiled then, took his hand in hers, and pulled him out of the bathroom and toward the bed. "When I first saw this bed," she said, casting a look over her shoulder at him and capturing his gaze, "I thought of you in it with me."

The duvet was already tossed aside from where she'd been sleeping before she heard Wade taking a shower. She'd thought that a mischievous monkey might have turned the faucet on.

No way had she envisioned that she'd find a naked man washing up on the wood deck—a hunk of a jaguar shifter whom she'd already fantasized about showering with there.

She released his hand and crawled into bed, while he continued to dry himself slowly, working on his hair first and showing off his exquisitely tanned body, every muscle group toned, his cock stretching out to her.

After he'd finished drying himself, he tossed the towel on the tile floor and stalked toward the bed. He climbed onto the mattress as she scooted over to allow him room. Pulling the netting around the bed shut, he half covered her body with his, like a big primal cat, as he began kissing her all over again.

The heat and sounds of the jungle surrounded their private, glassed-in cottage hideaway. The primitive, feral side of their nature thrummed in her blood as she cupped his head and kissed his mouth with desperate need and desire.

His hand slid over one breast, cupping, stroking, his thumb circling the nipple, and her breasts ached and swelled with his touch. His legs straddled one of hers, his knees spread wide as his thickening cock pressed against her hip, sliding, stroking, adding his musky male scent to her body, claiming her.

She knew he wanted her as badly as she wanted him.

No elephants trumpeted here like they did at the shifter club, and no music played as a backdrop to their heated moves this time. The only sounds were the tropical birds twittering, howler monkeys calling out to one another, and two shifters' hearts beating hard as one. Yet she felt the same heat and passion and craving between them as she'd experienced on the dance floor when he held her tight in his embrace. Clothing was all that had separated them then. Not now.

She ran her nails lightly down his muscled back like a cat in ecstasy as a low growl rumbled deep in his throat. She loved the primal sound, the connection with their feral side, and arched against his body, offering her own.

He lowered his face to lick her nipple, his hand sliding down her flat belly and making her tense with anticipation when his fingers combed through the golden curls nested between her legs and touched the knotted part of her that was sensitive and receptive. She couldn't help bending to meet the onslaught.

He looked up at her, his eyes heated, predatory, a jaguar's blue-green gaze like a shadowy jungle filled with dark secrets. She could smell his wild, musky male scent driven by ravenous desire.

She scraped her fingernails lower down his back to his buttocks.

He gave a raspy groan and slowly, deliberately ground his rigid cock against her thigh. She'd never felt this needy, craving to have his wicked flesh embedded deep inside her, moving in and out, taking her to a world of feral indulgence.

He slid a finger between her feminine folds, deep. "So wet," he whispered, licking her nipple. "So hot."

So needy, she wanted to whisper back, but she could barely breathe as he plunged two fingers into her. She was weak for him. She knew if he stopped, she would beg for more. No one had ever had such an effect on her.

His mouth was again on hers, sweet and not sweet, plundering and backing away, taking and offering. She couldn't fall for him. Not when he was her first shifter. She couldn't. But she wanted this—to quell the raging fire burning deep inside her. Just like the one he'd stoked within her when he was dancing with her at the club.

She bucked against his fingers as they stroked her, played her, and made her gasp as sprinkles of hot, white light flitted across her senses, her body's ache climaxing with guilty pleasure. Guilty because she shouldn't feel this much ecstasy from a man she hadn't given her heart to.

But she didn't want this to end.

Feeling as though Maya was a clawed wildcat beneath him, Wade fought for control, unwilling to give in to the madness he felt—the jungle fever—the desire rocking his body as she writhed and bucked at his touch.

He'd never felt this out of control. If she pushed him from her bed now, he'd have a devil of a time walking away. Her hand skimmed down his arms as he straddled her leg, his hands on the mattress as he loomed above her, the predator in him coming alive. His body demanded he finish this, that he thrust between her legs and take her for his own.

Yet some part of his brain screamed at him to wait. To come back for more when she truly wanted him and *only* him in her bed.

He growled as her lust-filled golden gaze studied him, her tongue licking her lips, her whole posture saying she was waiting, anticipating his next move.

He shook his head, trying to clear it so he could make the right choice, a human one, not a jaguar one. The jaguar in her was submitting to him. The human was not.

"Don't you dare leave me like this," she growled softly, her voice ferocious.

He fought smiling, knowing she could back up that threatening glower with deadly teeth if she decided to shift beneath him.

She lifted her head without warning and nipped his shoulder, not enough to break the skin and not in anger, but in a cat's way of courting before the mating. The fury in her eyes said she'd bite him again if he thought of moving off her. *Harder this time.*

He smiled, knowing that his expression was that of an extremely appreciative, hungry male who hadn't wanted to rein in his jaguar half. In a pure male jaguar display of ownership, he pressed his teeth gently against her neck. He pushed her legs apart with his knee, settled against her, and then thrust his cock deep between her folds in one slick move.

His mouth was alternately on hers and then sliding down her throat, licking and kissing, as her body arched to his thrusts and savage hunger drove him deeper. The smell of her—citrus fruit, orchids that she'd brushed against, and pure sex—filled him with hot need.

Her nails scored his buttocks this time and increased the intensity of the pleasure she aroused in him. He felt as though he was taking a hellcat in the jungle, surrounded by the rainforest noises—the wild animals, the bugs, the flow of a waterfall in the distance—and sweet, musky scents. The feral pleasure they took in each other was only a part of the sensations he was drowning in. He felt the tenderness, too. Her wide-eyed innocence when she'd come made him think that the humans she'd been with hadn't made her blood heat like this.

Smugly, he smiled as he kissed her again. Their tongues danced to the jungle beat of their hearts as he slid her legs around his hips and thrust again.

She was so hot, her sheath stroking him like wet velvet. When he felt her come again, he muffled her cry of release with a kiss and exploded inside her. He rocked inside her for a few seconds more, relishing the intimacy between them, before he rolled onto his back and stared up at the curtained ceiling of the bed. Hell, she might have been all wide-eyed innocence about being with a shifter for the first time, but he was feeling just as unsteady as he tucked her under his arm, her cheek against his chest, her golden hair tickling his bare skin.

For a long time, he didn't speak, just luxuriated in the satiny feel of her, breathed in her sexy scent, and enjoyed the whisper of her breath against his chest. "I wanted to swim with you in the Amazon River in the worst way," he finally said quietly, in case she'd fallen asleep.

"When?" she asked, her voice soft and caressing.

"The last time we were in the jungle together. I wanted to be the one brushing up against you instead of the pink dolphins."

"You were there?" Then she cleared her throat. "Of course you were. Guarding us. Ensuring no one sneaked up on us while we were swimming."

"I couldn't understand why you would let Connor kiss Kat."

She gave a little laugh. "I was his *sister*."

"I didn't know that then. Although in hindsight, I realized I'd never seen you being intimate with Connor. That he'd only been that way with Kat."

"You followed us to Bogota and knew exactly when we reached the hotel there, didn't you?"

"Yeah. Once you were safely on the plane, I returned to Pensacola." He stroked her silky arm, loving the citrus fragrance she'd washed with.

"What about the men you're after?"

"It's not good news. Remember Bettinger and the guy you called Lion Mane from the club?"

"Ohmigod, they are here? As jaguars? The smugglers captured them?"

Wade snorted. "They're in on it."

Maya lifted her head and stared at Wade, her eyes wide. "You're not serious."

"Yeah, I am. A couple of hunters arrived earlier. I believe Lion Mane and Bettinger are serving as the trackers. I wonder now if you did actually see them earlier at the airport. They probably planned to meet the buyer at the club before they took off. Then they saw you."

"The dark-skinned man. He was with Lion Mane and Bettinger. Maybe he was the buyer."

"I took a picture of all three of them and sent it to my boss. Hopefully, he'll be able to identify them."

She snapped her mouth shut.

"That's what I do, Maya."

"I never saw you do anything like that. Did you take a picture of me?"

He chuckled and pressed her head to rest on his chest again, loving the feeling of her soft body pressed against his. "Yeah, but only so I can keep you close."

She seemed to ponder that for a bit while her fingers caressed his abdomen. If she kept it up, he was going to want to make her come all over again.

"And the other women at our table?" Maya finally asked.

"Yeah. It's my job."

She grunted. "Did you get just a picture of their faces or of their remarkable assets, too?"

He smiled, not believing she could be serious. She had nothing to be envious about. A woman who could shift and run with him through the jungle was high on his list of preferences for a mate. The way she was so kind and caring toward Kat, protective of her, taking her in like she was her own sister, spoke volumes to him about how she was toward an extended family. And she was every bit as close to her brother as he was to his. That Maya was beautiful and had her own pair of remarkable assets only added to the package deal.

But she was so much more than that.

Even now he hated leaving her. He needed to. He should've been searching for the bad guys, not snuggling with one helluva sweet-smelling feline shifter. David would probably never let him live it down after he'd waited and waited and waited for his brother to leave her cottage.

"I took pictures of everyone," he said, "but only in regard to whether or not they might turn out to be the bad guys."

"What about me? What if I was living a secret life?"

He kissed her forehead, then rolled her onto her back and straddled her. "Then I'll have to do a little more digging to satisfy myself that you're one of the good guys."

She gave him such a wicked smile as she reached up to tug at his shoulders that he knew she was ready for further exploration.

Chapter 12

MAYA WAS ALONE. SHE SENSED IT BEFORE SHE EVEN opened her eyes. Fingers of early morning sunlight stretched through the glass windows, and like a big cat, Maya extended her arms, yawning and slowly waking.

Wade had left her without a word. She told herself he had to go before her brother discovered him here with her and that his own brother was waiting for him. That he had a job to do. But the gnawing at her gut that he'd left her without saying good-bye wouldn't quit.

Before she could yank off her covers and head for the bathroom and a thorough shower, a knock at her door and her brother's voice shook her from her thoughts, startling her. *Connor*.

"Maya, are you okay? Breakfast is served."

She groaned. If her brother smelled Wade on her—and he would if she didn't shower—he'd have a fit.

"Sorry. Overslept. Be right down."

"Hurry. They won't serve breakfast for very much longer."

She jumped into the shower, scrubbed her skin and hair good, then dressed in jeans, a long-sleeved cotton shirt, and a pair of boots and hurried down to the lodge's dining room. This time the room was filled with guests, all mostly having finished their meals.

Kat smiled brightly at her and stood to hug her.

Connor was glowering at her. Maya wanted to ask if he'd slept on the wrong side of the bed. But she knew he figured something was up with her since he had reminded her last night when he dropped her off at her cottage that they would share breakfast this morning and had specifically given her the time.

"I ordered you the tortilla stuffed with egg and cheese, skipping the onions," Connor said as they all took their seats.

"Thanks, Connor. I appreciate it."

Waffles smothered with coconut and fruit rested on Connor and Kat's plates already.

"Sorry I was late." Maya tucked the napkin onto her lap.

"Bad night's sleep?" Kat asked, seemingly oblivious to the storm building between Maya and Connor. Or maybe she was trying to defuse the situation.

One heck of a great sleep! Sex could do that for a body. Cuddling against Wade for most of the night had been wonderful. "I guess I just needed more sleep this morning." Maya avoided looking at Connor. She knew he was watching her, judging her reactions, questioning what she'd been up to.

"We saw that jaguar in the jungle again," a woman said at another table. "We were so excited, but by the time we got our camera out, he was gone."

Maya's heart did a flip. She couldn't help but look in Connor's direction. He was observing her.

Had it been Wade, leaving too late from her cottage? Or David?

Her face burned with mortification. Knowing her brother the way she did, she was certain he'd investigate around her place right after breakfast, smell that Wade and David had been there, and learn the truth.

"Are you ready to explore the jungle a bit?" Connor asked.

"Like we are now?" Maya asked. She suspected Connor meant to take them much farther away before they shifted. "I'm ready, but I need to talk to you both."

"We'll meet you at your place after breakfast," Connor said.

"I'll meet you at *your* place," Maya said.

This time Kat and Connor exchanged looks.

Okay, maybe they both already knew about her and Wade, but Kat was trying to be gracious and pretend she was clueless. Maya should have known better.

<hr>

Wade and David loped in their jaguar forms through the rainforest as they made their way back to their cabana. They could have stayed in the jungle all day, searching for the smugglers and their guides, but Wade wanted to go to the main lodge and send a message to Martin about the latest news and ship off the dagger and T-shirt wrapped around it that had been in Mylar Cranston's room.

When they reached their cabana, David went in first, shifted, and threw on a pair of boxers as Wade headed for his bedroom.

"I thought you were only going to warn her about Bettinger and Lion Mane," David said, humor lacing his words.

"Don't start with me."

"Hell, Wade, I knew you were going to get caught."

"What do you mean?"

"What do I mean?" David headed into the bathroom and shut the door. "What I mean is that the day was breaking, and you still hadn't left Maya's cottage. Does that mean she's given up on spending time with other shifters?"

"How would I know?"

"Not a certainty, eh? Maybe you should have stayed longer."

"What did *you* do?" Wade asked, taking a seat on one of the floral couches. "Sleep all night?"

"Are you kidding? I went looking for that female jaguar that had been hanging around the treetop cottages. I found her and discovered she was all jaguar and not one iota of a shifter. You know how my luck has been of late. She batted me a couple of times in playful interest and was definitely in heat. She rolled over on her back, displaying her chin and her throat, showing submission and that she was totally receptive to breeding."

Wade gave a gut-wrenching laugh.

"Yeah, laugh about it, will you? I'm trying to fight off a willing jaguaress, and you've got the real thing in a nice soft bed." The shower came on and the shower curtain rings slid across the rod as David pulled the curtain closed.

"Sorry," Wade said, still laughing.

"Yeah, sure you are."

"I'm going to run to the main lodge and tell Martin what we've learned. I'll pick us up something to eat," Wade said.

When he reached the lodge, he called Martin. "It's

Wade. Any word about who the buyer is?" Wade asked, his voice dark and dangerous. He was ready to kill a couple of shifters and the buyer, too.

The market for rare animals was similar to the drug market—if people didn't buy them, the market wouldn't exist. Unfortunately, the exotic animals market was just as profitable as selling drugs. The difference? Smuggling the animals out of their countries was illegal. Selling them was not, with the right permits. And some sellers just didn't care about the illegality as long as they were paid.

Some of the animals were near extinction. What a screwed-up world they lived in.

"No word here about the buyer. You'll need to see if you can get the information out of the men down there. Once you discover the buyer's name, we'll take it from there. And Wade?"

"Yeah?" He knew what Martin Sullivan, the director of the special elite force, was going to say even before he said it.

"Try not to kill the smugglers this time before we learn who they work for. Okay?"

Try was the operable word.

"Okay." But his boss knew the score. If the men started shooting, all bets were off.

"Maya," Connor said, opening the door to his cottage as she joined him and Kat.

She held up her hand to silence her brother. "I told you Wade and David are nearby, searching for the smugglers hunting a jaguar."

"Closer than nearby," Connor said, nearly growling as he stood next to the couch where Kat had taken a seat.

"You're right. Wade came to see me last night. Both brothers came, but only Wade spoke to me."

"I suspect more than talking was going on."

She gave him her crossest look. "He told me about two of the men we met at the club, who are at the resort where David and Wade are staying now."

Connor's frown deepened. Now she'd gotten his attention.

"The men are in on this whole operation of trying to capture a jaguar."

"Shifters are involved?" Connor said, coming away from the couch.

"Yeah. But Wade and his brother still don't know who the buyer is."

Connor paced, then turned to face her. "Do they know you?" Connor sounded both angry and worried now.

"Yeah. I danced with one of them."

Connor let out his breath in exasperation.

She frowned at him. "The other also wanted to dance with me. I didn't know they were wild jaguars."

"Wild?" her brother asked.

"That's what Wade said we're called because we return to the wild on a regular basis. It means they know how to get around the jungle, understand the dangers, and can skirt them. It also means they can help the hunters locate jaguars more easily because they can smell their trails." Then Maya had a brilliant notion. "Actually, shifters tracking the jaguars works well for all of us. Not for the jaguars, of course. But the shifters hunting them will know we're shifters, too. As soon as they smell our scent, they'll leave us alone."

Connor frowned at her. "Except that you said the one was interested in you."

Two, but she wasn't mentioning that again.

Connor walked over to the patio door and stared out at the shadowed jungle, which sported every shade of green—from emerald to olive to sage.

"I think Maya's right. Once they smell we're shifters, they'll leave us alone. No way would they want to try to hunt us and take us hostage," Kat said. "I've been too sick since we arrived to do much exploring as jaguars, but I'm feeling so much better now."

"David and Wade are searching for the men as we speak. So really there are five of us against the four men involved in trying to grab a jaguar," Maya said.

"We'll go. During the night, we can stick close to the cottages when hunters won't be about, looking for jaguars. Or at any time of day, we can head deep enough into the jungle until we can detect no human scents, and then we'll shift," Connor said.

Connor packed a backpack with bottles of water and sunscreen and insect repellent. Once they were ready, they took off into the jungle as humans, following a path for about an hour, and then headed into the dense foliage away from any human smells.

Much later, they reached their destination—dense jungle untouched by mankind. The three of them took in the beauty of the green foliage, the colorful tropical birds, and a waterfall cascading over a velvety moss-covered rock wall surrounded by green vines and giant leaves.

Maya breathed in the orchid-scented air, stretched,

and wanted to lie down and roll around on the jungle floor, gathering up the scents on her skin to relish being back in a rainforest atmosphere, to listen to the jungle sounds, and to feel one with nature, even in her human form.

Connor had been like a worried nursemaid, constantly asking if Kat was okay, but Maya was glad to see him smiling at Kat's reaction to being at home in the jaguar environment. He'd made the right decision to take Kat to the resort before she was too far along with the pregnancy. They meant to take videos of the place while they were here to enjoy later when Kat had the urge to return to the jungle and they couldn't go there. Except they couldn't capture the scents so unique to the jungle.

They climbed into a tree and began to strip, placing their clothes in the single backpack.

Maya and Kat shifted, then jumped to the ground. Connor stored the bag, tying it firmly to a branch, and then shifted and joined them.

For three nights, they returned to this spot of paradise, soaking in the sights and jungle sounds, the waterfall, the river, and stretching their legs as jaguars.

They didn't see any sign of Bettinger or Lion Mane while they stayed away from any areas where they sensed humans had been. They slept as humans half of the day in their treetop cottages. At least, Maya slept half of the day. She didn't think Kat and Connor were doing much sleeping. She hadn't seen Wade or David since she'd encountered Wade in the deck shower, but she'd felt as though the brothers were watching them sometimes from the trees, hidden, quiet, protective.

Maybe it was only wishful thinking on her part. Wade had to be busy with his work, not idly watching her while she played.

Every night after they returned from their trek, Maya silently prayed Wade would show up again at her cottage, but she was giving up hope. She couldn't quit worrying that he or David might have gotten into some kind of trouble with the hunters, though she reminded herself how vast the jungle was and how Wade and the hunters could be anywhere. And that both of the Pattersons were well trained for this kind of job.

For two nights in a row after supper when Kat and Connor were at it again in their cottage (Maya was certain the jungle did something to their libido), she went on a run as a jaguar by herself just a short distance from the cottages. The overwhelming need to see if Wade had been anywhere nearby was making her crazy. The longer she didn't see him, the more anxious she was becoming. Besides, Connor had agreed that the hunters wouldn't be out hunting at night. It would be dark soon.

She was only about two miles from the resort, not having meant to wander that far, when she heard a man shout, "The jaguar's down! We got her! Whoa, watch out for those claws! She's not out!"

Maya's heart jumped.

She… female… the jaguar that had been seen around the cottages? Maya glanced behind her. It couldn't be Kat. Unless the ones who grabbed the cat weren't shifters and didn't realize Kat was a shifter. But Kat and Connor couldn't have come looking for her yet. And Connor would have been with Kat. It had to be the non-shifting female jaguar.

Maya was afraid to go to her brother for help. What if the men took off with the jaguar, and she and her brother were too late in returning to rescue her?

Her heart drumming, all Maya could think of doing was rescuing the jaguar herself. She'd get close, then wing it.

"Holy shit! Where'd *he* come from?"

A roar met her ears. She paused. It wasn't her brother's roar. Was it David or Wade trying to rescue the female cat?

She wasn't in the Service or elite forces Golden Claw, but she damned well wasn't going to let the men take the cat from her environment. She'd kill them first.

She moved silently through the jungle, her spots rippling across her muscles and making her golden skin appear to mix and meld with the dappled leaves of the rainforest. Lifting her nose, she paused to smell the air. There was no breeze, the air perfectly still.

Dogs began to bark some distance away.

"Shoot him!" one man said.

"I don't have any more tranq darts!"

"Kill him, damn it!"

She ran full out, no longer using caution.

"Wait, got one!"

A dog yelped. The cat roared again.

A pop sounded. The cat screamed.

A chill raced along her spine. Then she got a whiff of wet smelly dog, and her hackles rose. She could easily kill a dog, though she preferred not to. They could smell her scent, and they'd probably give chase if they weren't being confined. No matter what, she had to get to the cats.

After climbing onto a branch, she leaped from one tree to another, then jumped to the ground again and ran through the dense foliage until she was close to where the men were speaking and stopped dead in her tracks. Hidden by leaves and vines and two fallen trees, she quickly scanned the area.

Beyond her hiding spot, she saw two jaguars down.

Wade Patterson. She barely breathed. He was lying on his side in his jaguar form, breathing in and out, his heart rate slow.

Anger welled up inside her, and she fought the idea of attacking the men that instant and risking all the jaguars' lives.

A female was down also, not a shifter. Not Kat. Both were drugged, their tails twitching slightly. Thank God. Not dead.

And the men—there were two of them. One she didn't know. The other—she clenched her teeth together. *Bill Bettinger*, the bastard. Dressed in camo clothes as if he was in the U.S. Army, in combat boots with a billed cap tugged tightly over red curls, he was staring at Wade as if he was trying to figure out what to do with him. He couldn't take a shifter back to the States, pretending he was a jaguar. He couldn't leave him here and remove the female from the jungle, knowing Wade had his number.

But if Bettinger killed Wade now, the other man would see Wade turn from a jaguar to a human. Dark hair fell to the hunter's shoulders, his eyes gray-blue, his clothes a more worn version of what Bettinger was wearing. He looked like bad news.

"The buyer is going to love this," the human said.

"We could sell him both cats. If he kept them for a while at his ranch, the male might breed with the female and then if she had cubs, he could have some more to hunt later. I don't blame him for feeling there's more sport in hunting a wild beast of prey rather than a deer."

Bettinger snorted with disdain. "How are the hunters going to kill the jaguars? Riding ATVs? Or are they going on foot with a bow and arrow? Not much sport if they're going to gun it down from a protected vehicle."

She was surprised to hear the pride in Bettinger's voice when he spoke about jaguars, considering he was selling them out.

The human shrugged. "They see themselves as big-game hunters. Who knows how they take down their prey? As long as the buyer pays us, that's all that matters. If he doesn't want them, we'll just sell off the cats to the highest bidder at any of the dozens of auctions across the U.S. What do I care as long as we get the money for them?"

Bettinger smiled. "To think we could still be in the drug trade, risking our necks." Then he turned icy-blue eyes from the cats to the man and said, "Mylar, I need you to leave, now. Go see to the dogs."

"But…"

"Now, damn it. Go!"

The man looked at Bettinger like he was crazy. "What are you going to do?"

"Kill the male. And *you* if you don't get your ass out of here."

"What? You're only going to take one of them? We could sell both. We could get twice the money."

Bettinger turned the rifle on Mylar. "*He's rabid.* We

can't take him with us. I'm... not... going... to... tell... you... again. *Go. Now.*"

"How do you know he's rabid? He looks fine to me."

Bettinger settled his finger on the rifle trigger, and Mylar looked back at him, his eyes rounded. Then he let out a grunt, turned, and headed in Maya's direction. She quickly crouched behind the trees, listening to his heavy footfalls as he walked past her fallen tree barrier, headed in the direction of the barking dogs.

Wade's eyes opened for a fraction of an instant, widening when he saw her through the fallen trees. He looked groggy. His eyelids dropped into narrow slits. He was too tired to be of any help in this mission. She was on her own.

Bettinger was watching the other man's progress, waiting until he was out of earshot. She was getting ready to leap from her hiding place before he shot and killed Wade, but she hesitated when Bettinger said, "What the hell are you doing out here?"

Not that Wade could reply to him in his jaguar form.

He kicked Wade in the chest.

The jaguar growled, but he was so out of it that the sound was barely audible.

Maya bared her teeth in silent protest.

"This won't do." Bettinger raised his rifle to shoot Wade somewhere less vital, but he had to know that wouldn't trigger the shift. Only a kill would. "Maybe if I shoot you somewhere that'll hurt but won't be fatal, you'll want to talk? Tell me why you're here? I don't believe in coincidences. You must be in the Service. You and your brother. The other guys, too, that you were with at the club? Hell. Forget wounding you. Too bad for you that you weren't better at your job. I thought the Service only hired the best."

His finger moved to the trigger again as Maya roared and leaped for the kill.

Chapter 13

A SHOT RANG OUT. A THUNK SOUNDED AS THE BULLET hit something. Ignoring the gunshot, Maya didn't take her focus off Bettinger. She slammed against him with her huge jaguar paws planted on his chest. He fell back with a strangled cry. Eyes wide, his expression was full of disbelief and fear. Jaguars in the wild didn't stick together, unless they were a mother and her cubs. Then she'd protect them with her life. Full-grown jaguars? No way. So he hadn't anticipated another jaguar's attack.

Flat on his back, he smelled her and his lips parted in shock. He *knew* who she was.

"Let me shift," he begged as she stood on top of him, pinning him down. "Give me a chance."

A growl rumbled in her throat. Like he was going to give Wade a chance? And the female cat? The jaguar wasn't going to be allowed to live, but hunted to the death on someone's ranch.

And if Maya gave the bastard a chance, if she allowed him to shift to fight her that way, he'd be bigger and could easily kill her instead.

Bettinger knew Maya planned to eliminate him. She didn't have any choice. If she let him up, he'd fatally shoot Wade and her. They knew he was involved now, and he couldn't risk letting them live.

She growled softly, her face close to his, smelling his fear but unable to decide what to do with him. Killing humans who were out to murder them had to be done with finesse. If she terminated Bettinger in a jaguar way, crushing the head with her powerful jaws, investigators would know a jaguar had killed him. Then hunters would descend on the area to destroy the jaguar, which could mean any that they came across. They were all the same, after all.

"Hey!" a man shouted from behind her.

Her skin prickled with fear. Hell, the other man had come back.

"Shoot her!" Bettinger shouted, panic driving his words.

That's when she felt Bettinger pull a gun from a holster at his side, realizing he'd only pretended to be panicked to distract her. She didn't hesitate this time. It was kill or be killed.

And she had two killers to contend with now.

She swiped at Bettinger's head with a powerful slash of her paw. He dropped the gun, his head turned hard to the right, his neck broken, his eyes staring but unseeing.

She whipped around to target the other man, the hunter who was ready with a rifle aimed at her. Wade growled softly, and Mylar turned as if afraid the other jaguar—*the rabid one*—was ready to eat him alive. He wasn't. Poor Wade was struggling to lift his head off the leaf-littered ground.

But his action had given her the precious time she needed to take care of the other man.

She leaped, trying out Kat's unusual way of landing on the prey's head, and it worked. When her body slammed onto his head, he dropped like a rock and hit the ground hard. His neck was broken. She sniffed Mylar for any sign of a breath, listened for a heartbeat. Nothing.

Now what was she to do? Lion Mane was most likely still in the area, and maybe even more of the men who were working with these bastards were around.

Wade was too drugged to leave the area under his own speed, and she couldn't move a cat as big as he was all on her own. The female couldn't be left alone like this, either. Not in the lethargic condition she was in.

Wade opened his eyes again, looking at her. If she could find his brother, David could help. She had no idea where he was but suspected he might be following Lion Mane and the others.

She stood as still as a spotted statue. Not even her tail was swishing as she considered her options in the shadowed jungle, listening for any sounds that would indicate men were approaching. Her heart was pumping hard and her body felt overheated. Unable to sweat like a human could, she began to pant, the only way for a cat to cool off.

She moved in close to Wade and bent down to nuzzle his cheek. She licked it, trying to get him to stand and shake off the drug. He sat up and shifted into one gorgeous naked hunk of a human male.

"Go," he said, his voice dark, deep, and… sleepy.

She shook her head and nudged at him to climb a tree. He struggled to get into one, and it was almost painful watching him climb the liana—a drainpipe-thick vine-like plant—slipping and scrambling for purchase and pausing to catch his breath, as if every movement was the most wearing. When he reached the first branch off the ground, he shifted back into his jaguar form. Couldn't he have jumped up there more easily as a cat? Was he too out of it to be thinking clearly?

Now what to do with the female jaguar? Maya tore a liana with her teeth and dragged the plant over to the sleeping jaguar, allowing the water dripping from inside the plant to fall on her face. The liana was a common source of water for survival, pure and cleansed as it was filtered by the plant. If Maya could revive the cat enough, she'd have another reason to revere the life-giving source.

Wake up, she pleaded in her jaguar brain. If she could just get the jaguar to wake enough, she could attempt to move her away from the area where the dead men were lying. *The dead men*. She needed to deal with them, too. The female jaguar's tongue licked at the water droplets on her face, but she didn't sit up.

Wade was watching her, his head resting on the branch as if he couldn't lift it.

Maya jumped onto the branch next to him, and they stayed there until he seemed to be able to gather more strength and leaped to another tree farther from where she'd killed the men.

Then she had another horrible thought. What if Connor and Kat came to her cottage and found her gone? What if they both came looking for her here?

She had to get Wade to her cottage before they came for her and got caught in the crossfire. If Lion Mane came, he'd know just who she was, and he'd smell Wade's scent, too.

Connor and Kat always rendezvoused with Maya at her cottage at night, but he and Kat had taken a little more time than usual so he was late arriving at Maya's place.

He knocked on her front door. "Maya?"

At first he was thought she was with Wade, but he heard no sounds coming from inside her room. He didn't think Wade had come back for her since that night he'd visited her. She had never told Connor that Wade had been with her, but Connor knew, just from her blushes and Wade's scent on her deck.

He'd also seen the way she'd watched for Wade when they were exploring the rainforest, looking for any signs that he was nearby. A couple of times, Connor had thought Wade was following them, watching their backs, being protective like he'd been when they were in the Amazon.

Connor paced in front of the door, then knocked again. "Maya!"

When there was still no response, he went around to her deck. He smelled that she'd been here recently, but the trail led down into the jungle. He opened the door to her cottage and quickly searched the place.

Maya *wasn't* there. She had obviously decided to take a run through the jungle by herself while he and Kat had been busy making love. *Again*. He wasn't happy about Maya exploring the jungle on her own. He understood Maya's restlessness and the fact that she probably was feeling like a third wheel. And that being this close to the jungle pulled on their wild-cat urges.

Back at his cottage, he found Kat straightening up their bed and said, "Stay here and wait for Maya to return, Kat. I'm going to look for her."

"She's gone again?"

"Yeah, like last night. I'll be right back."

"Can't I come with you this time?" Kat asked.

"No. I don't want to worry about you being out there

if she's gotten herself into trouble. Stay here and I'll return soon."

He kissed her and hugged her tight, knowing she didn't want to be left alone. Last night, Maya hadn't been far from the cottages. He hoped he'd find the same thing tonight.

Returning to Maya's deck, he removed his clothes and shifted in a blur of tanned skin to golden fur, nails to claws, and much bigger teeth. Then he leaped from the deck and took off to find her most recent trail. She'd been exploring the jungle in a happy-go-lucky way as they usually did, carving her nails into a tree, rubbing off strands of fur on another, but then her path and the scent she left changed.

That had him worried. Dogs were barking somewhere in the distance as he moved a mile away from the cottages.

Then he smelled Wade and the other female jaguar. What the hell?

And the odor of men. Two of them.

He could tell from Maya's scent that she was terrified. The men had to be hunting the jaguars. Connor was trying to keep a clear head where Maya was concerned, but his blood was racing through his veins, his heart pumping hard as he feared for Maya's safety.

He moved through the jungle, smelling the ground and low tree branches, sniffing the air. Unable to contain himself, he roared for Maya.

She immediately responded, her jaguar's roar sounding like music to his ears.

He'd covered another mile from when he heard her roar and discovered two dead men with Maya's scent

all over them. He looked more closely at a place on the
ground where a jaguar had lain, his body pressing the
grasses down into a mat, and smelled the scent—Wade
Patterson's. A female jaguar was still sleeping on the
ground nearby.

His heart hammered his ribs. Where the hell was
Maya? And Wade?

—⁓—

Maya had been so relieved to hear Connor's roar that
she let him know just where she and Wade were hiding.
Her brother would help get Wade to the resort, and then
she could assist Connor in moving the dead men and
hiding the jaguar female until she revived enough to take
care of herself.

Everything would be all right.

Before she could tell Connor where they were
again—she thought he probably had been sidetracked
as he checked out the dead men—she saw him staring
up at her and Wade as they sat on the tree branch together above him. Well, Wade was reclining, unable to
sit. Tension filled every one of Maya's muscles as she
worried about her brother's reaction.

Connor just waited, as if he was thinking she should
come with him now. Connor grunted at her. She licked
Wade's cheek, although Wade didn't take his eyes off
Connor. The two jaguars were ready to do battle. If
only Connor knew how unable Wade was to fight in his
current condition.

She jumped off the tree branch and landed next to
Connor. He nudged her as if telling her to return to her
cottage, but she nudged at him to go with her instead.

He followed her, and she led him back to Mylar and then pawed at the gun that the man had used to tranquilize Wade and the other cat. She waited for Connor to get it. She moved away from the dead man and pawed at the earth where Wade had been sleeping.

Connor sniffed at the ground, then stared at her.

He got it. Wade was not in any shape to help himself. She bolted back to the tree where Wade still waited for them, too drugged to move.

This time when Connor joined them, he shifted and folded his arms across his chest, looking up at Wade. "I take it you're too tired to move much at all."

Wade bowed his head.

Connor shook his. "I can't carry you. What do you want to do? Stay here until you're more yourself?"

Maya grunted at him.

Connor looked down at her, scowling. "You aren't staying out here with him all night. What if more men return to hunt down the cat that killed those men?"

They just might. That's what she was worried sick about! Lion Mane was still unaccounted for. She wasn't leaving a drowsy big cat out here to fend for himself. And Connor needed her help disposing of the dead men and helping the female cat to find shelter until she could safely leave the area.

"Maya," Connor said, exasperated. "You've got to come with me."

Maya glanced in the direction of the resort. She wasn't leaving Wade no matter what Connor wanted.

"Hell, Maya. All right, stay with him. I'll get us some clothes and we can carry him back to your place. Don't get caught."

She licked his hand, then jumped into the tree. He watched her for a moment, gave Wade a growly look, then shifted and tore off through the jungle.

She'd known her brother would come up with a solution. With tension filling every muscle, she reclined on the branch with Wade, hoping that they didn't encounter more trackers, the hunters, or any other humans. Or that anyone would find the dead bodies.

She thought they were relatively safe up in the well-shielded tree, but Wade appeared anxious, despite being so lethargic. He kept lifting his head, trying to turn, his tail twitching. She was apprehensive, too, and jumped down from the tree. Pacing between the two dead men, she wanted to move them to their final resting place, a nearby river. The crocodiles and piranhas filling the river ought to take care of the spoils of war.

Two rivers converged not too far south of here. She'd drag Bettinger, the shifter, there first. She gently bit into the gun belt strapped diagonally across Bettinger's chest and began to drag him over the rainforest floor. She was pissed off at the man for being one of their kind and leading hunters to jaguars. Not to mention that he'd planned to kill both Wade and her.

Wade grunted at her, sounding like he wanted her to stay. She couldn't, in the event someone came along who was investigating what had happened to the men. She also couldn't leave all this for Connor to handle. The quicker they took care of it, the better.

She heard water running over debris at the edge of the river some distance from her. A *woof* made her remember the dogs! She growled under her breath. She and Connor had to free them, too. They couldn't leave the dogs tied up where another predator could kill them, yet she wasn't sure how they'd manage that as the dogs would want to chase after the cats.

Dragging the body with her, she didn't think she'd ever reach the first of the rivers. She waited, watching for any signs of movement—people boating or swimming or fishing. Not this late at night. Unless it was a jaguar fishing.

If she had a flashlight, she could shine it over the water and see the red glow in the crocodiles' eyes. She heard something slither nearby and a splash.

Shit! She was bringing the crocs dinner, but she didn't want to be on the menu.

Chapter 14

CONNOR COULD NOT BELIEVE THE DANGEROUS MESS his sister was in. As stubborn as Maya was, he knew he couldn't budge her from protecting Wade and the other cat. Which put her in even more danger.

Now he'd have to face another female cat who was just as stubborn and would be just as much of a problem when he wanted to take care of this on his own.

"You're not going with me," Connor said as soon as he'd dressed on Maya's deck and found Kat waiting there for his and Maya's return.

The fact that he was alone said volumes.

"What's happened?" Kat said, her brows knit in a tight frown.

"Maya's in trouble. Wade, too. The female jaguar roaming around in our territory has been tranquilized, along with Wade in his jaguar form. There are two dead hunters in the vicinity." He rushed back to their cottage for a pair of drawstring pants for Wade, Kat hot on his heels.

"Of course I'm coming," Kat said, sounding annoyed.

He scowled at her over his shoulder as he pulled a pair of pants out of his drawer for Wade. "You're pregnant. It's too dangerous."

"Maya can't manage by herself. *You* can't manage this all alone, either. I'm going with you." She tucked her dark hair behind her ears, folded her arms, and looked about as furious with him as she could.

"I love you," Connor said frowning, "and I don't want you to come with me." She smiled so brightly that he groaned. "Kat, I really want you to stay." From her stubborn expression, he knew Kat wasn't changing her mind.

"We have to run the whole way back. The men were hunters. There are bound to be more of them. They've got dogs."

"I'll keep up."

"All right. Shift. It's the only way you're going."

She started to strip out of her clothes. As a jaguar, she could move even faster than he could. "Stay close to me."

She nodded. Once her blurred form had shifted into a jaguar resting on all paws, he hurried out to the deck. He climbed down the ladder, while she leaped from the deck. Then they were off.

God, he hoped they'd get back before anything else could happen.

Wade couldn't believe it when he saw Maya come to his rescue, saw the feral look in her eyes when she pounced on Bettinger. He nearly had a heart attack when he heard the hunter return and shout at her, trying to distract her before she killed the jaguar shifter.

With the utmost difficulty, Wade had lifted his head and growled, attempting to get the hunter's attention before he shot Maya, giving her just enough time to attack the human. After that, he'd had virtually no strength except to somehow manage to get into the tree.

Wade knew when she left him alone in the tree that she intended to get rid of Bettinger's body before anyone came looking for him. Wade hadn't wanted her to go. If she was caught dragging Bettinger's body off, she'd be hunted down. All of them would. Not that she wouldn't be killed if she was found here with a couple of dead men.

Connor was taking too long. Where the hell was he?

And Maya hadn't yet returned. He knew the river wasn't far off, but dragging a 175-pound man had to be slowing her down.

The dogs began to bark again. Someone or something had to be in the vicinity where they were tied up or caged.

He wanted to roar for Maya, to warn her that someone could be coming, but he knew she could hear the dogs as well as he could. Roaring would draw unwanted attention. Wade didn't want anyone investigating this location, not when he was half dead to the world, with the other man dead on the ground and the female jaguar sleeping like the dead.

Maya was so quiet, blending in so beautifully with the foliage, that at first he didn't see her return. Her spots rippled like a river current as she stalked toward the site. She glanced up at him, and he felt welcome relief that she was fine.

She listened, ears twitching, eyes focused on the direction her brother had taken, tail slashing the air back and forth, back and forth.

He was certain she was trying to decide whether to move the second body or wait until her brother arrived. He wanted her to stay. Not having a crystal ball, he couldn't know what the best option really was. But he wanted to keep her in his sights.

Then he heard voices in the distance where the dogs were, and his heart did a triple jump.

Maya didn't hesitate. She grabbed the human by his gun belt and began dragging him toward the river. If she managed to get him away from the female jaguar and Wade, the hunters wouldn't likely find them, not as dark as it was now.

Lion Mane was the problem. He could follow the dead men's scents and know not only that Maya had moved them but also where she'd taken them.

The brush rustled nearby, and he cocked his head to peer harder. Hell, it was *Kat* in her jaguar form. Where was Connor?

Maya was thinking a mile a minute. The human was just as heavy as Bettinger had been, and although she was able to dump Bettinger in the river, she didn't think she could do the same with this one.

"Bettinger!" a man yelled. "Mylar!"

Breathing suspended, she paused. The man shouting was still near the barking dogs.

She was struggling to drag the body toward the river when she saw a flash of golden fur and black rosettes in the plants nearby. *Kat*.

Glad it wasn't Lion Mane in jaguar form, Maya took a relieved breath. She released her hold on the body, ran across the dead man's chest, and greeted Kat. The two rubbed whiskers, then they worked together to drag the body to the river. A croc snapped near Maya, and she let go of the dead man and whipped around. It looked to be about thirteen feet in length but was no match for her powerful bite.

His long leathery needle-nose jaws snapped again at

her while she hopped back and forth, keeping her distance until she could go for the head and avoid his razor-sharp teeth. With a well-aimed pounce, she grabbed his head with her mouth and crushed his skull, tossing him aside to help Kat finish hauling the human to the dark river where he would be piranha and croc bait.

The crocs in Belize normally didn't attack humans, and like jaguars, they had a tendency to ambush prey at night, stalking them in the water. But when it came to fighting jaguars? No contest.

Kat rubbed against Maya's side, and the two licked each other's muzzles in camaraderie again. Then they turned and raced back to the site where the female jaguar and Wade were, and where Maya's brother had undoubtedly arrived by now.

When they reached the site, Connor had already hefted a sleepy female jaguar into denser brush. She was beginning to stir.

They would wait and protect her until she was awake enough to take care of herself. Then Maya saw Connor below the tree where Wade was resting, watching all of them.

Connor looked stern—worried, too. He'd hastily dressed in khaki pants and a long-sleeved shirt and his thick, sturdy boots. All he'd brought for Wade was a pair of black drawstring pants.

When Connor's gaze turned from hers to the half-asleep jaguar shifter, she swore her brother muttered a curse. He still didn't like the man, but she hoped her brother would come around.

The problem was that jaguar males were totally territorial. Connor didn't have male friends. It wasn't part of his nature. She suspected Connor would not be happy about any male crossing the line into his perceived territory. Even if the male was on their side. She hoped that Connor could overcome it enough that when she took a mate, he'd get along with him.

She sighed.

Connor said to Wade, "I take it you're Wade Patterson. Come on. Wake up and get dressed."

Looking groggy, Wade stared at Connor before turning his attention on Maya. He gave her a sleepy grin. Then he grunted at Connor.

Not a great start to developing a super family relationship.

Kat stayed back away from the situation to keep from stirring things up between the two males.

Maya jumped onto the branch and licked Wade's face, greeting him in a jaguar way. She shouldn't have done so in front of Connor because she knew it aggravated him, but she did it to try and stir Wade into action.

Wade smiled, showing off those great teeth that could take down an adversary or dinner, and nudged her face with his nose in a mutually caring greeting back.

"Come on, shrug it off," Connor ordered, sounding like he was ready to shift and knock the male cat from the tree. "Don't make me come up there to get you."

Maya was certain that Wade would have shifted already if he could. His lethargy was holding him back.

Finally, Wade shifted and she tried not to look at his nakedness again. Well, not really hard. He *was* glorious, all sleek muscles and sinewy strength, powerful even in human form.

Connor scowled at him. "You could have leaped down from the tree branch first."

That proved how much difficulty Wade was having in processing what he needed to do. He shifted back into his cat form, looking virile. He glanced at Maya as if feeling a little guilty that he was being so thick-headed. She sympathized, hating that he was feeling so out of it.

He licked her face as if wanting to annoy Connor and let her know he was interested in her, and then he leaped to the ground, forcing Connor to step back. He did it on purpose! She knew it and smiled. Touché! Wade was showing his alpha-ness even in his drugged state.

She didn't expect Connor to offer a slow, easy smile that said he was impressed with the big cat's reaction. Maya took a settling breath and stayed where she was until Wade shifted, slumping on his bare butt on the ground. Connor tossed his extra pair of pants on Wade's lap. "Get dressed. We've got to get back to the resort."

Poor Wade. He looked like a sloppy drunk who was trying to get a foot into one of the pant legs, the wrong pant leg, and wasn't making any progress. Connor watched him for what had to be the longest amount of time he could stand, glanced up at Maya, then shook his head as if to say, "The things I do for you."

Connor reached down to tug the correct pant leg over each of Wade's big feet.

She tried not to watch. Really she did. The whole scenario was almost comical.

Thankfully, Kat had left the show to watch over the female jaguar nearby.

Connor cinched the drawstring and offered Wade a

hand up. Wade didn't appear to have the strength to hold on to Connor's hand firmly enough.

"Fireman's carry," Connor said, not asking a question but stating a fact.

The significance was not lost on her or on Wade, as she could tell from his brief nod. Connor could have just grabbed him and thrown him over his shoulders, but he was giving him the respect of telling him what he intended to do first.

"Maya?" Connor said, glancing up at her.

She jumped down from the branch and stood next to him on the ground and rubbed his leg in a way of showing gratitude.

"Kat?" Connor added.

Kat grunted as the female jaguar rose to her feet, shook off the effects of the drug a little, and sauntered groggily away.

Then Kat and Maya led the way back to the resort while Connor hoisted Wade over his shoulders.

"Thanks," Wade said, his voice dark and slurred.

"I owe you one," Connor said.

They owed him more than that as he'd helped them out more than once. It was about all Connor could manage, considering how much he disliked another male invading his territory.

"Didn't... know... Maya... sister," Wade managed to get out.

"Save your breath," Connor said, annoyed.

Maya wanted to hear what Wade had to say and gave Connor a quelling look.

"Thought... Kat... shifter... too."

Connor snorted.

"Did," Wade said as gruffly as he was able. "Couldn't… have… two," Wade said, forcing the words out.

Maya looked back to see her brother's expression.

Connor frowned at her. "Sleep," Connor said to Wade, his word a command. "We'll talk later when I know the drug's not speaking for you."

Maya continued to move through the jungle on silent cat paws, Kat running beside her, believing Wade had succumbed to sleep. Until he said, "Not… drug."

She caught Connor's elusive smile.

Wade. Alpha male all the way. He wouldn't let Connor command him or have the last word either, no matter how worn out he was.

She loved her brother. He could be as hardheaded as the rest of them, but he still had a heart of gold. And Wade, well, tonight she definitely wanted to keep him close.

When she reached the tree where she'd hidden her clothes, she jumped onto the branch, climbed higher until she was on the branch where her clothes were stashed, and then shifted and began to dress. She said in a low voice, "Go, take him back to the resort."

Connor shook his head.

Stubborn man, but protective. He wasn't letting her out of his sight until he had her back at the cottage. Kat wasn't leaving her, either.

"I'm staying with him at my cottage," she warned Connor. She would take care of Wade. She wanted to ask him so many questions… when he was awake enough to respond. She had to know where his brother was. She was certain Wade was just as concerned about David and his whereabouts.

"No," Connor said.

She had expected Connor to say no, but she wasn't going along with it. "Okay, so he stays with you and Kat?"

Connor grunted. "Hurry up, Maya."

"I'm hurrying!" She pulled her shirt over her head. "Or Kat and I can bunk together, and you can sleep with Wade."

Chapter 15

"GET REAL, MAYA," CONNOR TOLD KAT.

She stifled a laugh. She could just imagine the two large men sharing a bed, fighting over the covers, and shoving each other away if one encroached on the other's side of the mattress. She laughed this time because the image proved just too precious.

Dressed and ready to return to the cottages, she climbed down from the tree and looked at Wade's sleeping face.

"Okay, so what is the plan?" she asked, as if letting Connor rule the roost, although he wasn't. Not this time.

He didn't say as they continued to walk through the thick vegetation until they saw the first of the cottages, Kat's and Connor's. Kat leaped onto their deck, shifted, and slipped inside the cottage. She reappeared wearing only a long pale-blue T-shirt.

The first thing out of Kat's mouth was, "Is he okay?"

That got a disgruntled grunt from Connor. Maya was sure that wasn't the question he wanted from Kat. Not when he was feeling somewhat unsettled about her interest in another jaguar.

Kat cast Connor an annoyed look and folded her arms. "You know, if you're always going to be worried about me and other men, *you've* got a problem. *Deal* with it." Then she stalked smartly inside their cottage and slammed the door with a resounding *thunk*.

"Hmm," Maya said.

"Don't say a word, Maya," Connor warned as he made his way with Wade through the jungle to Maya's deck.

"You know she has a point."

He gave his sister a cutting look. She tilted her head to the side. "So you stay with Wade, and I stay with Kat, and we have an all-night girl party where we dish impossible alpha males. *Or* you can go to bed with Kat and make it up to her, and I'll…"

"You're not going to bed with Wade Patterson, damn it, Maya."

She sighed. "I didn't say I was." Not that it was any of her brother's business. "But I want to talk with him." They climbed the steps to her deck. She unlocked the back door, and they walked inside. "We'll be fine. He's too sleepy to be any trouble."

As if they hadn't been there before.

Connor carried Wade up the stairs to her bed and dumped him on the mattress, rough enough to see if the guy really was sleeping or just playing possum.

Wade didn't stir a muscle and appeared to be out for the count.

Connor turned his hard gaze on Maya. "You tell me the minute he wakes. All right?"

She nodded. She would, truly. But there was awake and there was awake. As long as Wade had a hint of sleep about him, she wasn't calling Connor.

Besides, she knew how Connor would make it up to Kat. Maya wasn't about to interrupt them. Despite what he thought he wanted, she was certain Connor wouldn't appreciate it if she ran over to their cabin and stopped them in the middle of getting heavy and hot to tell him Wade was awake.

She could imagine Kat being angry with Connor all over again. And with Maya this time, too.

——∿∿∿——

When Wade woke enough from his drowsy state to have some idea of his surroundings, he felt a woman's arm draped over his naked waist as he lay in a soft, white bed, a ceiling fan spinning above. He was lying on his side, his back to her chest, when he took a deeper breath and breathed in her sweet scent.

Maya.

He turned to look at her. Her blond hair spilled over her bare shoulders and her breasts were naked, her nipples rosy. An ice-white sheet was draped over their waists and legs.

She was sound asleep, her breathing even, her expression peaceful.

His heart was hammering a hundred miles a minute. How, where… what was he doing naked here in bed with… he felt her bare leg touching the back of his… a very nude Maya?

Sunlight pressed against the sheers over the expansive windows in the living room, covering three walls, and he realized it had to be early afternoon. He didn't want Maya having to explain why he was here, should Connor come pounding on her door. Hell, what *was* he doing here?

"Maya," he whispered, wanting to be here with her like this as much as she obviously did with him. But the last memories he had were of tracking Bettinger and his hunter minion in the jungle, hearing they'd taken down the female jaguar, and rushing to her rescue.

Maya opened her eyes, looking sleepy and sexy and cuddly.

"Hmm," she said, and tried to snuggle closer against him.

"Maya," he whispered, turning onto his back, pulling her into the crook of his shoulder, and stroking her long, silky hair. Then he recalled having been shot. He vaguely remembered a growly Connor helping him into a pair of sweatpants. After that, nothing.

He wasn't wearing them now. He suspected he'd removed them sometime during the night, not used to wearing anything in bed. Or… he looked down at Maya… she had removed them.

He leaned over and kissed her, just a sweet brush of his lips against her sexy mouth. Not expecting her to respond, he was startled when she reacted as if she was starved for affection, kissing him back, sliding on top of him, and molding to him.

She was kissing him so frantically that he suspected something was wrong. "Maya." He tried disengaging from her, pushing her shoulders back gently so that he could see her expression.

Her eyes were filled with tears, and she looked stricken.

"Maya," he said consolingly and pulled her close against his body. She sobbed against his chest, her tears falling freely on his bare skin. "It's okay. We're okay."

"You could have been killed," she choked out, her hand clenched in a fist against his waist.

She could have been killed, and he would never have forgiven himself.

"I… would never have seen you again," she said, swallowing hard.

He drew her clenched hand to his mouth, kissing her fingers until she spread them like a flower opening its petals. Then she cupped his face, her teary eyes gazing into his. She lowered her mouth to his, and this time they kissed slow and hard, her tongue in his mouth, his in hers. Her hands slid over his hair, her body pressed fully against his.

He combed his fingers through her silky tresses as their kissing went back to soft and gentle. He swept his hands down her back and felt her shiver a little, then reached down to spread her legs for him as the hunger for her reared up inside him.

Tears clung to her lashes like dewdrops as she sat up, straddling him, her mouth curving up, her breath coming quickly, her breasts heaving. Her skin was golden all over, her nipples mouthwatering pink rosebuds. The golden curls between her legs pressed against his darker hair, his erection stiff and resting against her belly.

His whole body was tense with need, and he wanted to roar like a jaguar calling for his mate. With her hand, she stroked his cock, making him growl with pent-up desire. His hands slid up her thighs, his thumbs parting her feminine lips, and she groaned as she rubbed her sex against his erection. One of his thumbs flicked against her clit, and she arched back with a gasp. He slid into her with a well-placed thrust.

Seeing their bodies joined together turned his blood into a molten torrent. Guiding her with one hand, he thrust inside her, his free hand rubbing her sweet spot as he drank in her delicious scent of wild cat and citrus.

With her skin flushed, her body toned and tanned, she was beautiful. He didn't think he'd ever seen a lovelier sight as they made love among the white bed linens. The mesh surrounding the bed created the feel of a screened pleasure dome in the jungle cottage. The monkeys howled in the rainforest as birds twittered, insects buzzed, and a gentle fall of rain pattered on the thatched roof.

Breathing hard, their skin covered in light perspiration, he sped up his thrusts, digging into the soft mattress with his heels. He felt her climax drawing near, the tension in her body, and the shudders of her core clenching around his cock and rocketing with orgasm. She groaned with pleasure, and he reveled in the sound of her passionate response.

Before he came, he quickly rolled her over onto her back and continued to pump into her, kissing that sweet mouth of hers and reveling in the scent and the feel of her. He wanted the sweet ecstasy of joining with her to last forever. For the moment, she was *his*, body and soul, and he didn't want to give her up for anything or *anyone*.

Wade moved Maya's legs over his shoulders for deeper penetration, and she loved it. Loved him. As their hearts pounded like the steady beat of the rain on the roof, he rubbed his body against hers, covering her with his scent, claiming her. Thrusting into her with his face taut with concentration, he drove into the very core of her.

The heated look in his gaze intensified as he captured her mouth with his, plunging in with his tongue. She was lost to him, despite wanting to keep some semblance of balance. To keep her heart intact. But how could she when this felt so right? So perfect? So damned good?

He ground his body against hers and twisted, the sensation of him buried deep inside of her making her want more... making her need more.

He whispered her name against her lips, a half groan, desperate and resolute. Her hands swept down his back, feeling his muscles hard at work as he pleasured her and pleasured himself.

Her touch seemed to propel him on as he thrust deeper into her. Her lips parted as she tried to catch her breath, the sensation of him rubbing against her clit pushing her to the edge. As if he saw her open mouth as an invitation, he licked her lips, then thrust his tongue into her mouth again with feral abandon.

With primal need, she felt the erotic sensation of his tongue pushing into her mouth, casting her over the edge again, and she cried out his name, her word absorbed by the wild jungle sounds all around them.

His eyes were nearly black as he drove into her again and again. Then with one final plunge, he groaned his satisfaction, his warm seed filling her. He lay there quietly for a moment on top of her, breathing hard, capturing her, not making a move to let her go.

Some part of her reveled in that notion, and for now, she gave herself up freely to the sensation.

Feeling satiated and drowsy, she dropped her legs away from his shoulders, his cock still buried in her as he licked her breast, then took her taut nipple between his teeth and teased it with a gentle nibble, as if he wasn't quite ready to let her go yet. Then he kissed the top of her head.

"Maya," he said finally with the utmost tenderness, and she felt the tears collect in her eyes again. Bettinger could have killed him.

Wade gazed into her eyes, saw the tears gathered there, and brushed her cheek with his fingertips. "We're all right, Maya." He slid off her and took her into his arms. Together they snuggled in silence.

Maya was annoyed with herself for falling apart over what could have happened. She wanted him to enjoy sex with her and to help relieve some of the tension she'd felt ever since she'd discovered the trouble he was in. The danger all of them had been in.

She hadn't meant to get all teary-eyed over it when they first began kissing. Or now, all over again. She loved his gentleness when he seemed to understand and hadn't pushed her away. Ha! He'd conquered her, making her feel desired above all else, forcing her to reconsider seeing anyone other than him. She had to admit he was doing one hell of a job of convincing her!

Wade let out his breath. "I wanted to be close to you again like this, but not at peril to you, Maya, which was why I'd fought staying away from you—unsuccessfully."

She smiled a little.

"Whenever I couldn't find the shifters who were trying to capture a jaguar, I slipped off the beaten path to find you and your family." He stroked her arm. "I told myself I did so to watch your backs, which was true to an extent, but… I loved seeing the three of you as jaguars at play. It reminded me of my brother and me." He chuckled. "You and Kat would both gang up on Connor as he was nosing around at the scents on the ground and suddenly tackle him, and I had to stifle the urge to laugh out loud."

She smiled up at him. "You should have joined us."

Instead, Wade had envisioned himself being the alpha male and deliciously tormented by two female cats. What he wouldn't have given to be the one Maya was pouncing on, playing with, growling, batting, and biting. But he hadn't wanted her in danger. He took a deep breath and kissed the top of her head again.

"You never said what happened to your father," Maya said, her fingers making little circles on his chest.

"He finally came to terms with his grief, realized his sons were gone, then sought to reunite with us. He's proud of what we do but still regretting that he'd left us to our own devices when our mother was killed." Wade combed his fingers through Maya's satiny hair, loving the feel of it, loving the feel of her, loving the way she touched him.

"Hmm, I seem to recall there was some mention of the two of you getting yourselves into hot water," she murmured.

Wade caressed her shoulder, stroking her soft skin and smiling reminiscently. He chuckled a little.

"So?" she said.

"Nothing that bad. Okay, so one time we took it upon ourselves to leap off a bridge."

"As humans or jaguars?"

"Humans. As jaguars, we would have gotten into a lot more trouble."

"I take it you weren't injured," she said, looking up at him with those golden eyes that could stop his thoughts as he gazed into their crystal depths.

"No, but the third time, we got caught."

She shook her head. "You'd think you'd learn."

"We didn't get caught the other times."

"And after you got caught? You didn't do it again, did you?"

"Not at *that* bridge."

She chuckled. "I can see that you and your brother have an incorrigible streak."

"That's what our boss said when he took us on, but he said he was still hopeful he'd knock it out of us."

She laughed. "What else?"

"Are you sure you want to hear any more?"

"Yeah, I'd like to know what I'm getting into."

Wade chuckled. "I think I could really fall for you." He already had. Any woman who would come to his rescue without regard for her own safety had to be the one for him. How many jag shifters could claim they had a woman like that in their corner?

She smiled up at him, her eyes gazing into his, and she wasn't pulling away from him. Maybe she thought he was kidding.

"All right. Then there was the time David and I needed to withdraw some money from the bank, but he wouldn't come in because one of the bank tellers had the hots for him and he was afraid of her. So he sent me in instead. Guy at the next teller handed a deposit slip to her, and her skin turned pasty. The guy growled under his breath, 'Do it.'"

"He was attempting to rob the bank?" Maya asked, wide-eyed.

"Yeah. I could have used David's help. I glanced around to see if anyone else might be with this guy, and sure enough, another man was standing near the door, watching a security guard and looking nervous, his hand tucked in his jacket like Napoleon."

"You shouldn't have done anything. All they wanted was the money. Right?"

"Right. And I wouldn't have done anything heroic, worrying someone might get killed. Me, even. The robber near me growled, 'Now, lady, or you're dead.' About that time, my brother walked into the bank. I thought he believed I was taking too long, but I should have known better."

"He knew."

"Yeah, saw the getaway car, called the police, and came in to help me, in case I planned any heroics. I really didn't."

She smiled, looked down at his chest, and ran her fingers over his ribs with a featherlight touch. "I can't imagine that."

"Well, I thought about it, sure. But with just one of me and two of them, it was too risky. *Now* there were two of them. And two of us. David was close to the guy by the door. I was close to the one demanding the money. I shouted, 'Now, David!' Then I lunged for the guy near me, taking him down. He hit his head hard on the waxed tile floor, knocking himself out. Women screamed. Men yelled. The security guard shouted, 'Hold it right there!' He was waving a gun at David and the man he'd tackled, taking the guy to the floor. Police got the getaway driver and the two would-be bank robbers. As soon as David was standing, the teller who had the hots for him was all over him. I almost felt bad for him, considering he'd come in to save my butt."

Maya laughed. "You're so bad."

"Yeah, it was his fault he'd used his charm on her earlier, though. We were given an award for citizens' heroics and Martin had heard enough. We didn't know anything about him and his organization or that he'd been following our shenanigans with interest. We were either being taken in by the police or doing police work. He wanted us to work for him, or else. So we agreed."

She didn't say anything for a moment, just resettled her head against his chest, her fingers tracing a circle around his nipple. "He's damn lucky to have you."

"God, Maya," Wade said, hugging her close, hating that Maya had been in such danger and he couldn't protect *her*. "Bettinger could have injured you, killed you. I'm sorry I got you involved in this."

She shook her head. "You were always there for us... for Kat and Connor and me. Why shouldn't we have helped you this time?"

He snorted. "Because I was supposed to be doing my job. What did Connor say to you last night about the whole fiasco?" He figured Connor would have said plenty.

"He was angry and told me not to get near you." She smiled up at Wade with the most sinfully seductive look.

He chuckled, threading his fingers through her hair. "You didn't listen to him." He swept his hand over her bare arm.

She ran her fingers over Wade's chest with a tender touch, making his blood heat. "I don't always listen to what my brother tells me to do or not to do."

A rapping at the patio door made Wade's heart skip a beat. He peered through the gauzy mesh surrounding the

bed and saw a shadowy figure at the back door, hidden
by the drapes.

Chapter 16

"CONNOR?" MAYA WHISPERED, PULLING AWAY FROM the bed and Wade. The figure was definitely a male as tall as he was, and Wade was instantly on guard. "You stay in bed," she said, grabbing a white terry-cloth robe off a chair and pulling it on.

Wade wasn't sitting still, despite what she wanted. He quickly left the bed to protect her in case it wasn't Connor, watching her move down the stairs and through the living room, ready to shift into his much more protective jaguar form.

She pushed the curtain aside before she opened the door, then turned and, smiling, said to Wade, "It's *your* brother. And it looks like he brought us a late breakfast."

Wearing khakis and a light-blue shirt, David stood grinning at the door.

Relieved to see his brother and not Connor—or one of the bad guys—Wade snagged a towel out of the bathroom and tucked it around his waist, then joined them in the living room. "What the hell are you doing here? You're supposed to be getting your half of the bad guys."

David chuckled as he carried in the tray of food, kissing Maya briefly on the cheek, then setting the tray down on the coffee table. "Compliments of your brother and me, Maya."

"You spoke to my brother?" Maya asked, her brows furrowed.

"Yeah. I couldn't find Wade and got worried. Then I figured if he was goofing off again, he might be here."

Wade smiled a little at his brother and shook his head.

"I ran into your brother and his wife as they were on their way to breakfast. I assumed that the three of you had brought Wade back here."

"Yeah, not of my own choice," Wade said as he sat down next to Maya and looked at the food on the tray. An omelet made his stomach rumble with hunger. French toast made of Creole bread had been prepared for Maya.

Shaking his head, David sat down on the couch opposite them and glanced at Maya sitting in her robe. "Coming back here with Maya," he said, then glanced at the bed and again at Maya, "would have been *my* choice if I'd been *you*."

"Believe me, you would not have wanted to go through what I did to end up here."

"Thanks, David. What a treat." Maya smiled warmly at him.

"I was worried when you didn't rendezvous with me at the appointed hour back at our cabana, Wade," David said, watching him eat.

"Sorry about that."

David frowned. "I knew you had to be in trouble."

Maya looked up from taking another bite of her French toast. "Connor and Kat came to our rescue and we came straight back here."

David ground his teeth. "Okay… When Mylar and Bettinger didn't return to the cabana last night, Lion Mane and Smith were pretty shook up about it. Lion Mane knew we had searched the cabana, and he discovered the tranq darts and the scent of the female jaguar in the jungle. No sign of the guns or the men. No sign of the jaguars—you or the female. Lion Mane was sniffing at the scents left behind by Maya—who Lion Mane knew—and Kat and Connor, who none of us knew. He located the scents of Mylar and Bettinger, and the river where their scents ended."

"You followed them to the site?" Wade asked.

"Yeah. I was trailing them when they returned to the cabana and discovered we'd been there. Then they returned to the rainforest to find the others. I guessed that they were supposed to meet back at the cabana, but like you and I meeting, it didn't happen."

"So what do we do now?" Maya licked her fingers.

Both Wade and his brother watched her tongue sliding over her fingers. Wade knew what he wanted to do. Take her back to bed.

David cleared his throat. "Um, this is a Special Forces mission."

She snorted. "You wouldn't be sitting here talking to Wade if I hadn't helped out a little."

Wade and his brother shared looks.

"She's right," Wade said, finishing his omelet.

"So, what's our next move?" She sat back against the couch, folding her arms. When neither brother said anything, she let her breath out in exasperation. "Okay, look, if David didn't take down Lion Mane, the guy knows I'm in on this with the two of you. He'll also know that Kat and Connor are involved. He might want revenge, or he might decide things are getting too hot for him and leave. Or, he might risk going after the female jaguar again since he's already put this much effort into it and still wants the money. In any event, we're all involved in this now."

"Connor mentioned taking you and Kat home early," David said, his tone cautious.

Her mouth pursed as she raised her brows at him.

He shrugged. "Kat wouldn't hear of it unless you wanted to go home, too."

"No, I don't want to go home yet. If this guy wants revenge, he could drop by our garden nursery anytime. If he wants to go after the cat, the more of us there are to stop him, the better," Maya said.

David turned to Wade. "If you don't keep her for yourself, I'm not guaranteeing she's going to be free much longer."

Maya smiled and cast a glance in Wade's direction, but not before he could wipe the scowl off his face.

"Since Lion Mane knows about all of us, I assume it would be better if we all stayed at the same resort tonight," David said.

"There wouldn't be enough room at the cabana we're staying at. Enough beds, but not enough rooms for privacy," Wade said. He smiled at David.

Maya slid her hand over Wade's towel-covered thigh. If she did much more, she was going to get a rise out of him.

"So what were you thinking?" Wade asked his brother, taking hold of her hand and pulling her close. He tucked her soft, terry-cloth-robed body securely underneath his arm.

"A couple is moving out of their cottage this morning. You and I could stay there. I already reserved the place, just in case."

"Okay, sounds good. We'll figure out sleeping

arrangements later." Wade kissed the top of Maya's head. As long as Maya was agreeable, he intended to stay with her here until she left for home.

"You know we're leaving the day after tomorrow?" Maya said. "So we only have today and tomorrow to stop these men."

On her schedule. But not on David's and his.

"I managed to tell Martin I found you safe here," David said. "The main lodge here has really spotty reception, but I got through. I told him about Bettinger and Mylar. He wanted to know if you learned who the buyer was before Bettinger died."

Maya spoke up before Wade could say anything. "Bettinger had the gun and was asking all the questions while Wade was a jaguar at the time. So no, Wade didn't have a chance to ask him who he was working for. But Wade is alive and I figure that ought to count for something."

David smiled at Maya. "Martin better not cross claws with you. He's fine with it, only because Lion Mane is still running around. I sent him a picture of the dude to see if Martin might be able to learn who he is. As to Bill Bettinger, he said the man had a wife and two kids."

A knock at the front door gave Maya a start.

"Maya, are you finished with breakfast yet?" Connor asked through the door. "We need to talk."

Looking guilty as sin, Maya jumped up from the couch.

Wade shook his head. Her brother was bound to know he and Maya had made love. She raced up the steps to the bedroom, grabbed some clothes out of the dresser and closet, then scurried into the bathroom and shut the door.

"She's fast," David mused.

"Coming!" Wade shouted to Connor.

"Have you got any clothes?" David asked.

"Yeah. A pair of pants."

"I'll get the door. Why don't you put the pants on?"

"I'm fine," Wade said, heading for the door. "I need to take a shower anyway before I get dressed."

David sighed. "You like to live dangerously."

Wade opened the door, wearing only the towel around his waist, and raised a brow at Connor, whose eyes narrowed as he took in Wade's scent. Even if Wade had been dressed, he couldn't have hidden the smell of Maya on him—or of their lovemaking in the bed that was open to the view of the living room.

Connor glanced in the direction of the bathroom where the spray of the shower was going full blast. "We need to make some decisions here."

He took a seat on one of the floral upholstered chairs while David sat back down on the couch and Wade sat opposite him on the other couch.

"Yeah. Maya says she wants to help with our investigation," Wade said, not liking the idea. "Maybe you can talk her out of it."

"Are you kidding? Both women are going to help us with this. Lion Mane is trouble for us. We can't let this go. The other man? The hunter? Unless the shifter gets him involved in trying to take us down, he's not a problem."

"We don't take civilians on a job," Wade said, giving his brother a look. David nodded in agreement.

"All right, listen. We're involved. Once Maya saved your ass and Kat and I had to come to your rescue, we became part of the team. Now… we can work together, or we can work separately. But we *are* going after this shifter. His buddy would have murdered Maya. Lion Mane most likely would have opted for the same solution. Don't you agree?"

"We don't know that for sure. We don't know his background, his real name, nothing," Wade said, not wanting Connor and the two women involved. He did understand where Connor was coming from. But that didn't change how Wade felt about it.

Connor stretched out his long legs and leaned against the chair back. "Fair enough. Since you're the Special Forces hotshot jaguars, what do you propose we do? Serve as bait?"

"I don't like that idea," Wade immediately said.

"If Lion Mane—hell, I wish we knew the guy's real name—but if this bastard wants to take Maya out, no matter what we do, she could be his next target," Connor said.

"True," David said.

Not liking where this was headed, Wade cast his brother a disgruntled look. David was supposed to be on *his* side.

David shrugged. "Connor's right. You know it, Wade." To Connor, David said, "How about you stay here for the time being? I doubt he'd chance a confrontation at the cottages. Too many people around. Wade and I will return to our cabana and the place they were staying. We'll look for the bastard, and if we can't locate him, we'll return with our luggage. You take the women on one of the tours in the area. Something where we can watch your backs. If he doesn't try anything, then we'll have to take him on back in the States. But if you and the ladies take a jungle excursion, he might attempt to get to Maya. And we could take him out then."

"Too risky," Wade said.

"There are several excursions," Connor said, ignoring Wade's comment, although he smiled a little at Wade, looking somewhat pleased that Wade was concerned about Maya and not willing to use her as bait. "They have cave tubing, kayaking, Mayan ruins exploration, caving, zip line, and horseback riding. Horses aren't really fond of us. Zip line is no good because of Kat's condition. Kayaking would be hard for you to follow us. Cave tubing might work or the Mayan ruins exploration. Before all this had happened, we'd planned on the cave tubing. We'll have quite a bit of jungle hiking and trek-king through the caves. But also a gentle tubing ride. It should be easy enough for you to watch our backs."

Both men looked to see Wade's take on it. He didn't want Maya used as bait. Period. Too many things could go wrong.

Connor continued, "If this doesn't work and we miss him here, then maybe we can check out the dance club that you all went to. Your brother said those involved in the smuggling were meeting there. What if we all went there? David said a woman he danced with knew the shifter Maya killed. Maybe if David could dance with the woman again, he'd learn more about the other shifter."

"Yeah, we could try that," Wade said. "Our mission is to stop Lion Mane from leaving here with the jaguar, though. If he's hightailed it out of here, we'll go. If he's still trying to grab the jaguar, we're staying, and we'll leave when the situation is resolved."

"In the meantime, where will you be staying?" Connor asked Wade.

"Here. At your resort. It would make sense not to split our forces."

"Here," Connor parroted.

"Someone needs to protect Maya. She killed his partner, Bettinger."

Connor frowned. "All right. And David?"

"David is getting a separate cottage," David said and sighed dramatically.

"We need to return to our resort and grab our bags. Before we come back here, we'll make a last-ditch effort to find him before you go on the excursion," Wade said. "Will you take care of things here?" He meant Maya, but he knew he didn't need to get that specific.

Connor nodded. "Will you go as jaguars, or do you need to borrow some boots and a shirt?"

Wade hesitated to answer. He and his brother should stick together on the return to their resort in the event Lion Mane thought to ambush them. Just as he knew that Wade and David had visited Mylar's place, he would be able to find Wade and his brother's scent trail back to their own cabana.

They didn't have any idea what Lion Mane was up to. If he was smart, he'd leave the area. But being part jaguar, he also would be territorial.

"We'll run together as jaguars," Wade said. "We'll return here as soon as we can. If we catch wind of the men, we'll hunt them down. That would be the best possible scenario."

"All right." Connor rose from his chair, as did Wade and David.

"One last thing." Connor's amber eyes narrowed on Wade. "What are your intentions toward Maya?"

The shower shut off and all the men looked in the direction of the bathroom, listening for Maya. She wouldn't come out right away. She'd have to towel dry, then dress, and Wade suspected she wouldn't leave the bathroom until her brother was gone.

Wade turned to Connor. "Honorable. She doesn't want to see me exclusively, though."

Connor's brows rose in disbelief.

Wade shrugged. "She has father issues. You should know about them."

Connor grunted, sounding like he had some of the same issues. "What about you? Do you want to see other women?"

Wade smiled what he was certain was his most feral look. "After being around Maya for any length of time? No way."

Connor allowed a small smile. "Good. I don't want to see her hurt."

"She's safe with me," Wade assured him. "I'm not sure about the other way around, though."

"You mean if she finds another shifter she likes better?"

"Yeah." Wade didn't like where this conversation was going. He scrubbed his hand over his whiskery chin. "We need to head out."

"Are you going to say good-bye to Maya?" Connor sounded protective of her again. "She kept hoping she'd see you for the last several days. She didn't say so in so many words, but she was worried about you."

"I was keeping an eye on the three of you."

Connor openly smiled this time and slapped Wade on

the shoulder as if he'd suddenly been welcomed into the family. "I knew it. I never saw you. Never smelled you. You're good at it. But I knew it just the same."

David shook his head. "No wonder he kept saying he had to run farther south than where the men had been."

When no one made a move to depart from the cottage and Maya apparently wasn't planning to leave the bathroom while everyone was there, Wade said, "I'll be just a moment."

He headed for the bathroom and knocked once. Last time, he'd left without saying good-bye properly to her, and he had regretted the decision even though he'd told himself she was sound asleep and he didn't wanted to wake her.

This time he wanted to do it right, but not with his brother and hers standing in the next room listening to everything.

Chapter 17

WADE OPENED THE BATHROOM DOOR AND SMILED AS Maya yanked the towel she'd been using to dry her hair around her sweet, naked body. He stepped inside and closed the door.

Taking her face in his hands, he kissed her soundly. "Stay with your brother and Kat until I return. No exceptions." He didn't want her searching for him again, should she think he was in trouble.

"Be careful," she whispered, wrapping her hands around his neck and kissing him again.

He jerked her towel off her body, dropped it, and ran his hands over her breasts. She smelled like oranges, strawberries, and pineapple. "Hmm, Maya, about this exclusivity when it comes to seeing others…"

She smiled against his mouth, rubbing against his body and purring. "Return to me quickly."

He groaned and tongued her mouth, then kissed her cheek, hating to leave her. "Stay safe."

"And you."

When he left her and shut the bathroom door, he found his brother had already piled his clothes on the coffee table and shifted. Connor was looking out the patio door at the jungle.

Wade said, "We'll return." He dropped the towel around his waist and shifted, then headed for the patio door.

Connor opened it for them. "See you in a while and we can firm up plans."

Wade bowed his head in acknowledgment. Then he and his brother leaped from the deck into the brush below, blending into the dappled rainforest like two spotted shadows.

The two brothers continued back toward their cabana, searching the area as they went, looking for any sign that either man had been anywhere nearby recently. Wade and David swung around to the scene where Wade and the female jaguar had been drugged. They found the scent of the shifter from the previous night and the trail leading to the river where Lion Mane had stood on the bank, most likely searching for his dead companions.

There was no sign of any bodies in the daylight. The sun was beating down on the dark river, the trees stretching over the water, while a couple of dark grayish-brown crocodiles basked on the opposite shore. An egret spied the jaguar brothers and took flight.

Wade and his brother headed back toward their resort. It was daylight and not safe for them to run around in their jaguar forms. Anyone could be taking a day trip into the rainforest and catch sight of not one, but two big jaguar males.

Nudging at his brother to stay hidden in the relative safety of the rainforest, Wade loped out to the bathroom window of their cabana and leaped in through the frame. Fortunately, they'd left the bathroom door shut, because insects now filled the small room.

He shifted and opened the bathroom door, then closed it so he could check out the cabana. He heard a thump in the bathroom as David slammed against the toilet, making a splashing noise, and Wade chuckled.

He didn't smell Lion Mane or Smith in the place. He suspected they were afraid to come near the cabana.

David soon joined him, one foot dripping wet. Wade said, "Didn't miss the toilet, eh?"

"Damn thing moved since the last time I jumped through that window."

Wade chuckled. "Yeah, it has a way of doing that. They haven't been here. Let's get dressed and check out Mylar and Smith's place."

"We should have looked for Bettinger and Lion Mane's trail after they dropped in on Mylar and Smith and then left." David was already sitting on his bed, the box springs·squeaking as Wade was doing the same thing in his room, pulling on his boots. "I figured that the men had just arrived in the country like we had. When I thought it over, I assumed the shifters wouldn't have stayed with the humans."

"You're right," Wade said, heading out of his room. "So we check out their old place and then see if we can find a scent trail to another cabana."

When they arrived at the backside of Mylar's cabana, David provided security while Wade peered through the bathroom window before he entered the place. He shook his head. "They've left. Nothing's on the counter. Place is clean, fresh towels on the towel rack. No toothbrushes, shaving kits, nothing. It looks as though Smith vacated the place after they discovered Bettinger and Mylar were dead, and he took Mylar's stuff with him as a precaution, maybe dumping it somewhere along the way."

A gnawing feeling of dread filled Wade. He'd rather they found the bastards and ended this right here and now.

———

Maya finally left the bathroom, her hair pulled back in a ponytail and dressed in hiking boots, jeans, and a cotton top. She frowned to see her brother still there and expected to get another lecture from him.

He was sitting on her couch, waiting. His gaze held hers. "Did you hear the plan?"

"I did. For what it's worth, I think it's a good plan."

Connor nodded. "Kat and I were talking about what we'd do with our remaining time here, since we can't run as jaguars."

Maya let out a heavy breath and joined Connor on the couch. "Is she disappointed?"

"A little. But she'll be fine. She just wants to make sure she gets her fill of the jungle before we return. We won't be coming back until after she's had the twins, and not until they're a little older. She's been doing really well."

"Yeah, when she's a jaguar, you said."

"The cave-tubing trip is a tour-guided activity that includes a seven-mile water ride. I think she'll do fine on the water ride. It's just the hiking through the jungle and the cave as a human that might be a little much. But she's in excellent shape from being in the Army and running as a jaguar. She insists she can do it."

Maya bit her lip. "Okay, let's plan on her keeping to the jungle in her cat form. We'll carry anything she needs for the cave tubing."

Now they just had to wait for Wade and his brother to come back and hope that nothing bad happened to them while they searched for Lion Mane and the other smuggler.

—⁓—

Wade and David spent a couple of hours searching for the scent of Lion Mane and Smith, but they couldn't locate either in the jungle or around the cabanas.

"They have to have taken a vehicle—a bus or rental car—out of here," David finally said. "They might have packed up their bags and gone somewhere else. The Amazon, even."

Wade didn't feel right about it. He stared past Smith's cabana at the jungle beyond. "Bettinger and Lion Mane were together at the club."

"Yeah."

"We were together. Maya's cousins, Huntley and Everett, were with one another," Wade reasoned.

"Yeah, so…?"

"You and I are brothers. So are Huntley and Everett. If Maya had been with anyone else when she went to the club, she would have been with her brother and sister-in-law, had they been home," Wade said. His thoughts were headed down a dark path that he didn't want to consider.

"I don't follow you."

"We're thinking these guys, Bettinger and Lion Mane, were cohorts in a criminal act. They're shifters. But what if they were *brothers*?"

"Shit," David said, turning pale. "If he was close to Bettinger…"

"Lion Mane might want revenge for his brother's death. I was thinking he was just working with the guy, no great loss. They might have been friends, but not friends enough to get himself killed over. A brother? Possibly." Wade would if someone killed *his* brother.

David stared at Wade, recognition in his eyes. "He might have left the area already. The evidence points in that direction. That he's gone."

"What if he's not?"

"We're back to the plan of trying to catch him if he attempts to go after Maya on the excursion," David said slowly. "We need to get back to her place."

Wade was already heading in the direction of their cabana. "I'll get our bags. You go check us out."

David stalked toward the main lodge while Wade went to their cabana. He hastily packed and then, with their bags in hand, he pulled open the door. A man stood in the doorway, his gun pointed at Wade.

Narrowing his eyes, Wade took in the tall, scrawny man, his blue jeans muddy from the knees down, his camouflage shirt smelling of sweat and ripe body odor. The man's hair was plastered against his scalp, greasy and long, around the balding crown.

Wade took a deep breath, smelled the man's odor again, and said, "Smith, I presume."

The hunter who'd been staying with Mylar was just as dangerous as his now-dead friend.

Wade had no intention of attempting to reason with the man. He backed up as if agreeing to whatever Smith had in mind. He had to get the hunter inside the room. Once the guy shut the door behind him, Wade lunged like a jaguar shifter in human form. Smith's pale blue eyes rounded, his mouth gaping as he tried to raise the gun.

The human was too late. Wade struck him hard in the nose, breaking it with a crunch. Smith screamed in pain but didn't release the weapon.

Wade grabbed for the man's arm, yanking it so quickly and sharply behind the man's back that he heard a snap—the arm breaking. The gun clattered to the floor, the muffled pop of a round striking the mahogany leg of the coffee table.

With the constant jungle chatter, Wade was certain he and Smith wouldn't draw attention with any noise they made. At this time of morning, many guests would have already started out on day treks and wouldn't be in the vicinity. Only animals with keen hearing would hear a scuffle.

Smith collapsed to his knees, tears streaming down his cheeks as Wade finally released his arm. "Who sent you?"

The human glowered at Wade. Either he was acting tough, or he was just too stupid to believe Wade wouldn't punish him more.

Wade, standing in front of Smith, tilted his head to the side and scowled at the bastard. With the rap sheet he had, the guy was probably the one usually towering over a cowering victim. "You know where Mylar went, right?" Wade asked.

Smith's eyes widened.

"Yeah. You got it. You could join him next, though I'm sure there's not much left of him. The crocs and piranhas aren't choosy."

The man swallowed, his Adam's apple bobbing.

"Who… sent… you?" Wade demanded.

The sound of the window being yanked up in the bathroom had Wade twisting around to look.

Smith lunged for the gun with his uninjured arm. Grabbing it in his left hand, he turned to shoot Wade.

"Damn it." The guy must be ambidextrous, Wade thought. He seized the man's left arm, fully intending to break it as well, but the gun went off.

The man collapsed, clutching his chest. Not hesitating, Wade jerked the gun from the man's hand and aimed toward the bathroom down the hall.

"Just me!" David said, hands in the air. "I heard the fight and didn't want to get shot coming in through the front door." He looked down at Smith. "That must be Smith."

"Yeah," Wade muttered, looking back at the human, who was now lying on his back, his eyes open and sightless.

Wade pushed the man with his booted foot. The guy was dead, damn it to hell and back.

"Where's the bullet wound?" David asked, peering down at the man.

Wade pushed the man over with his boot, saw no sign of blood, and reached down to feel for a pulse. None. Wade let out his breath in a huff. "Hell, there isn't any bullet wound. He must have had a heart attack."

David gave an exasperated sigh. "Don't tell me you didn't learn who the buyer was."

"I didn't. Nor did I get a name from him as to who Lion Mane is. Let's drop him off at the river and get out of here. Are we checked out?"

"Yeah." David helped carry Smith through the

bathroom, and the two of them shoved the body through the window into the jungle out back where it was less likely to be seen. "We need to dump him and get back to Maya's resort. Any sign of the shifter?"

"No. That's what has me worried. I'm thinking that this guy was left behind to take care of us when we returned, while the shifter might have gone after Maya."

"The shifter's smart. He probably thinks Maya is easy pickings compared to the two of us," David said. "What if he has a gun like this guy did?"

"They'll think of something." Wade didn't want to second-guess the situation. He just wanted to dispose of the body and get back to Maya and the others quickly.

"Take it easy on Lion Mane if we get hold of him, will you?" David asked in a teasing manner. "I really want to get on Martin's good side this time."

Wade shook his head as the two carried Smith to the river. He knew David didn't care about getting on Martin's "good" side. In a situation like this, all he cared about was that Wade and he came out on top— alive and uninjured.

And right now, all they were concerned about was getting rid of the evidence and getting back to the Andersons in time.

Chapter 18

FRANCISCO, THEIR GUIDE, AND THE GROUP WERE ready to hike to the cave tubing site and anxiously waiting on Maya, her brother, and her sister-in-law.

Maya was staring out her window at the jungle, hoping that the plan to draw Lion Mane out would work, but she thought Wade and his brother had already taken too long to return to the treetop cottages.

She was wearing a bathing suit under her jeans and T-shirt and had a couple of water bottles, a waterproof camera, and a hand towel in her backpack sitting on the table. Connor and Kat would arrive any minute. It was now or never.

A knock at the door gave her a start, and she rushed to ensure it was her brother and Kat. It was. She opened the door. They looked as anxious as she did. Connor had one backpack between them.

"They're not here," Connor said, glancing at Maya's living room and stating the obvious. "We've got to go."

"But shouldn't we wait for Wade and David?" Maya asked.

"We'll miss the excursion if we wait. But I had another idea in case David and Wade didn't arrive on time. You go with the guide, and we'll join you at the site. At least that's how I've explained it to the guide. Kat and I will go in jaguar form, hidden in the jungle as your personal escort. Stay near the back of the group.

We'll watch for any signs of a jaguar. At the caving site, we'll shift and join you. I have a change of clothes in my backpack. You can add whatever you had in yours to ours and carry it."

"The guide won't like that you're going to join us at the caves, will he?" she asked, transferring her stuff to Connor's bag.

"I explained that Kat and I have taken the trip many times, but that I wanted you to have the guided tour. A little extra money convinced him to allow us to join you later."

"I'd rather it be me hunting down Lion Mane than Kat."

"If that's his game, he'd be after you, not Kat. If he thinks you're not with us and more vulnerable, he might take a chance to tangle with you. Kat can handle the hike better in her jaguar form. And she's a good fighter. Either that, or we return home and risk having him come after you when we're least expecting it. He could get reinforcements back home, too. Of course, this is just speculation. He might not be interested in dealing with you at all."

"What about Wade and David?"

"They know where we're going. They can join us if they're able to."

She hated the dark tone of Connor's voice.

Kat said, "I think Connor's right. We can give this a shot and see if it works. Just write Wade a note that you're going on the tour by yourself. That I'm not feeling well and Connor's staying at the cottage with me. That you'll meet him for dinner. That way, when he gets here, he'll know we left on the tour. He'll know Connor and I wouldn't have let you go alone. And if someone else reads the note, they won't realize that Wade and

David intended to watch our backs. Or that we won't be with you."

Unsure about the whole plan, Maya hastily wrote a note for Wade and left it on the coffee table.

"Go. The group and guide are ready to hike. We'll join you in a minute," Connor said, lifting his backpack to Maya's shoulders.

Maya kissed him on the cheek, gave Kat a hug, and then Kat said, "Be careful, okay?"

Heading outside, Maya hurried to join the excursion group.

She greeted the guide and the twelve other cave tubers, and then they began their hike through the jungle. The guide, Francisco, had near-black hair and eyes and a big white-toothed smile. The other cave tubers were of various shapes and sizes.

The men and women were quiet as Francisco walked ahead of the party, talking about the jungle, pointing out the importance of the plants, and identifying birds, insects, and reptiles. He guided them along the semi-worn path—as worn as any jungle path could be where the vegetation grew wild and couldn't be tamed, even by man.

Maya soaked up the feel of the hot, muggy rainforest as she tuned the guide out and watched for any sign of Lion Mane. Her brother and Kat would also be in the rainforest, but they would be elusive, trying to keep out of another jaguar's sight, if Lion Mane was following her. She would have been comforted to know that they were close by, but she couldn't stop worrying about Kat.

The tourists in front of them eyed the trees as the tour guide pointed out a bright green, poisonous tree frog, a boa constrictor coiled nearby, and colorful parrots high above. The tourists immediately began plying him with questions, but the chatter died down quickly because the men and women had to save their breath for the rigorous hike.

Maya thought she spied a jaguar's movement. She stopped, staring into the jungle, but it was too late. Whatever movement had caught her eye was now well hidden in the foliage.

By the time they reached the cave nearly an hour later, everyone was sweaty and breathing hard, except for the guide and Maya. No one had attempted to attack her, and she hadn't heard any fighting in the jungle.

She left the backpack hidden off the trail for her brother and Kat to find and rejoined the others.

The guide said they had reached the spot, and they could see through the blue-green water clear to the rocky bottom where fish were diving for food. Maya took a deep breath and stared at the pristine beauty.

"For over two thousand years, the Mayans used these caves for ceremonies," Connor said, taking in the wondrous site.

She whipped around to see him and Kat together, hands entwined and Connor now wearing the backpack. He gave her a small smile.

Maya was so glad to see them safe that she immediately embraced them both. "What did you see?"

"Trees," Connor said. "Nothing else."

Then the movement Maya had seen must have been Kat or Connor. She was glad Kat and her brother hadn't encountered any trouble.

"It's beautiful." Kat looked as though the long hike

as a jaguar hadn't bothered her in the least as she peered down at the water.

The jungle and whitewashed cliffs surrounded the river, boulders rising high above where the group climbed before removing their outer clothing and shoving it into packs. They each grabbed an inner tube and tossed it into the placid water. Then one after another, they jumped in to join their tubes. Each also had a life jacket and a headlamp to use in the darker parts of the cave.

The melodious mix of bugs chattered, mosquitoes buzzed, monkeys howled, and colorful birds of paradise sang, while gray doves cooed.

"Ahh," Maya said, as she settled into the tube and paddled over to where Kat was sitting in her own tube, a big grin on her face. "This feel so good. How are you doing?"

"Wonderfully," Kat said. "I couldn't be better."

"No sign of anyone?" Maya asked.

"No. We didn't smell any other jaguars in the area."

"Good."

They floated with the others into the cave. Water dripped from stalactites hanging down from the cave ceiling, and stalagmites poked out of the water at intervals. Sometimes the water flowed and they didn't need to paddle. At other times, it was still as glass.

Francisco pointed out stones that appeared to be in the shape of animals and humans. "The Visual Serpent," he said at one point. "The Celestial Bird," he remarked later. "And there, pottery shards from ancient civilizations. Do not touch. It is against the law. They are considered national treasures."

Natural windows carved into the rock allowed sunlight to pour into the cave, penetrating through the wet mist in the air. The tourists continued their way down the river until they reached a waterfall.

Here, everyone played in the waterfall, splashing and having the time of their lives, and then they continued into the crystal cave, where the walls glittered like diamonds.

A small colony of bats clung to the ceiling high above, twittering a little when the people's voices echoed off the cave walls, and a woman gasped.

"They eat fruit and insects," Francisco assured the group. "They're not vampire bats."

Maya caught sight of a spider crawling across the cavern wall and crustaceans feeding nearby, while catfish swam in a pool of water.

"Jaguars sometimes come in here to drink the cool water rising from underground springs or to hunt a gibnut, a nocturnal rodent," the guide said.

Maya looked at Connor. He was frowning. Would Lion Mane have come here in search of a jaguar? Certainly not during the day, because jaguars wouldn't hunt in the cave while people were around. She relaxed. She hated that the shifter had turned against their jaguar cousins and that he might make Kat and Connor worry during their otherwise enjoyable outing.

The group spent the rest of the afternoon exploring and floating on the inner tubes until they had to make the long hike back.

The guide spoke privately with Connor, glanced at Kat and Maya, then nodded at Connor. Francisco didn't seem really happy, but Connor had paid for their special accommodations. Connor and Kat headed into the jungle with his backpack, just beyond the tourists' and the guide's view. Then while everyone finished turning in their life preservers and tubes, Maya hurried off to grab Connor's bag and return to the group.

Maya was torn between wanting Connor to take care of Lion Mane, should he come after her, and craving one last quiet jungle hike, though she would have preferred touring the jungle as a cat, not stumbling over tree roots and vines as a human.

Wade and David had never arrived, at least that she knew of, and that made her worry even more.

Ever vigilant, she remained at the tail end of the group, watching for any signs of danger.

With the weight of Kat's and Connor's clothes and especially his big sneakers stuffed inside, the pack felt fuller and heavier, Maya thought, particularly after the day of exercise. She was unintentionally falling behind.

They still had another half hour or so to go when someone shouted, "Jaguar!"

"Stay together," Francisco told them. "Don't run. Just stay together. They don't go after humans."

Maya was looking around, trying to see if another cat was in the area besides her brother or sister-in-law—an all-jaguar cat or Lion Mane.

Her heart was already pumping hard from the exertion, but she felt a little hope that the jaguar might be Wade or David.

The pink ribbon of sky peeking through the thick canopy had all but faded, leaving a dark blue ceiling sprinkled with the Milky Way. It was getting darker, and they still had a long way to go, so most of the people were turning on their headlamps.

"Keep talking. Make a lot of noise," the guide told them. "The cat will stay away. Just don't run."

They should stand still if approached by a jaguar. The tour guide opted for getting them back to the resort before the jungle became inky black like the cave had been in sections.

Maya wanted to tell them to be quiet so she could hear where the jaguar was and ensure it was one of her own family that had spooked everyone. But the tourists tromped through the jungle with so much noise that holding their tongues wouldn't have mattered. She assumed the jaguar had to be a shifter. No all-jaguar cat would come this close to a bunch of noisy humans.

She tried to listen for sounds of a jaguar moving about in the brush that only her jaguar hearing would pick up.

She lifted her chin and smelled the breezeless air, noticing that the temperature was dropping with the coming of night. Nothing but the smell of wet earth, of leafy plants and fragrant flowers, of…

She turned her head just as a woman screamed several yards ahead of her.

People raced along the path far in front of her. She'd fallen behind again.

"Walk!" Francisco commanded them. "Don't run. If you do, the jaguar will chase you."

It was too late. Everyone was running to avoid the imminent attack of the jaguar. No one wanted to be the last one trailing behind, the weakest link ripe for the predator's picking.

Except for Maya. She couldn't run after them, not with the heavy pack on her back. She wouldn't run, knowing that was the worst thing anyone could do. Cats loved to chase. And pounce. Then bite. And she was the last one left behind. Easy prey.

A hiss and a growl emanated from somewhere in the jungle, but she couldn't see what was going on. She stood still, alone now, heart pounding, her blood rushing through her veins.

The guide would get the panicked people back to the resort, hopefully not losing anyone else in the process but her.

She wanted to ditch the backpack and shift. As a jaguar, she would feel a whole lot less threatened.

People were still making a full-scale ruckus as they fled north of where she was, screaming, wailing, and stomping the ground.

"This way!" the guide yelled as some of the panicked people ran in the wrong direction in the dense jungle. She could imagine them being lost forever.

She barely breathed, concentrating on the world close to her, the knocking sound of a frog on a leaf nearby, something scurrying around on the rainforest floor near her foot, something slithering on a branch near her head. She moved then, walking in the direction of the cottage.

She walked slowly. She would not run; she knew better.

Another hiss. A low, growling rumble off to her left. She wanted to stop. She wanted to go. She wanted to shift, feel her balance with the jungle, and be part of it, not stand out like a human did.

A figure moved out of the leaves as if it had been part of the vegetation. "Kat," she breathed, feeling relief at once to see her sister jaguar, to smell her scent.

Kat grabbed at the backpack strap dangling in front of Maya's waist with her jaguar teeth and gave a pull.

Her urgency made Maya walk quickly with her toward the cottages.

"Where's Connor?" Maya asked, as if Kat could tell her in her jaguar form.

Kat kept tugging, kept moving her in the direction of where the tourists had disappeared. Kat wouldn't leave Connor behind unless he told her to go with Maya. So where was Connor? Facing off another jaguar shifter?

Maya's heart was thudding hard, and she could hear Kat's heart pounding just as quickly. Connor had to be keeping another jaguar away from them. She kept looking over her shoulder, but Kat wouldn't let her stop. Her mission, it appeared, was to get Maya safely back to the cottages.

Fine. Maya picked up her pace, hurrying now to reach the resort. She'd make sure she got Kat safely to the cottage and insist she stay behind. Then she'd shift and return to help her brother.

~~~

They were getting closer to the resort. Connor still hadn't joined them, but Maya was walking as fast as she could, watching that she didn't trip over the liana crisscrossing the path back to the cottages.

Kat was running alongside her until they heard their guide say, "Wait. Don't go to your cottages or the lodge yet. I'm still trying to get a head count. Two are missing."

"Can you go around through the jungle and reach your cottage without anyone seeing you?" Maya asked Kat, her voice low.

Kat bumped her with her head and rubbed her leg. Maya took that as a yes. "Okay, go. I'll let Francisco know that we're all fine. That you and Connor already returned to your cottage."

She waited for Kat to leave, but instead, Kat jumped into a tree to watch her.

Maya sighed. "Okay, so you stay and protect me." She began walking toward the guide, though she still couldn't see him through the jungle foliage. "Connor and my sister-in-law already returned to their cottage," she hollered. "I'm coming!"

That's all she got out before she felt a claw swipe at her arm. She cried out in shock. Her shirtsleeve shredded, and she felt slices of throbbing and stinging pain streak up her arm. Before she could react to the angry cat, the large furry form hit her body, taking her down, his teeth bared.

"Lion Mane," she gasped, grabbing at the skin at his throat, knowing she couldn't keep him from biting her with his powerful jaws.

Just as quickly, another jaguar slammed into him, knocking him off her, snarling and hissing. *Connor!*

The cats' angry hisses were loud enough that the tourists must have thought Maya was being attacked and torn to shreds. She could hear running feet as the people scrambled to get to their cottages and safety. *Forget the head count.*

She couldn't catch her breath as she scooted away from the fighting males. Kat had jumped down from the tree and was standing protectively over Maya, who couldn't get to her feet because of the weight of the backpack. Before she could get it off, Lion Mane ran away.

Connor poked his nose at her, sniffing her arm and licking at her. "I'm okay," she said, reaching up with her uninjured arm to stroke his head. Lion Mane hadn't hurt her badly, just scared the crap out of her. Kat purred next to her, her head bent to inspect the damage.

"All right, everyone's accounted for," the guide said, watching for her.

Her heart still thundering, Maya hurried as fast as she could to the guide. She had to let him know she was safe. "Are you sure everyone's back?" she asked. "You said someone else was missing."

"Another person whose wife said he'd fled to their cottage before I could count him."

She could sympathize with the man—truly. "Is the wife okay?"

"She's about as growly as the cat. Are you okay?" Francisco asked, looking Maya over. "I… I thought maybe it attacked you." He was waving a stick in his hand, but it wouldn't have done much if he'd wanted to get the big cat off her.

When he looked down at her sleeve to see that it was torn and blood trickled down her arm, he gasped.

Shaken but trying to appear as though the experience hadn't rattled her, she clasped her hand over the wound. "Just a scratch." By morning the claw marks would have faded to scratches.

"Let me take care of it," Francisco said. "I've got a first-aid kit."

"No, that's okay. My brother's got medical training. He'll see to it."

"If you're sure…"

"I'll be fine." She hurried to her cottage to clean up, change, and meet Connor and Kat for dinner. They'd eat, and afterward they'd make plans to search for David and Wade, hoping to God that Lion Mane and his companion in crime hadn't already killed them.

She unlocked her door and walked inside, then shut the door, locking it. She tugged off the backpack and dropped it on the floor, relieved to finally have the weight off her back.

Turning on the light, she could see the claw marks down her left arm. Not pretty. She rummaged through her suitcase, and when she realized she didn't have any bandages, she hurried to the bathroom.

She yanked off her T-shirt and washed her arm with soap and water, grimacing and gritting her teeth as the claw marks stung. Intending to take a quick shower, she kicked off her boots and had barely yanked off her socks when she heard a key shoved in the lock and the door opened. She twisted around and left the bathroom, figuring it would be Connor.

But it wasn't. Wade loomed in the door frame, bag in hand, face grim, and his blue-green eyes darkened to nearly black.

Chapter 19

"THANK GOD YOU'RE OKAY. CONNOR'S ALL RIGHT, isn't he, Wade?" Maya asked quickly.

Wade set the bag down, pulled the door shut, and stalked toward her. "Hell, Maya," he swore under his breath, his heated gaze going from her face to her bloodied arm.

"I'm all right. Is Connor—"

"He gave me the spare key to your place and told me to check on you. He's fine. He's getting cleaned up and dressed." Wade sounded irritated and worried at the same time. "I'd kill the shifter that did this if Connor hadn't insisted that I stay and watch over you."

She parted her lips, unable to say anything for a moment. "Where were you? We waited as long as we could, but then we had to go or miss the excursion."

"Chasing down Lion Mane. Only he led us on a damn wild-goose chase. We lost him at the river. We kept trying to catch his scent and where he had gone to, hoping to end this. We finally gave up and headed here, worried he might have come after you at the resort." His gaze moved down her injured arm again.

"I've got to hurry and shower before they close the dining room."

"Yeah, but this won't wait." His voice was rough with need and frustration. Wade took her arm gently and considered the claw marks.

"It's okay," she assured him, not wanting him to fuss over her. "You know how we heal."

He pulled her roughly into his arms and kissed her hard, his tongue penetrating her parted lips. She was surprised at his passionate reaction. He rubbed against her like a cat needing to put his scent on her, growled when he smelled Lion Mane on her, and kissed her some more.

She was still stiff in his arms, worried about her brother and Kat, when Wade stopped kissing her and placed his forehead against hers, his breathing labored and his hands clenching her shoulders. "Okay. Go take a shower. I'll be all right."

She chuckled, then kissed him on the cheek, and hurried into the bathroom.

She took an ultrafast shower, and then she quickly dried and rushed to get some clothes.

Wade was showering on the back deck. She watched him for a moment as he ran his soapy hands over his naked body, his eyes closed. Transfixed, she couldn't take her eyes off him. God, he was a beautiful specimen of a wild cat. Grabbing a pink-and-yellow strapless sundress from the closet, she slipped it over her head and shoved her feet into a pair of jeweled sandals.

When she was done, he was drying himself. He pulled on a pair of Bermuda shorts and a T-shirt and sandals, then headed inside. He stopped when he saw her and smiled.

"You clean up nicely if you don't mind the cliché," he said, stalking toward her. She thought he was going to begin kissing her all over again.

Instead, he took her arm and examined the claw

marks. They had stopped bleeding, and he kissed them gently. "I suppose you don't have any bandages."

"No, afraid not. I thought I had some in my suitcase." She envisioned David and the ladder of colorful, fanciful bandages across his forehead. She was almost glad she didn't have any of *those* bandages.

"Okay, let's go. David has a first-aid kit in his bag." Wade caressed her back with his hand, and she thought that if they didn't leave the cottage quickly, they'd end up in bed together instead.

"Just plain old bandages?" she asked.

Wade smiled down at her and kissed her nose. "We'll have to add some fancy ones to the kit just for you. Your brother didn't expect us for dinner, but he and Kat and my brother are saving us seats."

She felt her face heat. "I take it you're planning on staying here this evening." She motioned to Wade's bag as he escorted her past it, hoping he was planning on sleeping there. "And you're not taking off after Lion Mane in the dark."

She didn't feel comfortable being alone if Lion Mane had any intention of returning to finish what he started.

"Oh yeah. If I hadn't insisted on it, your brother would have. He doesn't want you to be alone until he gets you home. He tested my resolve first, though."

"Tested you?" she asked, puzzled, as Wade led her down the walkway toward the lodge.

"Yeah. He said David and I could stay in your cottage, and you could stay with your brother and Kat. I said no."

Maya looked up at Wade, saw the determination on his face, and smiled. She smelled the aroma of red fish and stewed pork cooking and sighed. "I'm hungry. Is Connor really okay?"

"Yeah. He took a bite out of Lion Mane, though."

Her mouth gaped for a second. Then she nodded. "Good. What about the hunter who'd been with him?"

"He's joined the other one in the river."

Maya pulled Wade to a stop. "What happened?"

"He held a gun on me at our cabana. I believe he'd been ordered to hold David and me hostage until the shifter returned. He didn't figure on me not going along with the plan."

Maya stared at Wade, then took a deep breath, tears misting her eyes. He pulled her under his arm and walked again with her toward the lodge. "Everything turned out all right. We just need to get Lion Mane now."

"Did you get the name of the buyer?"

Wade chuckled. "No. I mean, it's not funny. But you're the third person who's asked me that tonight."

"Your brother and mine," she guessed.

"Yeah. I only have my boss to add to the list when I call him."

When they reached the dining hall, several of the guests were still arriving after cleaning up, some looking a little shaken from their ordeal with the jaguar.

"There had to be three or four of them," one woman complained. "At least. They were roaring and screeching, and I was sure the lady…" She looked up to see Maya walking in with Wade and snapped her mouth shut.

Wade escorted Maya to the table where David and Connor rose from their seats. Kat remained seated, looking a little pale.

"Are you feeling all right, Kat?" Maya took a seat, and the men followed suit.

"I'll be fine once I have something to eat." Kat was already nibbling at a garden salad. She looked at Maya's arm, which was burning like crazy. "What about you? Are you okay, Maya?"

Without any bandages, Maya hadn't wanted to wear a sleeve that would rub against the open wound. David was already rising from his seat as the waitress approached.

Once they ordered their food, David said, "I'll get a bandage for Maya," then hurried out of the dining room.

Everyone was quiet for a while, then someone started talking again at another table about the jaguars attacking them. Maya said to her tablemates, "We saw the most beautiful crystal cave today where the Mayans held some of their ceremonies. A treasure trove of ancient pottery was strewn about. When we come back here, maybe you and David could see them with us."

The conversation at the other tables died.

"It *was* spectacular," Kat agreed.

David raced back into the dining room, breathing hard. He had to have run all the way to his cottage and back. He shoved a roll of gauze and tape at Wade, then retook his seat.

"Thanks," Maya said to David. He smiled at her and winked.

Everyone waited for Wade to bind Maya's wounds. She wished they would just talk and get all the attention off her. Her whole body was heating to sauna levels despite the cold air circulating in the dining room.

"Oh yes, and the cave tubing was so much fun," Kat said, perking up after finishing her salad, *finally* starting the conversation again. "The water was just the right temperature."

"I'd love to visit the cave." Wade finished binding Maya's wound, then took her hand in his and caressed it, gazing into her eyes like an adoring puppy instead of a hot-blooded cat.

She smiled at him, deciding she liked him both ways, a *lot*.

She noticed that both her brother and Kat were watching the way Wade was caressing her hand, and her whole body heated all over again. She pulled her hand away from Wade's and dipped her spoon into her soup.

"We won't be coming back for some time," Connor said, running his hand over Kat's belly. "Too difficult with twins on the way."

Poor Kat. Every eye in the place turned to look at her stomach.

Maya sighed a little, grateful that Connor got her out of that one. Until he said, "But you and Maya could visit in the meantime, Wade. I wouldn't want her to feel that she couldn't enjoy the rainforest just because we can't go."

Maya glowered at her brother. Spending time totally alone with Wade was *not* a good idea.

Wade grinned. "Sounds like a deal."

She could have kicked her brother under the table. Then she saw David smiling at her, and she had a brilliant thought. "David could go with you, Wade. Since he hasn't been there, either."

"If he wants to come along for the ride, sure," Wade said, not about to let her slip out of that one so easily.

The entrées were served, and they got busy eating,

the whole room quiet except for the clinking of silverware or the pouring of fresh water into glasses.

Thinking back to what their guide had told them, Maya said, "The cold crystal-clear water was coming up from natural underground springs. I didn't expect to see the catfish in the pools of water or how clear it would be."

"And a jaguar hunts there, too," the woman who'd spoken about Maya earlier said.

This time Maya frowned at her, irritated that the woman kept harping about the jaguars. "He wouldn't come out until night and only to hunt big rodents, not people," Maya finally said, annoyed.

The woman motioned to Maya's arm. "You didn't have those claw marks before. One of the jaguars did that, didn't he?"

Wade placed his arm around Maya's shoulder, but she didn't need protection from the woman who scorned their kind. Maya tapped her long nails on the table and then showed them to the woman. "He did. But when I clawed him back, he took off running."

Everyone chuckled.

"Laugh, but she could have been killed," the woman said, frowning. "And where were *you* when I was left alone out there in the jungle?" She scowled at the man sitting beside her, no doubt the husband who'd escaped to the cottage and confused Francisco's head count.

The woman hadn't been left alone in the jungle. She'd been standing near the guide with all the other tourists.

"Unlocking the door of our cottage for you, dear, so you'd have a faster escape," the man said, sounding sour about it, though he was attempting to keep his voice level. She probably had already given him hell for it and wouldn't let him live it down for the rest of their married lives.

Several tourists looked like they were fighting smiles.

Wade leaned over to kiss Maya's cheek and nuzzled his mouth against her ear with tenderness. She felt her whole body tingle with need and looked up into his solemn gaze. He'd been playing the role of a man taking a woman to a family gathering for dinner, but now she could see he was still disturbed about what had occurred between her and Lion Mane.

She might pretend that the exchange between her and the shifter had meant nothing, but his clawing her had meant something. Danger, possession, or a wish to kill her. She wasn't clear about his intentions, but since she'd brushed him off at the club and killed two of his partners in crime, she suspected she was on his terminal list. She was used to dealing with armed drug runners in the Amazon. But not anything like this. A chill slid up her spine.

"What's on the schedule for tomorrow?" David asked.

"Resting and packing up," Connor said. "The long bus ride, wait at the airport, and three-and-a-half-hour plane trip will be wearing enough for Kat."

Wade leaned his head against Maya, his arm tightening around her shoulders, his whole body saying he wanted her.

She felt her face heat, hating that she was so transparent.

David blushed himself and said, more to the table than anyone, "Yeah, I've got a lot of resting up to do. I'll call our boss and tell him our plans—if I can get through, considering the spotty reception in this area."

Everyone looked at Wade. He raised his brows. "My brother and I will take the bus when you do," he finally said. "Our flight won't leave until the next morning, which means we'll have to stay in a hotel in the city." Wade looked at Maya. "Since we didn't resolve the situation here, we've got a club date after that."

Maya didn't have much time to think about that because everyone was saying their good-nights.

Maya and Wade barely made it into her cottage before he was kissing her, shutting the door, and locking it. They never made it up the steps to the bed.

With their mouths fused, she was yanking off her sandals while he was kicking off his own with one clunk and then another. He swept his fingers along the sweetheart neckline of her sundress. A frisson of heat winged through her blood as he slipped the top of the silky dress down, freeing her breasts and allowing the cool air to whisper across her heated flesh. Her nipples were already peaked, and he smiled at the sight of them.

"No bra." His eyes were smoky with lust, his hands moving over her breasts.

"Corset built into the dress." She smiled at him, reaching up to fluff her hair around her shoulders as he watched, engrossed.

He smiled. "I *like* this dress." His voice was gravelly with need. He began kissing her. His hands stroked her bare shoulders, but she wanted them on her breasts again, doing wicked things to her libido. She took one of his hands and curved his fingers around her swollen breast. He moved his other hand down, too, so he was covering both her breasts, skimming over them almost reverently, then squeezing them gently. His mouth was rough on hers, and the light stubble covering his face grazed her skin as he rubbed his cheek against hers, then kissed her lips again.

He slid his hand up her thigh underneath the short dress but paused when his fingers reached her hip and he hadn't found any panties. He grinned down at her. Tickled, she smiled back.

He tried again, only this time sliding his hand between her legs, giving her an even more wicked grin when he found she truly wasn't wearing panties. He slipped a finger inside her, smiled, and pulled his finger out. "Wet," he said, his mouth capturing hers. His kisses and touches were desperate and unchecked.

"Wade," she breathed against his mouth, loving the feral side of him as he sank his finger deep into her wet sheath again, his other hand pressed against her lower back, holding her steady as he kissed her harder. More passionately. No holds barred. Claiming her in a way he hadn't before.

He moved her toward the couch, inching their way there and not stopping the sensual assault on her senses. The smell of his arousal, his maleness, the jungle, and the citrus soap he'd used in the shower were a tantalizing aphrodisiac. Before she expected it, he had positioned her next to the couch and lowered her back onto the soft cushions. Then he was tugging her skirt up, bunching the silky floral fabric at her waist and leaving the rest of her bared for his pleasure. *He* was still fully dressed!

He feasted on her for only a moment, his cock so hard that she could see the rigid outline against his silky shorts and marveled at the size of him and his control. She wanted him inside her now.

He jerked off his T-shirt and tossed it aside, then nestled between her bare thighs. The satiny feel of his Bermuda shorts slid against her thighs, her mound, caressing and enticing her. His arousal was stiff and ready for her, and his hot, bare chest was pressed against hers. He had to want release as badly as she did.

Instead of yielding to the lust, he cupped his hands on her face, and she gave in to the gentle kisses. His lips brushed her eyelids, her cheeks, her mouth. He was like shadow and light—dark and demanding, then subtle and soliciting. He was already between her legs, and her ache below lessened as he rubbed his erection against her, hard and compelling.

She slid her hands beneath the elastic band of his shorts and cupped his cool buttocks. He groaned against her mouth and rubbed his whole body against hers, slowly, methodically as if he was already plunging deep inside her.

He brought her knees up, her feet planted on the couch, legs spread, as he rubbed her crotch with punishing deliberation, making her want him all the more. His mouth moved down her throat, licking, kissing, tantalizing her. Then he took a mouthful of her breast, suckling, teasing, and nipping it. She throbbed with need and moaned. She squeezed his ass, licking his mouth, parting her lips, and begging him to take her to the top as she felt she was almost... Just... a... little... more...

She let out an exalted cry of release and scored his buttocks lightly with her nails.

―⁓―

"Ahh," Wade groaned, ready to come in his shorts with the way Maya was responding to his kisses and rubbing that sweet body of hers against his. He smelled her fragrant arousal and tasted wine and lime pie on her lips and tongue. Agonizingly, he fumbled to slide the shorts down over his hips. When he finally managed, his cock sprang free.

With Maya, there was no going slow. No partial commitment. It was all or none. And he wanted it all. Wanted all of her. He couldn't have stopped this if he'd tried.

His fingers brushed against her clitoris, and she gave a little gasp. She was wired. He thrust his cock deep into her wet heat, his damnable shorts at his knees, but he couldn't do anything about that now. He was too far gone. He pounded into her with a need so great that he couldn't quench the compelling urge to claim her.

Delicious heat spread through every nerve ending as his blood sizzled. He ground against her as she dug her heels into his buttocks. He pushed deeply, hard, fast, thrusting until he felt he was ready to come. Then he held it, held her still, and gazed into her beautiful golden eyes that simmered with passion... and love, he thought.

"More," she said, as he groaned his release, and she was close to coming again.

Wanting to please her, he kept it up, thrusting until she came, her lips parted on a purr of pleasure. He gave her a quick kiss and a thorough tonguing. He pulled away from her, yanked his shorts off the rest of the way, and dumped them on the floor. Before she could protest his abandoning her, he gathered her up in his arms and this time carried her up the steps to the bed.

He had every intention of making love to her again. And again.

Morning would come way too soon.

―――∞―――

Wade and Maya snuggled, her soft body curled against his chest as he stroked her hair.

"There's something you're not telling me," Maya said. "You seemed more than worried last night when you saw me before dinner. More than was warranted just because Lion Mane clawed me."

Wade snorted. "His clawing you had me seeing red, Maya. *Hell.* Although you're right. I am concerned about something else. Nothing's for sure, but just speculating, what if Lion Mane was Bettinger's brother?"

Maya didn't say anything for several moments. "Great."

"Yeah. Not good. If he decides he wants revenge…" Wade didn't need to finish the thought.

"Okay. I'm glad I know what I might be up against."

"He might not be Bettinger's brother. But the possibility exists."

She nodded. Then, to his surprise, she asked, "What do you think of our garden nursery?"

Wade kissed her cheek and gave her a long look. Maybe she was having doubts about seeing other shifters. He could only hope. "Your brother asked me the same thing."

She stiffened and tried to pull away. He held on tight and nuzzled her face until she relaxed. "He'd better not be acting like we're… well, we're…"

"A couple?" Wade supplied. "He just wondered what I'd do if we got hitched. He was concerned about how you'd feel. Stay in Texas. Move to Florida."

"That's not for him to discuss. Or you. We're not a couple."

"Maybe not, but he doesn't want to lose you. That much was evident."

She settled down. Two alpha male cats in the house wouldn't work well. But when she looked up at him, he could see the worry in her expression.

Wade understood how she felt—the closeness she shared with her brother and sister-in-law was important to her. He didn't want her to give that up. "I wouldn't take you away from your brother or Kat or their kids."

"Then what?"

He fought a smile. She *had* been thinking about it. "Connor says you have plenty of land. A lake, even. We could build a place on the lake. You could still work at the nursery. Your brother said he and Kat couldn't do it without you. And he wasn't talking about your menial labor, either."

"What would you do?"

"My job," he said honestly. "But I'm not gone all the time. I wouldn't mind helping with the garden when I'm around."

"You?"

"Planting seeds. Digging around. It could work." And he wasn't talking about the garden, either.

She nestled against him. "I'm not saying yes about anything."

He nodded. "I told you it was your choice." But he had every intention of changing her mind. He did have a thought, though. If he could get some of his friends to take her out and prove how much better of a choice he was for her... He shook his head. He couldn't do that to her. Besides, what if one of the guys he knew appealed to her?

"You don't really mean it about not minding that I'm planning to see others," she finally said, her fingers caressing his chest.

"Sure I do," he said, not even trying to be convincing. She already had him figured out.

She smiled up at him. "You're making headway."

He smiled back at her. She was *not* going to date anyone else if he had any say in it.

———

Maya couldn't believe she'd slept most of the day. Then again, since she and Wade hadn't slept most of the night, they'd had some making up to do. They finally managed to pack their bags and have their last meal together at the dining room where David, Kat, and Connor were already waiting for them.

Maya tried hard not to blush as all eyes were on her, but that part of her being just wouldn't cooperate. It was one thing knowing they knew she'd been making love to Wade half the night and this morning. It was another thing to face them in person.

Everyone but David seemed tired. Too much late-night activity for the shifter couples. Poor David.

No one said much of anything during the meal. Not even the other guests, some of whom were also headed home.

Once they were on the bus to Belize City, Maya

realized she hadn't once eaten anything in the jungle as a cat, like she normally did when Connor and she visited the Amazon. At least she'd had several nights to run as a jaguar.

The club date was the next big adventure, and she worried just how that would turn out. Fighting in the jungle was one thing. Dealing with a shifter in a city was quite another.

Chapter 20

WHEN MAYA KISSED WADE GOOD-BYE AT THE AIRPORT, she felt as if he was going off to war or something—or *she* was. Maya couldn't help feeling awful, but she was annoyed with herself. What was wrong with her?

As soon as she entered the plane, she knew what was wrong. In her heart she was already falling for the hunky jaguar shifter. Afraid that she was going to be like her mother and her father with their doomed relationship, she was trying hard to keep her emotions intact and maintain some distance from the cat who made her hot with just a whisper of a kiss or a caress of his fingers across her bare skin. Distancing herself from him wasn't working.

The problem was trying to figure out what made for the perfect couple. As she and her brother and Kat flew home, Maya stared out the window at the majestic cotton-white thunderheads hanging aloft in the clear blue sky.

Connor and Kat's relationship was close to being perfect. Sure they'd argue sometimes, but making up seemed to be wonderful. She hadn't seen Connor this happy in years, and Kat was so much like family that it was if she had always been with them. Being with Connor was home for Kat.

Maya couldn't believe that Wade would be willing to move to Texas to live near her family. What was not to love about him? The notion that he'd want to return with her to Belize when Kat and Connor couldn't was just as appealing.

She sighed and glanced over at Kat, who was sitting in the middle seat beside her, watching her. Connor had closed his eyes, head leaning against the reclined seat, his hand clasping Kat's. He was in his shielding and territorial male jaguar persona—sitting in the aisle seat, claiming this row, protective of his wife and sister. As *if* anyone was going to bother them on the flight. Still, it was an instinctive part of his behavior.

"What?" Maya mouthed to her virtual sister, wondering what she wanted to discuss because Kat wouldn't be staring at her if she didn't want to talk about some issue—most likely one that Maya wasn't interested in discussing. At least not on the plane while Connor listened in.

Kat smiled. "You love him. Don't deny it."

Maya frowned at her, *really* not wanting to bring the topic of Wade up right now. She was too unsettled about her thoughts concerning him. "He's pretty nice."

"But?"

Maya sighed. "What if it doesn't last? What if after the babies came…"

Connor's eyes popped open, and he turned to look at Maya. Kat's lips had parted, her expression one of surprise.

"I'm not pregnant," Maya whispered harshly. "Sheesh, we just met. I'm just saying…" She scowled at her brother. "Go back to sleep. Or something. Quit staring at me. Kat and I are having a private conversation." As if they could when they were seated next to each other in such a confined space.

Connor shook his head, closed his eyes, and leaned against the seat back again. But she knew he would be listening to every word.

"Your mother and father had issues, obviously. They weren't a match." Kat reached over and squeezed her hand. "If it's to be, it'll be. Don't project your parents' relationship onto yours. You and Wade are two totally different people."

"He wanted to meet you in the beginning. He was obsessed with getting to know you," Maya insisted.

"We'd corresponded. He thought I was a shifter. When he came to Connor for the spare keys to your place, he told me that he would *never* have changed me. He would have wished me well, thought it was nice that I loved jaguars so much, but that would have been the end of any blossoming relationship."

Maya stared at her, trying to see the situation in a new light. She stopped short of saying "oh" and let out her breath instead.

Kat smiled at her. "He wished *you* hadn't been Connor's wife. He said it really hit him hard to learn you were Connor's sister instead."

Connor didn't open his eyes, but he smiled a little.

Maya frowned at her brother. If he hadn't been so overprotective, she might have met someone earlier. Probably everyone who saw them together had the same misconception. "What if… well, if we tried it, what if the relationship didn't work out?"

"What if it didn't?" Kat said. "It wouldn't be the end of the world."

True. Maya tended to think in terms of all or nothing. "What if I had kids?" Maya could see feeling like her mother, stuck with twins and no one to help out. No father to assist in raising them or love them.

"You'd love them to pieces. I'd become an aunt. Connor would be an uncle, and we'll have that extended family you always wanted. And you could look for another mate. Your mother isolated herself from others of our kind. She didn't want another mate, from what Connor says. Seize the moment. Make the most of your relationship with Wade. If it doesn't work out, at least you can say you gave it your best try."

"I don't know."

"You know, maybe your mother pushed your father out of the house," Kat said, her words soft as if she was trying to cushion the blow. "Maybe your father wanted to stay."

Maya shook her head.

"There are always two sides to every story."

"Okay, so if he wanted to be with her, why didn't he at least keep in touch with Connor and me? He never did. We were born, and he left."

"He left after you were born or when he learned of the pregnancy?" Kat asked.

Maya hesitated. Would it have mattered?

His eyes still closed, Connor said under his breath, "When he learned of the pregnancy."

Kat pondered that for a moment and then said, "What if they had agreed not to have kids and she'd broken the promise? Or what if you weren't *his* kids?"

When Maya and her brother and Kat arrived home, they were dead tired, Kat especially. She went straight to bed.

But Maya couldn't help wondering if Kat was right. Was Connor and Maya's father not truly their father? If he had learned her mother had gotten pregnant by some other man… oh God, what a mess. Then another thought hit her. Everett and Huntley wouldn't be their cousins.

Connor had to have heard Kat's question on the plane, yet he hadn't said a word. Had Kat and her brother already discussed the issue? And he was afraid to mention it to Maya?

Her thoughts scattered when Bear, one of the men who worked for them when they were away, hurried to meet with her and Connor. His wary expression warned her something had gone wrong while they were absent.

He bowed his head a little, looking nervous as the other workers packed up their belongings and placed them in the pickup truck. "We had trouble as soon as Miss Maya left for the airport that morning," Bear said to Connor.

Connor glanced back at the gardens. "Not another busted water pipe."

The last time the water bill had cost them a small fortune.

"No, no. A man by the name of Thompson was asking about cats."

"Cats?" Connor said, his face darkening.

Maya's heart began racing. Connor had to know that Bear wasn't talking about the wild kitty cats that meandered through their gardens.

"Jaguars." Bear looked down at the gravel beneath his feet, as if he was afraid of mentioning the jaguar word to a jaguar god and goddess.

Connor and Maya suspected Bear and his family, who were originally from Columbia, knew they were jaguar shifters, but still, there wasn't any way they'd come out and tell them the truth.

"The stolen jaguar from the zoo," Maya reminded her brother.

"Oh, that." Connor waved the notion away. "No problem. No stolen jaguars here."

"No." Bear looked around at the woods as if he was afraid someone might be listening.

Maya glanced around, her eyes narrowed as she watched for any movement other than the leaves fluttering in the hot, humid breeze. She'd never seen the man so anxious before.

Bear swallowed, his eyes on Maya, as if she'd been the one who'd invited all the jaguar gods to the gardens. He whispered, "He said there were four male jaguars. *Four* of them. One black." He waited for Connor to acknowledge the sighting.

Connor looked down at Maya as if she was the cause of all the trouble. She shrugged and said, "Thompson must have been drunk."

Connor nodded. "That would explain it."

Bear looked from Connor to Maya. But when she just sweetly smiled at him, he nodded and said, "That was it. But he'll be back. He asked when you were returning, and I told him."

"You did fine, Bear." Connor handed him a check. "We'll see you next time."

Bear gave a worried smile, then hurried to the truck and drove off with a wave.

Connor escorted Maya into the house before he began questioning her. "How the hell did Thompson see so many of our kind in the gardens?"

"Our cousins fought Bettinger when he came to see me."

"If you hadn't gone to the club in the first place, none of this would have happened."

Ignoring that, she said, "I had no idea Thompson was skulking around in our woods when it all happened. It's really late, Connor. I'm going to bed."

Connor shook his head. "Hell. What next?" He plodded off to his bedroom and shut the door with a clunk.

Maya thought about Wade and David. They wouldn't get in until sometime tomorrow afternoon. She already wished he was in her bed tonight. She glanced at the recliner where he'd slept. It seemed like so much longer than a week ago.

She peered out the kitchen window at the garden, which was peaceful tonight, and thought about her cousins fighting Bettinger in their jaguar forms. Watching the big cats fight in the garden, Thompson must have nearly had a heart attack. Served him right for spying on them. He wouldn't be able to prove a thing of what he'd seen. Thankfully.

Not that the whole situation *should* have ever happened in front of the human. They were just lucky he'd been alone. At least she hoped he had been.

Grabbing her bag, she rolled it into her bedroom. She collapsed on her bed and pulled out her phone, then texted Wade.

We're home. Missing you already.

She paused before she sent it. The message sounded too needy. Too personal. Too intimate. Too permanent. She erased Missing you already and tried to think of how to end it. She thought about mentioning Thompson, but that would only concern the brothers, and they were still in Belize City and unable to do anything about him.

See you tomorrow evening at the club. Night.

How to end it? Maya? Love, Maya? Too intimate. She sighed. She was overthinking it. Or TTYL, as in talk to you later. That could work.

She stared and stared and stared at the message as if it would tell her how to sign off. Hell. She signed it: Maya.

"We have our marching orders," Wade said to his brother as he put away his phone before boarding the plane.

"Is Martin okay with us setting something up at the dance club?" David asked.

They showed their boarding passes to the airline staff. "Yeah. He doesn't want Kat there, though. With her being pregnant, if something goes wrong, he's afraid she might be injured."

"Connor won't want to leave Kat home alone, but he won't want his sister in the fray, either."

David and Wade took their seats on the half-empty plane.

"The good news is that Martin got hold of Maya's cousins, Huntley and Everett. They're arriving this afternoon. They're going to help with our case," Wade said.

David smiled. "Whose idea was that?"

"The brothers. Martin went along with it, but if he'd

wanted to give them another case to work on instead, they weren't buying it."

"Good. So… are they meeting us at the club or taking care of Kat?"

As the plane took off, Wade leaned against the seat and closed his eyes. "They wanted to drop by the Andersons' place, meet Kat and Connor, and bring Maya to the club if she's willing."

"Are you going to dance with Candy if she's there?"

Wade opened his eyes and looked at his brother. "Now, how am I going to win Maya over if I'm chasing some human woman at a club?"

David smiled at him. "Just thought you were up for the game of trying to learn more about Bettinger since he'd given her his real name and asked her out. Besides, maybe if you danced with Candy, Maya would change her mind about seeing other guys."

"Or be so annoyed with me that she would see *only* other guys."

David shook his head and ordered a cup of orange juice from the hostess.

"Two," Wade said, holding up two fingers.

"Have Huntley or Everett heard back from their sister, Tammy?"

Wade frowned at David. "Why? You're not hoping to meet her, are you? She wouldn't come to the club the first time because she was busy having a date with a human."

"No. Remember what the brothers said? They were having her look into the situation concerning the missing jaguar from the Oregon Zoo."

"Thompson," Wade said, recalling the man who was

searching for the stolen jaguar. "Hell. I forgot all about him. Connor will have a fit if the man bothers them when they get home."

"At least Connor won't allow Thompson to badger Maya any further. Maybe Tammy's got some good news. If she's found the stolen jaguar, that'll be the end of that problem. Besides, surely Thompson wouldn't be hanging around all this time while the Andersons were in Belize, waiting for their return. Don't you imagine he'd be off somewhere else looking for clues?"

"Yeah." Wade leaned his head against the seat. If Thompson had been a shifter, Wade would have liked him for his obvious concern for the missing jaguar. But because Thompson had targeted Maya, believing she had something to do with the stolen cat, Wade was ready to tear him apart if he harassed her any further.

As if he was afraid to ask the most important question until last, David finally said, "Did you hear from Maya yet?"

"Yeah."

"What'd she say?"

Wade smiled at his brother.

"Well? Was she all gushy? Saying she missed you terribly? Or is there hope for me yet?"

Wade knew his brother was teasing him. He shook his head and drank his orange juice, but didn't say. It was what Maya didn't say that made him smile again.

When they arrived in Houston, they got a rental car and drove to their hotel.

Dumping his bag on the floor of the economy hotel room, Wade noted the two queen-sized beds with standard floral bedspreads, the television, writing desk, and

black-out curtains for sleeping late. He checked his
phone to see if he'd gotten any messages from Maya
or Martin.

"I'm taking a shower, then getting some sleep,"
David said, "before we have dinner and go to the club."

"Just texting Maya to let her know that we're here."

Maya,

David and I arrived early. We're staying at the
Santa Anna Inn in Houston. Look forward to
seeing you soon. Wade

He heard the shower end.

David walked out of the bathroom, drying his hair
with a towel. "Did she respond?"

"That had to be the quickest shower you have ever
taken."

David usually used up all the hot water before Wade
could take a shower when they shared a room. He
wondered if David was afraid he'd miss out on hearing
from Maya.

"I wasn't very dirty," David said with a gleam of
amusement shining in his eyes.

"There was no response from her. She might be out
checking on the garden."

Wade headed for the bathroom, and David pulled his
phone out.

"Don't you text her, too," Wade said, a warning in his
voice. Before he closed the bathroom door, he saw his
brother gave him an evil smile.

Chapter 21

THAT NIGHT, WHEN WADE AND HIS BROTHER ARRIVED at the club, Wade couldn't help but look for Maya. Maybe he should have been more concerned about watching for Lion Mane, Candy, and whoever else might lead them to clues about the buyer, but Maya had been all he could think of since he left her at the airport yesterday afternoon. He half expected to see her and her hulking cousins, but there was no sign of her.

"She can't be here yet," David said, bumping Wade's arm as he motioned to an empty table. The club was filling up fast. "Huntley and Everett's flight wouldn't have arrived that early, and then they still had the drive out to her place. She won't be here for another hour or so."

"We should have picked her up."

"They wanted to meet Connor or Kat. They'll be here."

Wade hoped they'd all be more prepared tonight. Martin had checked out Houston and the surrounding communities for any other place that the buyer might go, but he'd concluded that as territorial as cats were, this was it. He'd also researched Thompson's background and discovered he had been rescuing animals from hunters from the time he was ten years old. He was definitely one of the good guys where wild animals were concerned. If the zoo man had been a jaguar shifter, Martin would have already recruited him.

The music was playing and the drinks flowing while

David and Wade spent more than three hours observing the crowd. Then Wade smelled Maya's sweet fragrance and instantly stood up from his seat. Despite the mob, he glimpsed her headed in their direction.

He just gaped at her. She was wearing a sexy red minidress with a low-cut bodice showing off the swell of her breasts. Wade wished he could take off his shirt and cover her, feeling that she was way too exposed for this horde. Before he could greet her, Maya rushed between him and his brother, brushing against them the way cats would in greeting when they didn't move out of her way fast enough.

They just stared after her before they followed her, Wade wishing she hadn't left her sweet scent on his brother, too.

"Where are your cousins?" Wade asked, just short of tacking on a "damn it."

"They're late. They texted and said they couldn't make it on time and would meet me here. Flight arrived late, and they missed their connection."

"Your brother let you come here alone?" Wade took a seat next to her.

Maya's lips parted for a second, her amber eyes darkening, and then she snapped her mouth closed. Looking around the room, she turned to Wade and said, "Get me a Singapore sling, will you?" Then she left the table, walked over to another where two men were eyeing her with interest, stretched out her hand, and asked one to dance.

Wade stared at her in disbelief.

"I wonder what that's all about. Maybe she's still serious about seeing other shifters." David shook his head and waved for a waitress. "Two beers and a Singapore sling." While he was placing the order, he saw Candy, and so did Wade. "Why don't you dance with her?"

"I think I will," Wade said, getting up from his chair. He was trying his damnedest not to look in Maya's direction, wondering what she was so angry about, while he approached Candy. She flipped her hair off her shoulders and smiled up at him.

"I see your girlfriend is still dancing with others. Want to dance with me?"

He shrugged. "That was the general idea." Wade meant to dance with Candy away from Maya, to question her in as subtle a manner as he could about Bettinger, but he found his feet drifting in Maya's direction. The guy with Maya kept putting his hand on her ass, and she kept moving it to her waist.

Wade was about to rip the man's arm out of his socket when Candy tugged at his belt and said, "I've missed you since the last time. Where you been?"

"Hunting."

Her eyes widened. "Really? I have a couple of friends who hunt."

"What do they hunt?" he asked, getting interested. He was trying to focus on Candy and not on Maya, but it was killing him not to look and see if the asshole dancing with her was molesting her.

"Cats," Candy said, smiling up at him.

"Really? I hunt cats. Lions, tigers, leopards, jaguars."

Candy's eyes sparkled with interest. She moved closer and whispered, "Ever capture one and want to… sell it to someone?"

"You know someone who'll buy?"

"Maybe."

"You said that Bill Bettinger had asked you to date him. Are you still seeing him?"

She shook her head. "I learned he's got a wife and two kids. Bastard. If a guy's got a wife, it doesn't matter to me. I figure it's her fault she can't hold on to her man. But when he's got kids, I draw the line."

"What about Lion Mane?"

She narrowed her eyes at Wade.

"Aren't they brothers? And he's single?" Wade pressed.

"Why do you want to know about him?"

"I heard he's a hunter, too."

Candy stumbled. He smelled fear emanating off her beneath the flowery perfume she wore. "He's... he's dangerous."

Bill Bettinger was dangerous, too. Or rather he *had* been.

Wade shrugged and glanced around the room to see where Maya had gone with her dance partner. Hell, now she was sitting at the two men's table, ignoring him!

He ground his teeth. Candy looked at where he was glowering and laughed. "Looks like she's found some place else to sit." She pulled Wade back to his table, motioning to the Singapore sling, and said, "Oh, for me?"

"It's for Maya." David grabbed it and headed over to the table where she was sitting.

Still unsettled about Maya's behavior and what he'd said wrong to her, Wade took a seat beside Candy and ordered her a margarita.

"Is your brother also a hunter?" Candy asked.

"Yeah, he is."

"Thought so." She leaned back on the chair covered in leopard print. "It looks like he's got Maya's attention."

Wade turned to see what his brother was up to. He was taking Maya to the dance floor, leaving her drink sitting on the other men's table! On one level, he knew his brother was really in protective mode, taking care of her so the other clowns didn't think they had a chance with her. That didn't change how Wade was feeling about her.

Where the hell were her cousins? And why was she so mad at him?

"So, you want to split and go somewhere else... less noisy?" Candy asked.

Maya was having the worst night. She wanted desperately to dance with Wade, but first her cousins said they couldn't make it to her place on time, and then her brother and she'd had a big fight over her coming to the club alone. She knew he only had her best interests at heart, but she also figured that if she helped Wade and his brother out on this case, maybe they could track down the buyer of the jaguar and Lion Mane.

That a buyer for jaguar flesh was still out there was bad enough, but Lion Mane was another story.

The only way she could think to make this work was to act angry and make a scene in front of Wade. It was killing her to do so. He looked so upset with her, like he wanted to shake some sense into her and murder the human she was dancing with. She was grateful when David came to her rescue and asked her to dance.

"Humans," David said as he moved her across the floor, careful not to hold her too close and stir up his brother's ire.

She didn't say anything. Sure, the guys were humans, but she hadn't wanted to dance with shifters. She'd noticed several eyeing her, a couple that she'd seen the last time, but no sign of Lion Mane.

She didn't want to tell David the truth—that she was doing this so Wade would have a chance to learn something from Candy—and have him spill the beans to Wade.

"He's upset," David said quietly, studying her.

She looked down at his shirt. "I'm upset." Looking up at him, she said, "Okay?"

"With Wade?"

She swallowed hard. David smiled. Damn it. She didn't have to say anything, and David would know the truth. She glanced at Wade. He was watching her but sitting with Candy, who was looking smug.

As soon as Candy saw Maya look in her direction, the woman ran her hand over Wade's hand resting on the table near his beer. Wade looked down at Candy, and she whispered in his ear. Maya wanted to jerk the woman off her seat and toss her to the floor.

When Wade shifted his attention back to Maya, she put her arms around David's neck, moved closer, and kissed him on the mouth.

"Hell, Maya, what are you trying to do to me? My brother's going to kill me," David said, not appearing terribly upset about the consequences.

She smiled at him in the most wicked way. Of course she didn't want Wade to kill his brother, but if she was going to make this real, she had to do something. Wade wasn't taking the bait.

Then Wade was on his feet, dragging Candy along with him. His face was dark with anger. He was supposed to be *dancing* with Candy, not stomping across the dance floor to intercept her and David.

"Uh-oh," David warned. "That kiss did it."

Wade was going to ruin it. "Fine. Let's return to the table." She started to pull away from David.

"No, I don't think so. I don't know what your game is, but I'm letting Wade call the shots before I get myself killed over this." David tightened his grip on her waist.

She rolled her eyes. "He loves you as a brother."

David snorted. "When it comes to you, that notion goes out the window."

The dancers moved out of Wade's path as if they sensed the big cat's anger.

When he reached Maya and David, Wade hauled Candy over to his brother, offering her arm to him. "She wants to dance," he said, his voice dark.

Then he took hold of Maya's hand and quickly moved her away.

"What the hell is going on?" he growled.

"You are screwing everything up." She glowered up at him, tears in her eyes.

The tears undid him. Immediately his hard-set jaw and scowling features softened. He began to kiss her, and she half expected David to pull them apart and tell them to get a room.

But Wade's kisses were *not* hot and molten like before. Instead, he was tender and caring, and she had the damnedest time not crying. "I missed you," she said, tears in her voice and eyes as she slipped her arms around his neck and he pulled her close against his body.

"Strange way of showing it," he said, kissing her hair, her cheek, her lips. Yet his voice was no longer growly, as if the cat in him knew she was back to being his.

"I'm worried about Kat and my brother, about Lion Mane going to the nursery with the intention of killing me, and them becoming collateral damage. I wanted to help you learn more from Candy if she showed up, and she did. She was near the front door when I arrived, then followed me in. I knew if I said hi to you in the way I wanted, we'd… we'd end up like this. You needed to dance with her and learn what you could from her. She needed to believe I was breaking up with you."

Infuriatingly, he smiled and shook his head. "We can't be breaking up with each other if you're not seeing me exclusively."

"You know what I mean."

"I missed you," he said softly against her ear, as if he didn't care about anything but showing how much he wanted her, needed her in his life—as if anything else was half as important. "It was killing me not to make the two-hour drive to your place and pick you up. I wish your cousins had let me know they weren't arriving at the airport in time to bring you."

Getting back to the topic they needed to discuss, she asked, "Did you learn anything?"

He snorted. "That I can't stand the sight of anyone else's hands on you. That human was about to lose both his arms if he made any more moves on you."

She gave Wade a tentative smile. "I meant about the *case*."

"Candy knows a buyer. Maybe not the one we're after. But maybe."

"Good. Shouldn't we still be fighting?"

"Hell, no," he growled. "If my brother had kissed you back, he'd have been sporting a shiner and a broken noise."

"He was only being protective."

"I know. It's the only reason we're not going to have words over it."

She sighed and ran her hand over Wade's arm. "I don't think I'll be returning to their table, and I didn't get even a sip of my drink."

"I'll get you three more, but you're sticking by my side."

She took a deep breath. "Wade, we have another problem. Remember Thompson? He saw my cousins and maybe you at the nursery garden… as jaguars."

Chapter 22

WADE COULDN'T BELIEVE THOMPSON HAD SEEN Maya's cousins in their jaguar forms. What next?

He kept Maya locked against his body, her head settling on his chest, their moves as one as the music continued to beat. He swept his hands over her back as hers wrapped around his waist, their scents mixing as they claimed each other, their body posture telling anyone who might be watching that they were a couple, together, in their own world, and unapproachable.

He understood her misguided need to push him away, to offer him a way to resolve the situation with Lion Mane, but he wasn't going to allow her to do it. He wanted the shifter to know he was Maya's protector, joined at the hip with her if need be. The bastard wouldn't touch her again.

His phone buzzed at his hip, and he lifted it off his belt, checked the caller ID, and saw that it was her cousin Everett. "Hey, we're at the club. Are you joining us?"

"We're visiting with Connor and Kat. Connor said Maya isn't answering her phone. Is she there with you?"

Wade rubbed her back, his body hard with need as she molded to him. "Yeah, she's here." Was she ever. In the flesh—hot, sexy, and all his, as far as he was concerned. Hell, he was ready to move into Connor and Kat and Maya's house to ensure he didn't lose Maya.

"Good. Keep her there with you until we arrive."

"I'll take care of her."

Maya purred.

Everett didn't say anything for a moment, then he asked, "Are you bringing her back here tonight?"

"We haven't decided yet. We have some making up to do."

Maya smiled up at him and shook her head.

The movement of someone big heading toward their table caught Wade's eye. "Oh hell. Thompson's here. If Connor didn't fill you in on the latest news concerning what a particular zoo man has seen, ask him about it. Got to go, Everett." He ended the call.

Maya turned her head to look in Thompson's direction. He waved at them as if they were old buddies, pointing at their table, and Wade nodded.

The zoo man sat down on one of the free chairs.

"Great," Maya said under her breath, her hands cupping Wade's buttocks.

"Hmm, Maya, we're really going to have to get a room. I'm not sure I'm willing to wait the two hours to get back to your place after we leave here." The ruby-colored dress was just too provocative, along with her scent and the way she moved like a slender, sleek cat rubbing up against him. He took a deep breath and kissed the top of her head. "I don't want you seeing anyone else."

There, he'd said it. He had wanted it to be *her* choice, but observing her with other guys made him ready to have one hell of a catfight, and he didn't think killing another man who'd had his hands all over her would encourage his relationship with her in a positive way.

"I don't want to be with anyone else," she said on a sigh.

Relief washed over him, and he smiled.

She quickly added, "It doesn't mean that I don't worry about… us and what will happen in the future. Or that I'm not anxious about whether I'm leaping into something that neither of us will be happy with in the long run." She looked up at him, and he saw the worry in her golden eyes.

"Maya…"

She shook her head. "Kat told me I'm projecting my parents' failure onto our relationship."

Wade kissed her forehead. "It doesn't matter. We are not your parents, and whatever happened between them has nothing to do with us."

"That's what Kat said."

"Good. I like Kat. She gave you some sound advice."

"I want to know the truth about our dad. Kat suggested maybe he hadn't fathered us and that's why he left when my mom was pregnant."

"We can look into it." Not that he wanted to learn anything she might be unhappy about, but he'd help her just the same.

"What are we going to do about Thompson?" she asked.

"That's another matter entirely. What do you want to say? Stick to your shifter story?"

She rolled her eyes. "Isn't your organization involved in keeping our status secret?"

"Truthfully, I haven't a clue as to how to handle this. Come on. The dance has ended. Let's go see what *he* has to say about us." Wade escorted a very tense Maya back to the table.

He nodded at Thompson, who stood and raised his beer to them, his eyes drifting to Maya and her dress, a slight smile curving his mouth. Then he said to Wade, "I hope I'm not intruding."

As if he really hadn't meant to.

"Not at all. It's good to see old friends."

Thompson smiled a little at the comment, but then a frown marred his forehead. He sat down and leaned forward against the table as if he didn't want the rest of the people in the club to hear. "I checked news reports to see if jaguars—male type—had been stolen from other zoos."

"And you found?" Wade asked, his fingers threading through Maya's as they sat across from him.

"None. But you already knew that, didn't you?"

"That you'd been searching for missing jaguars or that you had found none? How would I know that? Besides, we've been in Belize for the past week."

"Both of you?" Thompson said, sounding surprised. Then he narrowed his blue eyes at Wade. "Of course. A jaguar haven."

"Which is exactly where they belong," Wade said.

"And that's why three big males were roaming through Maya's garden center? Maybe even four of them?"

"They were?" Wade asked, squeezing Maya's hand. She looked cool and collected, but her hand was cold and clammy in his. "I'm sure Maya's customers would have reported it, and when she got home, she would have heard about it. Three, you say? Or four? So were the sightings reported? Since she's mentioned nothing to me about that—"

Thompson skirted the question. "I know what I saw."

"So it happened at night? Early morning? When we were gone? Before we left for Belize? I'm just trying to get a picture of it in my mind," Wade said, studying the big man.

Thompson sat back on his chair and regarded Wade coolly but didn't say a word.

Wade shrugged and took a swallow of beer, set the iced glass on the table, and considered Thompson further. "Okay, if you were there when the garden shop wasn't open, you must have been trespassing."

Thompson's face reddened. "I want my cat back," he said.

"Fair enough. Maya's already told you that she had nothing to do with your stolen cat."

Thompson tapped his fingers on the table, then lifted his beer mug. "They're dangerous predators. Not a feral animal you can truly train. Sure, circuses give the illusion they have the wild cats coached to do as the trainer wishes, but in the end, the beast is never tamed. You're fighting with fire when you let those big cats run loose. Someone's going to get injured. Maybe killed." He looked at Maya.

"You're right, of course," she said. "They're dangerous. No one would have let a bunch of jaguars loose on their property unless they wanted to suffer the consequences."

Thompson folded his arms, his eyes dark and troubled. "This is not something to joke about. I know you're involved. If I'd had any doubts, I wouldn't after what I saw."

Maya lifted her tall glass and took another sip of her drink. "Why do you think I have anything to do with the jaguars?"

Thompson left out his breath. "They were serving as

guard cats. One stood with you in the entryway of the back door of your home. They ran in and out of your place as if they belonged there. Hell, I was ready to run in and try to save you!"

Her lips parted a little. Wade couldn't help but admire the man for having been terrified but still wanting to protect Maya.

Thompson waited for Maya to respond. She sat silently. Even Wade didn't know what to say to that.

"You didn't report it," Wade finally said.

"No. You must have packed the cats up in your vehicles the next morning and taken off with them. There wasn't anything to report that anyone would have believed."

It wasn't good that Thompson thought they had a bunch of jaguars at the garden nursery, but he didn't have proof, and he hadn't seen any of them shift.

Wade squeezed Maya's hand. "There is no such thing as a trained jaguar guard cat. Maya and her family don't own any jaguars, male or otherwise. That's all we've got to say about it."

Thompson shifted his attention from Wade to Maya. "You remind me of a lady I know—Bella Wilder. She loved wolves and we're pretty sure she freed a wolf from the Oregon Zoo. I'd taken the female wolf to the zoo to protect her, and she was getting to know another red wolf when she vanished and a naked female—Bella—ended up in her place. Now, we're friends, but I still believe she and her husband had removed the wolf and freed her into the wild."

Wade didn't look to see how Maya was reacting to the news. Just because some crazy woman who loved wolves thought to release one into the wild, it didn't have anything to do with them.

"I'm beginning to think we have a similar situation here. Except wolves do run wild in Oregon. Jaguars don't in Texas," Thompson said.

David headed back to the table with Candy, his face dark. "Can I have a word with you alone, Wade?"

Wade was torn. He couldn't take Maya with them. Why the hell weren't her cousins here yet? He couldn't leave her here alone. Thompson was studying them, analyzing the situation.

"I'll be okay," Maya quickly said. "You guys go take care of business. Thompson and I can just talk about plants or something."

"We'll be right back." Wade kissed her cheek, gave Thompson a look that warned him not to upset Maya, then rose from the table. He squeezed Maya's hand, then left the club to speak in private with Candy and his brother.

"What's going on?" Wade asked Candy in the alley beside the club as David listened in.

Candy smiled up at him. "I called the buyer. He said we can meet him at another location tonight if you want to do some business with him."

Wade had two choices—leave his brother to watch over Maya and try to take down whoever the buyer was on his own, or take Maya with them. He didn't like either choice.

David must have been thinking along the same lines. "We can't take Maya with us."

"That's right," Candy said. "She can't go along for the ride."

Wade ignored her.

David cleared his throat and said to Wade, "Our friend Thompson could take her home."

Wade knew what he was referring to. Thompson had protected her at the club before, and Martin had checked him out and determined he was one of the good guys. Wade still didn't like the idea.

"It's about our only choice."

"The buyer won't wait forever," Candy warned.

"All right," Wade said, hating to agree to this. But if they could take down the buyer, they had to do it. He wasn't certain that Maya would go along with the plans, but he didn't want her driving home alone, either. "Wait for me at the car. I'll be right back."

Wade stalked into the club and saw Maya watching for his return. He smiled at her, and as soon as he reached the table, he pulled her into his arms and said into her ear for her hearing only, "We've got a chance to meet the buyer."

Her eyes widened.

"I don't want you to drive home alone," he said out loud.

"I'll be fine."

"I've got to take care of business. I don't want you to be alone," he said again. "If your cousins were here…"

"I could wait for them."

"No, it could still take a couple of hours for them to get here." He glanced at the dancers in the club. He was afraid Lion Mane might show up still.

"You need me to take her home?" Thompson asked.

Not looking really pleased but knowing how important this was, she finally let out her breath. "Okay, Thompson can follow me home if he doesn't mind. We both have our own vehicles."

Wade gave her a searing kiss and another hug, then reached over to shake Thompson's hand. "Thanks. I owe you one."

"I promise you I'll see her safely home."

"Thanks." Then hating it, but pumped up about catching the buyer, he gave Maya one last squeeze and headed out of the club.

"Do you want one last dance?" Thompson asked Maya.

Yeah, with Wade. She looked up at Thompson. "Sure, but I want you to know we're the good guys."

"Good guys, how?"

"We don't steal jaguars. We love them. We would protect them with our lives, but we don't steal them."

"I don't understand. So you're saying you bought them? Don't you have to have a license to have them in Texas? Facilities to house them? They can't be running loose like I saw."

She danced with Thompson, her attention drifting to three men lurking at the edge of the dance floor, shifters. "Yeah, I agree. We don't have any jaguars. Despite what you think you saw." Before the dance ended, she said to Thompson, "We better go before there's another fight."

Thompson looked at the men who were lined up, eyeing her. "You're still popular, I see."

"I'm a wild cat. Didn't you know?"

He smiled down at her. "As in shifter. Like you told me before."

"Sure." She took his hand and skirted around the men, trying to avoid them. Without David and Wade or her cousins to run interference, the shifters zeroed in on her.

"Wanna dance?" one of the men asked, trying to block Thompson from moving Maya out of the club.

"No, thank you."

The man grabbed her arm. "Just one dance."

"Let her go," Thompson said, his words dark with threat.

The shifter released her. Thompson moved Maya quickly through the club. "They're following us," he said under his breath to her.

Not liking this, Maya picked up her pace. Thompson swiftly escorted her to her car. She stared at the tires, punctured, as if the rubber had melted against the hot pavement. Her blood iced with anger.

She glanced back at the club and saw the shifters hesitating at the doorway.

"Come on. I'll take you in my truck, and your cousins or your boyfriend and his brother can take care of your car," Thompson said.

She hated leaving her car, but she figured they could be in more of a mess if the shifters decided to play hard-ball with the human.

Thompson's truck was black and featured a pack of beautiful gray wolves howling against the backdrop of a snow-covered mountain in a custom airbrushed paint job. He really was a wolf person. It amused her to think that he'd tangled with a bunch of big cats. She was never so glad to be inside a vehicle as when she climbed into the passenger seat of the truck, and he jumped into the driver's seat, turned on the engine, and gunned the gas.

"Okay, tell me what this is all about," he said.

She chewed on her lower lip.

Thompson glanced at her.

She folded her arms. "I've already explained."

"That you're a cat shifter and so are your brother and sister-in-law. So what about the rest of the cats I saw? Your cousins? Wade and his brother?"

"You really don't believe that, do you?"

"No. I think you're involved in something. But damned if I know what. I mean, jaguars aren't train-able like that. Not so that they can serve as obedient guard cats."

She frowned as Thompson took an exit she hadn't expected. "This isn't the fastest way out of Houston to catch the highway we need."

"We're being followed." Before she could ask him anything further, he added, "I'm a hunter. I know."

Chapter 23

DAVID DROVE THE RENTAL CAR WITH CANDY IN THE front passenger seat and Wade in the backseat. Wade texted Martin about their whereabouts in Houston and asked for backup. He also texted Connor to let him know that Thompson was taking Maya home.

Martin responded that Maya's cousins were the closest to them and on their way. But they were still about an hour and a half away in driving time.

"So how did you get involved in all this?" David asked Candy as she gave him the location to go to.

She shrugged. "I knew the guy who was looking to buy big cats. Then I met Bill and Jim Bettinger."

Lion Mane *was* Bettinger's brother. Wade's blood chilled.

"Yeah. I met the brothers at the club. The buyer wanted me to check out the place. He said he'd heard rumors that hunters met there who liked to get money for hunting big cats and selling to any willing buyer. I just kept asking guys, like I did your brother, if they were hunters. When I got a yes, I'd ask if they ever hunted big cats. Since you were both headed to Belize, and that's where some of the jaguars live, I figured you might be on a hunting expedition for someone else."

"Jaguars are not on the list of legal hunting game in Belize," Wade said. "Did anyone seem irritated that you were looking for big-cat hunters?"

"A few. One told me he'd kill any bastard who thought to hunt the beautiful creatures. I went along with it. Go with the flow, I always say. Just told him I agreed and moved on to the next table of guys."

Wondering how long the buyer had been paying to have the cats brought here, Wade bristled. "I've heard that thousands of hunters flock to Texas ranches to hunt endangered exotic animals."

"The animals here are *not* endangered," Candy said, her voice taking on a defensive tone. She flipped her hair back off her shoulders. "Not in Texas. Besides, over a quarter million animals come from Asia, Europe, and Africa. Texas has more exotic animals than anyplace else in the world. And it's perfectly legal to hunt them. So what's the difference?"

"The difference is that they're raising dama gazelles and cape buffalo and other exotics alongside the Texas longhorn, and then the ranchers offer hunting at a price to cull the stock of the gazelles and buffalo to raise money to provide for the rest of the animals. But the jaguars aren't being raised here. They're being brought in to slaughter. And shooting them isn't legal. Isn't that so? The buyer's not just keeping the cats to breed, right?"

He was against what the ranchers were doing. Many people agreed with the ranchers—that by bringing the exotic animals here, they were maintaining stock so that these rare animals wouldn't be exterminated completely. But many, like Wade, felt that the exotic animals shouldn't be raised just so hunters could kill them.

Candy folded her arms. "I thought you said you hunted big cats. I thought that's what you were doing in Belize."

Wade ignored this. "I've heard that hunting a dama gazelle on some ranches that offer exotic animals for hunting can run $10,000. The cape buffalo costs hunters about $50,000 to hunt." He was trying to show he knew something about how much the hunters were paying for a kill. And he wasn't going to be cheated when selling a jaguar to her boss. "So what does a jaguar price out at on a hunt?"

She smiled at him. "If you have to ask, you can't afford it." She sighed. "Okay, here's the deal. I overheard Jim and Bill talking about the jaguars Bill discovered on your girlfriend's property. He was angry because one of the cats bit him. He couldn't have been injured too badly because he didn't go to the hospital, and he flew out to Belize the next day. But he swore he'd been at Maya's garden nursery when it happened. Jim was really irate with him when he learned his brother had gone there without him. I figured that was because Jim had the hots for Maya, and he told his brother several times that it served him right that the cat bit him.

"I checked out Maya's business and discovered she had a jaguar pictured in her greenhouse. I showed the website to the buyer, and he said it was a female. But Bill said he encountered three big *males*. One was a rarer black. I'm pretty sure Maya wasn't the one who captured them and brought them to the States. Her brother and sister-in-law are too busy with running a garden to be bringing in jaguars. But your brother and you were there that same night, Bill said. You were in Belize after that. And in the Amazon five months earlier. *So*, my buyer believes *you* brought the cats here. If you have a jaguar or two to sell to my buyer, we could make a deal."

"Who's the buyer?" Wade asked.

Candy cast a quick smile over the seat back. "If you thought you could deal directly with him, you could cut me out of the market."

"So you're the middleman, and we're really not meeting him." Wade forced a smile. "Do you know what they do with the big cats after the hunters sell them to the buyer?"

"What do you care? You just hand over the jaguar and get paid for it. End of deal. When you want to sell him another, you can offer him that one, too. He pays $50,000 upon delivery."

Wade shook his head. "That's too small a payment for us to go to all that trouble. It costs a hell of a lot to transport them here. We have to pay a lot of money under the table to get them across two borders."

"If you've got three males and a female, it seems to me it wasn't all that difficult for you to get them here."

"Looks can be deceiving. I never expected the middleman who arranged for the sale of jaguars to be a beautiful woman, either."

She smiled at Wade's compliment.

"So who actually gets to hunt the cat?" David asked.

"The buyer offers a drawing. Whoever wins the lottery gets to hunt the cat."

"Does he use dogs?" Wade hoped not.

"No dogs. Hunting with dogs is illegal. And so is baiting the animals," she said.

Like killing jaguars wasn't.

"There are about three thousand acres, and about a

third of them are covered in trees. Lots of woods like the big cat might be used to," she continued.

"The hunter is on foot?" David asked.

He'd like to get the bastard on foot, Wade thought.

"Some hunt on foot. The ones who really want to live dangerously. Others drive an ATV. It costs more to use the vehicle. My buyer figures that if the hunter doesn't want to put the real effort into hunting the beast, he can pay for the luxury. He doesn't let the hunter take home the pelt. Too dangerous if someone should ask where he got the skin, and the hunter couldn't keep his mouth shut."

"So the buyer sells the cat's pelt to someone else," Wade said.

Candy smiled at Wade. "I like you. You're smart."

"Do you watch the hunt?" Wade wondered if she had the killer instinct like the hunters did, or if she was just in it for the money.

She hesitated to say and David and Wade glanced at her, reading her body language. She fidgeted in her seat, avoiding looking at them. "No," she finally said, then changed the subject. "So why do you hunt?"

"For the money," David said.

"For the kill," Wade said, thinking of Lion Mane and just how he wanted to take the bastard down.

"Does he have a regular group of hunters that bring him cats?" David asked.

"Yeah, but Jim Bettinger came home and said he'd lost his brother and two of the men who help him hunt down the jaguars and then smuggle them into the States. He couldn't do it alone."

"Lost?" David asked.

"He wouldn't say more. But he was really angry, and he didn't bring back a cat, either."

"Why don't you care to watch the hunters kill the cats?" Wade asked.

David glanced in the rearview mirror, frowning at Wade.

"The buyer follows the hunt as much as possible, taking a video of it. The other hunters get to watch it for a nominal charge while the hunt is in progress, open bar at the same time. But it's really a case of man against beast, so the only ones out there are the hunter and the buyer... and the cat, of course. I just arrange for the sale of the cat."

"So what's the time frame we're talking about for capturing a jaguar and handing it over to him?" David asked.

"He really needs this cat soon. The buyer's party is this weekend, two days from now. The hunters are in the area, but they'll be leaving on international business trips and my buyer had to move the date up, promising he'd have the cats available by then. The Bettinger brothers pledged they would have the cat to him before then. When Jim Bettinger came home empty-handed, I had to go to the club last night and ask several guys if they hunted, but everyone said no. One guy said he'd heard of the trouble the other men had in Belize, and there was no way in hell he was going to take on a job like that. You had cats here, but you'd taken off for Belize."

"What if the buyer can't locate a jaguar in time for the scheduled cat hunt this weekend?" Wade asked.

"He's got a backup plan."

"What's that?"

"He's got a female cat, but she's not all that big, and she's not that aggressive. He wants one from the wild. He's afraid the female he has won't provide a real challenge to the hunter. He'd also have to cancel the other hunter's chance at the hunt. He hates refunding money. Believe me, these hunts can backfire in a heartbeat. The news spreads by word of mouth and then there's no more hunting here. Or the hunters will refuse to pay the higher fees even if they still want to hunt the cat."

Thompson's missing zoo cat? Wade texted Martin about the possibility of the zoo cat being offered for the hunt.

Martin texted back. If you're thinking of "selling" a shifter to the buyer to learn who he is and where this business is taking place, I say no. Too dangerous. And as for the location she's directing you to? There's no such place.

"Stop the car," Wade said to David, then turned to Candy. "What is it that you want us to do exactly?"

David immediately pulled up next to the curb and waited for further instructions.

"My buyer doesn't believe Jim Bettinger can return to South or Central America and pick up another cat in time. He'd have to get some other help, since he's lost his brother and the rest of his men. My buyer knows you have jaguars that attacked Bill. He must have tried to steal your cats and say they were his and then planned to sell them as his own to the buyer. You must intend to sell them to someone else, or you wouldn't have them hidden away somewhere."

"You know that for certain?" Wade asked.

"I went to the garden nursery while you were away to look around the place. So yeah, I know that."

"You thought to steal them while we were gone? Cut out the hunter in the equation?" Wade growled, doing his best to sound angered.

"No, I just was to verify that you had the big cats before I told the buyer," Candy quickly said.

"Get out, Candy. You might get hurt." The threat in Wade's voice was real.

"What… you can't leave me out here." She twisted around to scowl at Wade. "This is a really bad part of town."

She was right. He couldn't leave her here. "We weren't really meeting the buyer, were we? You just wanted to confirm that we had the cats and were willing to sell them." Wade was already punching in a message to Maya. Where are you?

David said, "You heard my brother. Hit the road."

Candy didn't move. "You *need* me to make the sale to the buyer."

Wade's phone rang, and he said, "Yeah, Maya, where are you?"

"All four of my car tires were slashed. I had to ride with Thompson. We're being tailed. Thompson's trying to lose them."

Wade swore under his breath. "Divide and conquer" came rushing into his thoughts as the adrenaline surged through his blood. "Give me your coordinates. We're coming to your rescue."

"What about the buyer?" Maya asked Wade, her voice anxious.

He didn't care about that as much as he was worried about Maya. "We'll take care of it later," he said harshly. "Got to take care of Candy, then get back to you."

"Who's after Maya, Candy?" Wade grabbed his door handle and shoved the door open, then jumped out of the backseat, ready to toss Candy to the curb.

"Lion Mane. Jim Bettinger."

"Shit."

"I don't know why everyone's interested in Maya. Must be good in bed," Candy groused.

Wade yanked Candy's door open. "Why the hell is he after Maya?" Wade was certain he knew. Maya had killed Jim's brother.

"I don't have any idea except that he wanted more of her than just to dance." Candy wouldn't budge from the seat.

Wade reached down to grab her arm. "You got a phone on you?"

She nodded.

"Then call a taxi. Or Bettinger can drop by and pick you up, but you're not coming with us."

She yanked a Taser gun out of her purse.

Narrowing his eyes, Wade tsked. "Give us the name of your buyer, and we won't dump you here."

"I'll be out of a job."

"Your choice."

David wrenched the Taser gun out of her hand. She cried out as he twisted her wrist behind her with his quick action.

She rubbed her wrist. "Okay, okay."

Wade got back in the car and gave Thompson's co-ordinates to Martin. David pulled away from the curb and hightailed it in the direction Maya and Thompson were headed.

"The buyer's name is?" Wade asked Candy.

"Gunther Smith." The woman frowned at Wade.

"Your name?"

"Candy."

Wade looked up from texting, and she shrugged. "It's the name my mother gave me. So sue me." She frowned at him. "What are you doing exactly? How are you learning all this stuff so quickly?" Her eyes widened. "Are you the feds?" She shook her head. "You can't be. We already checked you out."

"Your last name?"

She hesitated to answer, then asked, "Will you sell us one of the cats?"

"You're not with the police, are you?" That's all they'd need was for Candy to be an undercover cop, attempting a sting operation.

She laughed. "You think I'm going to say you're both under arrest for attempting to smuggle exotic cats into the country for the purpose of selling them? Hardly."

"We'll have to think further about selling one of the cats to you."

"If you say you definitely will, I'll give you my full name. Oh, and what happened to the other men? Bill Bettinger and the two smugglers?" she asked, sounding a little unsure of herself as if it was a dangerous thing to ask.

"They didn't make it back. The rainforest can be a deadly place if you don't know what you're doing." He gave her a warning look not to press the issue or she might end up where the others had.

"So you eliminated some of your competition," she said. "That's what we suspected."

Wade said to his brother, "Drive faster. We need to find Maya, now!"

Chapter 24

MAYA'S SKIN PRICKLED WITH ANXIETY. SHE WAS certain that Thompson wasn't going to lose the truck following them. The rig painted in camouflage had a Herd grill guard and bull bars in front, so if the driver chose to ram Thompson hard, he would lose control of his truck, guaranteed.

Maya pulled off her seat belt as Thompson made another turn downtown, trying to lose the tail. "What are you doing?" Thompson asked. "You should keep your seat belt on. It's too dangerous not to."

"Do you have a gun?"

He stared at her for a second, then watched his driving again. "Tranquilizer gun."

"Good. But it might not be enough. I'm going to shift. You *can't* tell anyone about this, okay? My brother would kill me if he knew. Maybe kill you, too. So we keep it a secret between ourselves, all right?"

"I don't believe any of this," Thompson muttered. "Who are those guys following us?"

"Taking a wild guess? Lion Mane and a buddy. Lion Mane was the guy I danced with at the club a week ago. You remember the guy with the blond hair?" Maya climbed over the seat, afraid she was flashing her thong, but hopefully Thompson was watching his driving.

Thompson snorted. "I never thought they'd go this far to get your interest."

She yanked her dress over her head and tossed it on the seat, then ditched her shoes.

Thompson swung a wild right down another street.

Maya lost her balance and fell against the seat. She quickly righted herself and slid her thong off. Thompson glanced up at the rearview mirror.

"Watch your driving." She unfastened her strapless bra and left it on the seat. "Don't watch me."

Thompson didn't say anything, but he was grinding his back teeth. "I don't believe any of this." But he sounded like he wasn't real sure of what he was saying.

"Believe what you will. We'll need every weapon we can use. Oh and, Thompson? Lion Mane is a jaguar shifter, too. If they stop us and we're out of options, open the door so I can get out of the truck and attempt to deal with them. Okay?"

Thompson stared at her. Thankfully, because of the seat, he couldn't see her nude body, only the swell of her breasts and naked shoulders. "All right? If you keep me penned up in the truck and they begin shooting, I won't have a chance to help us."

"All right." He sounded so unconvinced that she wanted to shift and give him a small nip to prove she wasn't making this stuff up. "I'll let you out if the time comes. And I'll have my rifle ready."

"I won't bite you. No matter how scary I might look, I know what I'm doing. I might growl and sound vicious and deadly. But you're one of the good guys. You love the jaguars as much as we do. You're on our side. You just can't let anyone, not *anyone*, know we exist."

Then she called on the need to shift, and in that blur between human and jaguar, warmth seeped through her body, through every muscle, through every tissue, through every cell. She felt the change from being a much less flexible human to becoming a golden furred cat, stretching and purring until the vehicle crashed with a bang.

Wade was getting a really bad feeling. For the past ten minutes, he'd tried over and over to reach Maya without success. "I can't get ahold of her," Wade told his brother. He contacted Martin. "Any luck with locating her?"

"None," Martin answered. "I've been in touch with her cousins. They're on their way to your location."

Wade was afraid they'd be too late. David drove around the area for another twenty minutes, until Wade was ready to shift and run through Houston searching for her.

His brother glanced at him. "You can't."

"Hell, I know I can't. But sitting in a car and not being able to search for her by..." He stopped short of saying scent. He wished they'd dumped Candy's butt at the convenience store.

"You wouldn't be able to locate her while she's riding in Thompson's truck," David said.

Wade knew that. He just hated feeling that the situation was so out of his control. They heard sirens, and David headed in that direction.

"Where are you going?"

"Anywhere. We haven't had word, and until we do, I have no idea where to drive to."

Wade watched for signs of emergency lights and finally saw the flashing, colorful lights partially hidden by a tall glass building. "Fire truck, police cars. Virtually no traffic down here."

When they drew close, Wade took in the sight of the crumpled truck, wolves painted on the side. Thompson's truck? Wade's heart thundered in his ears. David had barely slowed down to see what was going on before Wade was opening the car door.

"Christ, Wade, let me stop before you kill yourself." David jerked the car to the curb and let Wade out as a policeman hurried toward them to tell them to stay away from the scene of the accident.

"I know the driver and the woman who was with him, Thompson and Maya Anderson," Wade said to the policeman, trying to draw closer. "What's happened? Where are they?"

"Mr. Thompson suffered a head injury in the collision. It looks like another vehicle hit him, slamming his truck into the light pole, and then took off. There wasn't any sign of a… woman."

"Let me talk to him," Wade said, trying to get past the policeman, attempting not to growl too much. He really had to speak with Thompson.

"Sir," the policeman said.

"She's my fiancée, damn it!"

David had parked the car farther away and was running in Wade's direction.

The policeman cleared his throat. "You know this man well?"

"Thompson? Yeah, he's from the Oregon Zoo, searching for a missing jaguar. We've been trying to help him track it down."

"And your… fiancée was with him because…?"

Wade glowered at the officer. "He was taking her home."

"Sounds like police business to me." The officer waved for someone else to talk to them.

Wade glanced at the waiting ambulance as emergency personnel were strapping Thompson on a gurney before they loaded it into the ambulance. "I need to see Thompson."

"I'm Detective Oberton," the man said, then dismissed the other policeman. "I overheard you say you know the driver."

Wade quickly gave him the same spiel as he had the other officer. "I need to speak with Thompson. My fiancée was with him. Where is she now? If the man who forced Thompson off the street did it to kidnap my fiancée…"

The detective let out his breath and glanced in the direction of two officers who were checking out Wade's rental car. The men shook their heads, and one of them motioned that it was all clear.

Wade frowned at the policemen and then at the detective. He folded his arms. "I didn't have anything to do with crashing Thompson's truck into the pole."

"It appears you didn't." The detective continued to jot down notes on his notepad, then looked up at Wade. "Mr. Thompson has a concussion. He's incoherent, slurring his words, mentioning something about jaguars and Maya. I'm sure if he's looking for the missing jaguar from his zoo, he's confused about that and jumbling it together with talk about your fiancée."

"So let me talk to him."

"For just a second. They need to get him to the hospital." The detective walked with Wade to the ambulance, though Wade was ready to push him aside and sprint for it. He also needed to check out Thompson's truck.

"Thompson." Wade reached out to grasp the zoo man's cold hand. He squeezed it reassuringly.

Thompson's eyes looked like glassy blue lakes. He stared at Wade without comprehension.

"Was it that blond guy… you know, Lion Mane, who took Maya? Did he say where he was taking her? Thompson?"

Thompson's lips parted, but he didn't make a sound. Frowning a little, he looked confused.

"Thompson, tell me. Did he take her?"

"Mr. Patterson," the detective said, "he's just too injured to respond. Let them take him to the hospital. You can see him there."

"Thompson, did… he… take… her?"

Thompson shut his eyes.

Hell. "Okay, we'll check on you at the hospital in a little while. Hold on, buddy." For the first time since he'd met the man, Wade noticed that Thompson wore a wedding ring. "I'll get in touch with your family."

As the ambulance took Thompson to the hospital, Wade began to walk toward the truck, taking deep breaths and trying to smell Lion Mane's scent.

"You can't get close to the truck. It's a crime scene," the detective said.

"I'm not going to touch anything."

David was walking with him but stopped in his tracks to let Wade try and persuade the detective to let him get closer.

"The thing of it is…" the detective said, stopping Wade, "the situation's a little complicated."

Wade frowned at him. "What do you mean?"

"Well, you think Mr. Thompson is a friend of yours and Maya's, but maybe something else was going on… more than you might think."

Wade stared at the man, believing he was trying to tell him something without really coming out and saying it. Wade looked back at the truck and tried to imagine why the detective was so antsy about him getting close to the vehicle. What would be inside that would concern him?

Her clothes. Damn it to hell. She couldn't have shifted. Not in front of Thompson.

He turned to face the detective. The officer thought Thompson and Maya were getting it on when Thompson was already married and Maya was Wade's fiancée? Not that she was, but close enough.

"She had a change of clothes. She lives with her brother at Anderson Garden Nursery, and he doesn't like it when she goes to a club dressed in something kind of scandalous. Since I bought it for her, she wore it. She would have changed into jeans and a T-shirt before she arrived home. Were you worried about the dress she left behind?" He imagined she left more than that—panties and a bra, and how could he easily account for that?

"We did wonder." The detective's face turned a shade of mottled red, and he cleared his throat.

Wade was certain that the detective had probably seen everything anyone could imagine, but not a woman shifting into a jaguar. He was afraid one human had seen something he should never have. How they were to resolve that mess, he didn't know.

"Do you have a picture of the lady?" the detective asked, not sounding convinced after hearing Wade's explanation.

"Yeah. Hold on." Wade searched for the one he'd taken on his phone at the club when he first met her and she was wearing the T-shirt minidress, smiling, beautiful. "Here it is. That was taken just a week ago at the club."

The detective had Wade email him the picture. "And we can reach you where?"

Wade gave his information and Maya's home address where they'd be staying, although they were sticking around Houston while they tried to locate Maya. He also gave the detective her brother's contact information.

"Who was this… Lion Mane… character?" the detective asked.

"A man she danced with at the Jungle Cat Fever Club. He was interested in her. She didn't return the interest."

"I see." The detective didn't sound like he believed Wade. That maybe the lady had changed her mind. After all, if she was supposed to be Wade's fiancée, why was she dancing with other men? "You don't know what his real name was?"

"No. That was his club name." Wade wasn't about to give the detective Lion Mane's real name. Wade had to take care of this shifter to shifter.

"If anyone contacts you concerning Maya, here's my number. Call me directly—right away." The detective handed him a card.

"Thanks. I'll do that." Wade walked closer to the truck and smelled that a gun had been fired, and that Jim Bettinger had been here. Another man had been with him. Another shifter. He was sure the two of them had taken Maya.

His hands clenched into fists, Wade felt his temper escalate.

"We'll get her back," David said quickly.

Yeah, but alive? Or dead?

When David and Wade returned to the rental car, both brothers were silent, just sitting in the car and saying nothing.

"He won't hurt her," Candy said, and they both turned to look at her. She shrugged. "He had the hots for her."

Ignoring the woman, Wade said to his brother, "A shot was fired next to Thompson's truck. Since Thompson wasn't shot, I can only assume Maya was. She was… feral." He couldn't say she was wearing her jaguar coat in front of Candy. She wouldn't have a clue what being feral meant.

David shook his head. "She's not ready for city life. So where do we go now?"

"Where did Bettinger take Maya?" Wade asked Candy, his voice a growl, warning her to tell him the truth, or else.

Chapter 25

DRIFTING IN AND OUT OF A LIGHTLESS ROOM, MAYA felt warmth seeping through her blood, felt him hold her close. Dancing, so light on her feet that she was floating, their bodies as one. Moving, kissing, she licked her lips. He was touching her breasts, her waist, her buttocks, embracing, holding her tight, murmuring in her ear like a soft, warm summer breeze. No words, just a whispered brush of breath. Wade, she tried to whisper back, but she couldn't form the word. Only in her mind, his name drifting like a wisp of cloud just out of reach.

Wade. She wouldn't try to say his name then as she felt his warmth surround her, his love, his comforting embrace.

Maya stretched lazily as a cat—wondering when she'd shifted forms—and bumped into a clinking metal mesh. At the same time she smelled the odor of cat urine mixed with bleach and water, felt the hard concrete floor beneath her and the warm breeze flowing over her. Immediately she opened her eyes. The cat pee smell was strong, burning her eyes. Where the hell was she?

She tried to get to her feet, but all she could do was lift her head and stare at her cage. *Drugged.* She'd been drugged like Wade had been in the jungle. Only she wasn't in the jungle. He wasn't with her. She was in a big-cat run somewhere surrounded by a grassy meadow, trees dotting the landscape, and a heavy pine forest surrounding the area close by.

She stared at the steel, twelve-foot-tall mesh that surrounded the run, the rough concrete slab beneath her, the wooden box behind her that looked like a den to curl up in, and a slight overhang to provide shade. A security light pierced the darkness. She noticed another run next door and saw a female jaguar sleeping. The one from the zoo?

Then she remembered the truck accident, Thompson being injured, her attacking or trying to attack Lion Mane, and him shooting her with a tranquilizer dart. She'd nearly bitten him, then collapsed, a cat ready to rip him apart and then too sleepy to bother.

A man cleared his throat, and she swung her head around, totally thrown off by the fact that he'd been watching her and she hadn't known it. The drug running through her system had to be making her so clueless—so… unjaguar-like. She should have sensed him right away, though she did notice that the breeze was carrying his scent away from her.

She looked him over closely now—the lean tall form of him. About thirty-five, she guessed, his gray-blue eyes sharp, his dark brown hair mussed by the breeze. He was placing his weight more on one leg as though he was favoring the other. Then she saw the cane tucked behind him. Twice already, he'd moved, and each time he winced as though his leg was bothering him. But what really caught her eye was his face—half of it was scarred horribly, like cat claw marks running from his forehead down his throat. He was lucky to be alive after an encounter that left him scarred like that.

Had it been one of the big cats he'd bought to have hunted?

Served him right, if so.

His gaze remained on her, his mouth curving up slightly. "Jim said you're a wild cat, straight from Belize. Now I don't have to rely solely on that poor excuse for a jaguar." He motioned toward the other cat.

Jim Bettinger? He couldn't have sold her to this man so that he could have her hunted down. If the hunter killed her, she would shift into a human and he knew it. What was Bettinger thinking?

"He said you're real special. That you killed his brother and one of our smuggler friends. So we're going to ensure that you have a chance to really show what a tiger you are. Pardon the mixed cat reference."

She wanted to tell him that whatever cat had clawed him so grotesquely deserved to be rewarded. But she imagined the animal had died long ago.

Maybe his injury was the reason he arranged for the hunting of big cats—to get back at the one that had disfigured him so badly.

"He promised me a big male, too. And I've decided to throw in the other female. Three hunters at one time. It'll be the hunting sensation of the year."

Maya glanced at the other cat. Had Bettinger managed to capture the female jaguar his brother lost in Belize? Bettinger had said Maya was a wild cat. So did that mean the other wasn't? Was she the zoo cat Thompson was searching for?

Maya's advantage over a jaguar that didn't shift was that she knew something of the way hunters thought. She was both a hunter and a human. If she were strictly a cat, she'd try to avoid the hunters. That's what they couldn't anticipate: Her unpredictability. The hunted hunting *them*.

"The price is going way up on you, missy," the man said proudly.

She heard someone coming, and he turned and smiled at the person just out of Maya's view.

As soon as she saw him, Maya growled low.

Jim Bettinger, aka Lion Mane, smiled broadly at her as he ran his fingers over the steel mesh caging her in. "Hello, beautiful cat. So we meet again."

The tip of her tail twitched, and her eyes narrowed as she focused fully on him. She so wanted to take care of him just as she had his brother.

"Better not get in her way," the buyer said. "She looks like she'd love to rip you apart and eat you slowly."

"Hmm," Jim said, running his hand along a corner pole. "She's welcome to bite me any time, Gunther. But just know this, beautiful cat. I bite back." He turned to Gunther. "Make sure she's locked up tight in there."

"You think she's going to walk out on her own?"

"Trust me," Jim said, looking back at Maya. "She's capable of anything. And if she can't do it on her own, she might very well have help. So you need to ensure she's not going anywhere."

Jim glanced up at a point on the cage above her head. "We'll be watching you."

She looked to see what he was talking about, presuming the place had security cameras. It did. She didn't give a damn who was watching, though. If she could buy her freedom any way possible, she was doing it, even if that meant she had to shift in front of the camera.

"I think you've done a good job," Gunther told the shifter. "I can tell just from the way she was watching you and now me that she's intelligent. She's going to be just perfect for the hunt."

"Yeah, she is," Jim agreed.

"Want some dinner? This calls for a celebration. I'll have some nice bloody steaks sizzling on the grill in no time." Gunther limped off.

He would be an easy kill, Maya thought, though they needed to send him to jail for all of his illegal killings, since he was human.

Jim still watched her through the cage and made a kissing motion at her.

She shouldn't have done it, but she wanted to scare the cockiness out of the son of a bitch. She leaped to her feet, thankful she could manage to shake off the grogginess this much, bounded across the run, and slammed against the cage door with her paws, growling and snarling, forcing Jim to jump back and let out a cry of distress.

Gunther laughed. "Told you she's smart. You'd better not be anywhere near the hunting grounds. If she could, I'd bet my lands she'd target you even if someone else was firing a gun at her."

Jim was watching her warily, and Gunther had stopped to observe her with a sly smile on his face, amused that the she-cat had frightened the superior hunter.

"Your ass is mine," Jim said, his eyes full of hostility.

"Only if you pay for the chance to hunt her," Gunther warned, the smile sliding off his face.

Jim nodded. "Let's get those steaks." Then he turned and headed in the direction Gunther was going.

She watched them disappear past the cement-block wall that blocked her view. She wondered if anyone was monitoring the cameras. If she could knock out a light overhead, they couldn't see her. But she'd have to shift first before she could use something on the light.

She looked around and saw a stainless-steel water trough and food dish.

The food dish might work. She'd have to wait until the men were gone or in bed. She glanced at the other cat. She was watching her, almost looking like she was smiling.

"I don't know where Jim Bettinger has taken your girlfriend," Candy said to Wade and David. Her phone buzzed and she texted back. "My buyer just bought a female cat from Jim Bettinger."

Damn it to hell. Bettinger had to have sold Maya to the buyer. What was Bettinger thinking? "Bettinger didn't have a cat to sell. And you know it. He stole one of mine."

Candy folded her arms. "Says you. How are you going to prove that cat was yours? Got papers?"

"I've got a picture of her posted on Maya's website. You know the one. You saw it yourself."

Candy's mouth dropped open. But then she quickly snapped it shut. "I don't know anything about it."

"I really don't give a damn if you do or don't. I want you to contact the buyer and tell him my brother's bringing you a trade. A male for a female," Wade said.

Candy smiled. "Interesting proposition, but he's surely already paid for the female. You can't expect him to pay you for the male and give up the female."

"No payment. Just an even trade."

Candy frowned at him. "I don't get it."

"She's my *breeding* stock, damn it." Maya would be thrilled to hear Wade say it.

"Let me call him." Candy touched the screen on her phone, then spoke into it. "Um, I have an offer from the other hunters. They say Jim stole their female cat, and they want to trade a male for her."

Candy looked up at Wade. With his cat's hearing, Wade heard the man say, "He does, does he? Jim's right here, and he says the cat's his."

"It isn't. Wade has proof it isn't," Candy said.

"Possession is nine-tenths of the law, Sis."

Sis? This woman was the buyer's sister?

"He's willing to give you a male in her place so he can use her for breeding stock," Candy said.

A long pause followed.

"Candy, Jim said no to the offer. He's going to deliver another cat—male this time. We're going to have three on the hunt. First time to have multiple cats to hunt."

"Won't that be dangerous?" Candy asked, sounding anxious. She was frowning, looking at the floor as if she'd forgotten Wade and his brother were there. "If you're going to do this, I don't want you out there in the field videotaping it. It's too risky."

"I'll be in the ATV. You worry too much."

"You know how dangerous the cats can be," she said.

"All too well. Jim and I are having steaks to celebrate his bringing me a wild jaguar and the other addition—tomorrow. You won't need to drum up any more business for a while. Unless you're just enjoying yourself. Come on home and join us, if you want."

"Thanks. I will. Bye." She hung up the phone and stuck it in her bag.

"Your brother," Wade said.

"What?" Candy looked stricken.

"Your brother. The buyer. He said no to exchanging a male out for the female because Jim is going to sell him another cat. Since he didn't bring one from Belize, that means he intends to steal another one of *my* cats."

She licked her lips and glanced from Wade to his brother. "I'm sorry. I… I don't know what to say."

"Give me your purse," Wade demanded.

"I don't have any money."

"Just give me the damned purse."

She handed it to him and he jerked it out of her hands, found a wallet, and looked for her driver's license. *Candy Lyn Jaemison.*

He brought out his phone and took a picture of her name, address, and ID photo. Now, if they could just find a Jaemison who lived in the area, probably some distance away from Houston, though. The ranch couldn't be too close in, not if they did big-game hunting.

She had several credit cards—looked like business was good—and the usual woman stuff—nail file, lipstick, pen, checkbook, a clutter of receipts. One was a gas receipt for the little town close to Maya's garden nursery. He read the address on the checkbook, same as the one on her driver's license.

He pulled out her phone next and called Martin. When he answered, Wade said, "Record the number. It's Miss Candy Jaemison's. The woman leading us to Maya's captor."

"Got it. Anything else?"

He read off all the phone numbers she had in her address book.

"All right, all right," Candy said. "Maya's abduction has nothing to do with my brother, though. If Jim took her, then I'll tell you what I know. I was supposed to meet George Tucker after we made a deal about the cat. You know, I mentioned him before. He was at the bar that first night I met you." She gave them the name of the hotel and David headed downtown.

"How do you know he's involved in this deal with Maya?"

"He and Jim were together tonight. Jim was ranting about his brother dying in Belize, and George was trying to calm him down. Jim said he knew Maya had returned to the club, and he talked about convincing her to go somewhere quiet with him. George said he'd help him. I was to meet him later at the club, and then we were going to the hotel. I had to call off the club date because of you two. I told him once I was done with business, I'd join him at the hotel. What are you going to do to him?"

"Convince him that he wants to let us know where Maya is."

When they reached the hotel, Wade and David rushed Candy up to the seventh floor. Wade and his brother stood away from the door of the room where George was staying while Candy knocked on it.

"It's just me," she called out.

Chapter 26

"WHAT THE HELL TOOK YOU SO—" GEORGE SAID, opening the door, wearing only boxers and a frown. His brown eyes widened as he saw David and Wade holding Candy's arms, and he took a deep breath and smelled the scent of the shifters in front of him. Angry shifters.

He tried to slam the door in their faces, but Wade had anticipated his action and blocked the door with his boot.

George raced across the room, grabbed a tranq gun, and fired it without aiming properly. The dart hit Candy. She squeaked, eyes wide, and crumpled to the carpeted floor.

Wade had the man by the throat in the next instant, walking him backward into the suite, while David quickly checked the rest of the place to make sure George was the only person there.

David nodded to Wade. "You can kill him now."

"Wait," the man said, eyes bulging as he grasped Wade's hands still around his throat. "What's this all about?"

Wade backed him up to the brown sofa in the sitting area and shoved him onto it. "Bettinger asked you to help him grab Maya for him."

"What? He wanted her. Sure. But then he changed his mind, called me, and told me to pick up a jaguar for him instead."

"He paid you to take a female jaguar where?" Wade towered over him, arms crossed over his chest, eyes narrowed.

The shifter glanced at David and then at Wade, his forehead pebbled with sweat. "What... what do you want with the jaguar?"

"She was *my* property. Bettinger had no right to her. What's your name?"

"George Tucker." He swallowed hard. "Jim said... the man stole the cat from him. He needed my help to get her back, and he was paying lots of money, no questions asked."

"That's the first thing that should have clued you in that you were doing something illegal."

"Illegal?"

"Where'd you take her? To the ranch? To be hunted?"

"Hunted?" George shook his head.

"Were you involved in crashing the truck Maya was riding in?"

"No, I never saw any truck. Bettinger handled the whole thing and had me pick the cat up from him at an abandoned building. I delivered her across town to another location where a waiting vehicle was parked. Bettinger was really paranoid that someone would come looking for the cat." George's jaw dropped open, and then he let out his breath. "Hell, no wonder he was worried someone could find the trail. He'd stolen the cat from two shifters."

"Where *is* she?" Wade growled.

"I don't know. I was supposed to transfer her to the trunk of another vehicle parked in a vacant lot."

"Okay, let's go. Don't try to cause any trouble for

us," Wade said, "or you'll damn well regret it. Get some pants on first."

"They're in there," George said, motioning to the bedroom.

David waved for him to get his clothes. "Nice and easy," David warned.

"You realize we're with the Service, right?" Wade said.

George swallowed hard. "I kind of suspected that when you barged in the way you did. I didn't know anything about jaguars being hunted. I swear it. It was just some quick, easy money. I should have known it was too good to be true." He slipped into the bedroom, quiet as a cat in the rainforest, and grabbed his clothes, then hurried out of the bedroom. David and Wade waited while George fumbled with his clothes in getting dressed.

"What… what are you going to do with me?" George asked, looking like his legs were barely holding him up.

"Just keep talking about what happened while you dress," Wade said.

"Okay, I assume that whoever was picking her up was watching because I had to leave the keys on the driver's seat and anyone could have stolen the car. I was told in pretty harsh terms not to wait around."

George yanked on his sneakers without bothering with socks. "If someone got to the car and stole it, the thieves would have a real shock. They'd have found a jaguar in the trunk. Once she awakened, they'd have regretted stealing the car, but it would have served them right."

"Name and make of the car? Color? License tags?"

George gave Wade the information in a hurry. "You can't kill me. I haven't done anything wrong, according to our laws." He tugged on a T-shirt.

David quickly texted the information to Martin.

"You conspired to supply a jaguar as prey for an illegal hunt." Wade said, raising a brow. "Grab Candy.
We'll take her with us. If we left her and she woke, she
could warn her brother we're out to get Maya back."

The man's eyes grew round as he stared mutely at
Wade. He suspected the man really hadn't known that's
why Bettinger was buying the cat. "I can't believe
they're going to hunt her. I... I thought Bettinger just
wanted his shifter girlfriend back and was plenty pissed
about her being with the other guy. You know how we
are. Possessive. Territorial."

David grabbed Candy off the floor and cradled
her in his arms, since George seemed too shocked to
react quickly.

Wade continued to tick off the charges as he shoved
George toward the door. "Taking a shifter hostage."

All the color drained from George's face. "I... I
didn't think of it as taking her hostage. She was just...
asleep. I was just returning her to Bettinger."

"...To use in a hunt where hunters have paid to kill
said shifter. Do you know what would happen if word
got out that a hunter had killed a shifter and that shifter
turned from cat to human when she died? All caught
on videotape?"

"My God," George said, shaking. "I... I didn't know
that's what he wanted her for. I would never have agreed
to anything like that. I thought he just wanted her back."

"*And* she happens to be *my* woman," Wade growled,
hand clenched around George's arm as he guided him
out of the suite.

"*Your* woman?" George looked like he was ready to

pass out. "I swear I don't know where they took her. I'll drive you to the place where I transferred her to the other vehicle, but that's all I know. What are you going to do with me?"

Wade and David flanked him as they hurried him out of the hotel. "We'll turn you and Candy over to our boss. He'll hand her over to the police once we're finished mopping things up," Wade said.

"Which group are you in? The Enforcers?" George sounded hopeful. No one who knew about their organization wanted a visit from the Avengers, who terminated shifters who were this much in violation of their shifter laws.

"Golden Claws." Which meant they did *everything*.

George stumbled. Wade tightened his hold on George's arm to steady him. "Easy, man."

"I… I heard Bettinger's brother and a couple of human smugglers were in Belize and didn't make it out of the jungle alive," George said.

Wade gave him a small smile. "You heard right."

"I don't… haven't ever done any of that kind of work."

"Our boss will investigate your claims," Wade said.

"Whose car do we take, or should we take both?" David asked Wade.

"These people trust George more than they do us. We'll take his car."

They all piled into George's car, David driving while Candy slept in the front seat and Wade sat in the backseat with George, who gave directions while Wade read his text messages. He saw George watching him. "What?" Wade asked, his tone harsh. He was ready to kill George for handing Maya over to Bettinger.

"I'll help you get her back. Whatever you want me to do, I'll do it. Anything."

"Anything?" Wade asked, his voice softly dangerous.

"Yeah. Anything. I didn't know she was someone else's woman, damn it. Or that they planned to hunt her. Hell, I'll kill Bettinger myself."

"That's my job," Wade said, noticing how late it was getting. He hoped the bastards weren't mistreating Maya. Just confining her in a pen would be bad enough.

"I don't know if it'll help any, but Candy said something about the big party being moved up to this morning."

His heart thundering, Wade stared at George in disbelief.

"Storms are predicted for the area all day."

"This morning," Wade said, the pit of his stomach dropping like a lead weight in the dark Amazon River. "We're running out of time."

~~~

He was with Maya now, loving her, kissing her, hugging her, warming her. She couldn't seem to raise her arms to hug him back. She tried, but she felt... lost. He didn't seem to mind, his whispered breath against her cheek, letting her know he was here for her. She wasn't alone.

Thunder boomed in the distance as the air crackled with the approaching storm, waking Maya from a sound sleep. The damn drug!

The weekend was only two days away and no sign of any sort of rescue. She knew Wade and everyone else would be looking for her. But would they be too late?

Last night, she'd intended to attempt an escape, but that bastard Bettinger had shot her with another tranquilizer dart after he'd eaten dinner with Gunther. After that, she'd been out for the rest of the night.

She'd only just managed to get to her feet and stood staring at the sheets of lightning flashing across the black sky in the distance, highlighting massive blue-black thunderheads that towered in the early dawn. Forks of lightning zigzagged to the earth, an explosive boom of thunder rippling into rumbling overhead afterward.

She was swaying on her feet, unable to keep her balance as the wind picked up. Twisting her ears, she heard what sounded like a truck approaching. Breakfast? At this hour?

Glancing at the cat run next to hers, she saw that the other jaguar was gone. Her heart fluttering wildly, Maya stared at the empty cage. Where was the cat? She'd wanted to save her, though she wasn't sure how she was going to do that. She needed to save herself if she was going to be any help to anyone else.

She saw headlights in the gloom and felt a chill race down her spine as her tail swished anxiously. If they opened the cage and didn't shoot her first, she would leap at them and run.

As the truck drew closer, she stiffened, with only the tip of her tail moving in a tight twist back and forth.

The engine rumbled. Maybe they meant to take her somewhere drier in the event the storm was really bad. Yeah, right. So she would be nice and dry for the hunt later.

The truck backed in toward the cage. The tailgate lowered like a lift. Then she saw the smaller cage sitting on the bed of the truck. Bettinger and a man she didn't recognize got out. She smelled the air. Human.

Bettinger smiled. "Glad to see you standing, though you look like you're ready to collapse, beautiful cat. Why don't you take a load off, and we'll take care of you?"

She stared at him, her feral expression reflected in his dark eyes. He smiled. "Have it your way, but I think you're going to want to cooperate. If you do, no more tranquilizer darts and by the time the hunt starts, you'll have a sporting chance to run. Not get away, but just… run. If you give us any trouble, I'm taking you down again. Then you're going to have one hell of a time waking up enough to attempt escape before the hunt starts. So I'm giving you fair warning."

She knew he wouldn't. He'd have hell to pay if he shot her full of dope and she didn't give the hunters the sport they had paid for. He was all bluster. She sure would love to take a bite out of him and end this game between them.

He began to rig up a fenced-in walkway between the cage and the run. She could slash and bite at the mesh, but it wouldn't do anything but make them jump back and maybe make Bettinger angry. She couldn't believe they were moving up the hunt. Surely they couldn't mean that she could run free for two days.

She looked at the mesh while the other man held a rifle aimed at her, just waiting for her to make a move. She glanced at the other cage. Had they taken the other cat and let her go free until the hunt began also? Or had they already killed her, and Maya's turn was next?

Bettinger was almost finished setting up the mesh walkway and glanced in the direction Maya was looking. "Don't even think of searching for the other cat.

She's on her own. You go to her, and you're going to forget watching out for us."

Us? She looked back at Bettinger. He smiled. "Oh yeah, I'm coming for you, beautiful cat."

The other man said, "You didn't pay to hunt her, Bettinger. You can't go out there."

"I've promised Gunther a male cat, and I'm going to be the one videotaping the hunt this time."

"Gunther always videotapes the sessions. He won't let anyone else touch his camera equipment."

"Not this time. It was my condition. One free, wild male cat for his hunters to kill, and I tape the show."

"You've got balls. I'll give you that."

"Yeah. I do." Bettinger patted the cage. "Come on. Up you go. Make it easy on yourself."

"She won't do it."

Bettinger smiled at Maya. "Sure she will, if she knows what's good for her."

Maya looked from him to the cage. It was so small. She'd be so cramped in it. No room to move, to even turn around. She'd have to back out when she got to where they intended to let her out. She didn't have much of a choice, and if it meant freedom even for a short while, she'd do it.

She ran through the mesh walkway and jumped onto the bed of the truck, then crouched in the cage, growling as she went.

"That wasn't so hard now, was it?" Bettinger said, jerking the cage door shut and locking it.

He climbed onto the bed of the truck and sat next to the cage.

"What are you doing?" the other man asked.

"I'm going to give the cat a pep talk." Bettinger's grin was as evil as they come.

Chapter 27

MARTIN CAME THROUGH FOR THEM. THE LICENSE-plate number George had given to Wade belonged to Gunther Jaemison, Candy's brother. A rural address was listed on a farm road two hours north of where George had put Maya in the trunk of a car, but Wade and David were now only ten minutes from it.

David was driving forty miles over the posted speed limit. Wade had texted the information to Everett, who texted back that they would arrive about fifteen minutes after Wade did.

Then Wade let Connor know what was up.

"I want him dead, Wade."

"You don't have to tell me. Bettinger won't live once I get hold of him."

George flinched next to Wade in the backseat. George was the only reason they had a lead to where the ranch was. As long as the rest of his story checked out, he was good to go, with a warning.

Wade wasn't about to let him off the hook yet, though. George had endangered Maya's life, and she could still die. He would put George's offer to help them to the test, no matter the sacrifice, if it meant saving Maya.

"What are you going to do?" Connor asked.

"Shift as soon as we get there. I've got to locate Maya. From what Candy told George, they're moving up the hunt to this morning. If they release her, no telling where she's going to be. I've got to try and locate her, and I can't do that running as a human."

"What is your brother going to do? Our cousins? Where are they?"

"My brother will direct operations at the ranch. He'll coordinate with your cousins to make an arrest of all the people at the ranch who are supposed to be watching the videotaping of the hunt. David and our other men will pose as federal agents."

"And that bastard who's with you?"

"George?" Wade glanced at him. "It's his choice. The ones waiting at the ranch are all hunters. More hunters will be in the woods. I'll let him decide where he thinks he can be of more use." Though if Wade didn't agree with him, he was calling the shots.

George's jaw tightened. "Tell Maya's brother I'll be with you. But I won't be looking for Maya. That's your job. I'm going after some hunters."

Wade smiled at him. "Got that, Connor? Two male cats and Maya. They'll only be expecting the two females."

George shook his head. "Bettinger said there would be another male cat to hunt."

Wade pondered that, then said to Connor, "Make that another male cat also. I don't know if Bettinger is counting on me, thinking that I might arrive to help Maya or…"

"Bettinger is planning on hunting Maya in his jaguar form," David said.

Wade swore under his breath. "Okay, I think David might be right. Bettinger's going after Maya—as a jaguar."

~ ~

Bettinger smiled at Maya as he peered through the mesh of her tiny cage. The truck bounced them over the rough ground. "You wonder why Gunther looks the way he does? Limps, too?"

She already half expected that she knew the answer.

"Gunther worked at a zoo one summer. He liked the big growly cats best. He thought he could look into their eyes and be their master. Cats don't work that way. But… he didn't know any better. He liked to stir 'em up. Make 'em growl. Make 'em restless. Prove he was in charge while they were caged. He thought the jaguar was sleeping when he entered his cage. The cat might have been, but as soon as he smelled Gunther's scent, the cat roared to life. Territorial, he lunged at Gunther."

Maya shook her head.

"He was lucky he lived. His sister nursed him back to health. You met her at the club. Candy?"

Maya growled low.

Bettinger chuckled. "Gunther was really angry that the zoo didn't kill the cat that had attacked him. But they wouldn't. Said he was in the wrong. Made him pay for his own hospital bills, which were considerable. Fired him from his job. And he couldn't get another. So now Gunther gets back at the jaguars. And Candy's happy to help him. He makes a great profit and shares a percentage with her. Believe me, he is truly terrified of big cats. As he should be. But he loves the thrill of the hunt."

The truck stopped and Maya's heart nearly stopped with it.

"We're here. Didn't take long, did it? Remember what I said. Fend for yourself. The other cat won't care anything about your fate."

She wondered how he was going to release her from the cage without worrying that she would attack him.

An ATV pulled up with Gunther driving. "You said you'd have a male cat. Where is it?"

"It's coming."

"Damn you," Gunther said. "He's supposed to be here as soon as you release the other female. You said you'd have the other one."

Bettinger spoke softly to Maya. "You have a sporting chance to run wild for a while. If you try to kill us, I'll shoot you. Drug you, then you won't have a prayer. Have we got a deal?"

She didn't make deals with the devil.

He cast her an elusive smile. "Okay, boss, I'm releasing her," he said to Gunther.

"You're a fool if you think she won't kill you," Gunther said, but he had his camera out and was ready to tape the kill.

Bettinger tried to act cocky, but Maya saw he was sweating. He jerked the cage door open while standing well out of her way. She could attack him and then attempt to attack Gunther. But the man in the pickup truck was still a threat. If she attacked Bettinger, she worried that Gunther would grab the rifle on the seat and forget taping the kill, shooting her instead.

She leaped off the bed of the truck and ran for the forest. Once she was there, she watched to see what was going to happen next. She still planned to kill both of the men if they gave her the opportunity.

The truck headed back to the ranch house. Good. One less gun to worry about.

Bettinger stalked toward the ATV. "Okay, the male cat's coming."

Gunther stepped out of the ATV and struck Bettinger in the head with the cane, his face red with rage. "You said he'd be here *now*. *Damn you*. The two hunters paid extra cash to hunt the three cats! You've lied to me for the last time!"

Maya closed her gaping mouth. She didn't think Bettinger would take that kind of abuse from a human.

She was right. He started yanking off his clothes.

"What the hell are you doing?" Gunther said, sounding shocked.

Shifting. Bettinger wouldn't be shifting unless he meant to kill Gunther. But if Bettinger eliminated him as a cat would, it wouldn't be good for the jaguars.

"What…?" Gunther said.

"Never strike a jaguar," Bettinger said. He was naked now, shaking with rage, right before he shifted. "Here's the male cat."

Bettinger turned in a flash into a golden jaguar.

"Holy…" Gunther dropped his cane and the camera, and stumbled backward toward the ATV.

Maya watched the jaguar knock the man unconscious. Instead of killing him with a bite, Bettinger dragged Gunther into the nearby lake and drowned him.

Heart pounding, Maya ran away from the lake through the woods. Bettinger would find her soon enough, tracking her scent, but if she could delay him long enough, maybe someone would have time to come to her rescue.

She glanced up to see the female jaguar in a tree. Maya growled at the cat, but she didn't move and just twisted her ears back and forth, watching Maya. Jaguars called to each other when they wanted to mate or growled over territory or called as males fighting over a female. Maya had no way of telling this jaguar she wasn't safe where she was. Then again, if the hunters chased Maya, maybe the jaguar would be secure up there.

Glad to see that the other jaguar was still alive, Maya loped away from the jaguar's hiding place. The problem was Bettinger. He could track the other cat by smelling where her scent led.

The sound of two ATVs, a pop of gunfire, and a re-sounding crack as the bullet slammed into a tree only inches from Maya's nose made her dash deeper into the shelter of the woods as her heart skipped beats.

The sky was beginning to lighten some with the ap-proach of daylight while dark thunderclouds still stretched across the area as Wade, David, George, and a tranquilized Candy arrived at the sprawling ranch. The grasslands were dotted with mesquite and oak, with the forest of mostly pine rising nearly a hundred feet above them. Wade noted the high fences, twelve feet tall. They'd have to cut through them.

"Wire cutters?" Wade asked George, his heart thundering.

George shook his head.

"We can't go in the front entrance. Not until we have backup." Wade contacted Martin. "We're here. No wire cutters."

"I've finally reached more of our people, and the men are on the way. They'll be there in a half hour. Get in any way you can."

"All right."

Wade told David, "You wait here for the other guys and coordinate their actions. And have someone take charge of Sleeping Beauty."

"Will do."

Wade turned to George. "You and I are going to shift and look for another possible way in. With the remoteness of the ranch, we should be good to go. But it'll be full daylight soon."

"Okay." George started stripping and so did Wade. Within seconds, the two had shifted into their jaguar form.

David turned off the car's overhead light, then opened the door for Wade and George. "Good luck," David said to Wade and nodded to George, wishing him the same.

Wade and George took off running along the fence, searching for a way in.

A mile beyond where they parked the car, they found that the fence was stretched across a lake. Cats wouldn't normally dive below the wire mesh. But as long as the fence didn't reach the bottom of the lake, Wade and George should be able to swim underneath it.

Wade took a breath, then dove. The mesh was only sunk two feet deep, and Wade quickly swam underneath it and up to the other side. If he could locate Maya, he'd bring her here where she could swim to safety.

When he surfaced, lightning flashed and a boom of thunder struck overhead. The rain came down in a torrent. *Good*. It wouldn't hamper the jaguars' movements, but the hunters would have a tougher time of it.

George came up beside Wade, and they paddled toward shore. Wade spied a body floating facedown in the water. One of the hunters? Maya must have had some luck. He was glad there was one less hunter to worry about, though he had hoped the hunters would be arrested for their crimes.

Once on the grassy bank, Wade and George shook off the excess water. That was useless with the rain pouring down, but it was a natural instinct they couldn't curb. They ran straight into the woods surrounding the lake, and Wade roared for Maya. If his calls brought the hunters down on him, so much the better. He'd distract them from her.

Maya's responding call sounded like the sweetest music to his ears. But the report of a rifle firing near her location forced his adrenaline to run hot through his veins. He and George leaped into action and headed for the distant sound of a rifle firing again and a man yelling, "Woo-hoo! Almost got you!"

The sound of an ATV's engine was headed away from Wade and George as the hunter tried to run down the jaguar he'd spotted.

Before Wade could go after the hunter, a growl from his left flank warned him that another cat was nearby. The deepness of the growl meant it was male.

Wade swung around to face the jaguar, just as he got a whiff of his scent and Bettinger attacked. Jaws clashing, claws slashing, snarling like wild cats, they came to blows with Wade fighting as he never had before.

While Wade battled the jaguar, George took off after the hunter armed with the rifle in the vehicle.

Lightning illuminated the forest in an eerie, ghostly way as the water poured from the dark heavens.

The two cats broke off, snarling and hissing. Another shot was fired. Damn it.

Wade was waiting for the cat to make a fatal move, but Bettinger seemed to be of the same mind. Wade had thought Bettinger would be eager to chase after Maya and kill her. But maybe Bettinger would take even greater pleasure in killing Wade first and then going after the she-cat.

Wade sprang with his powerful legs and landed on the jaguar's right side as Bettinger scrambled to get away. He bit into Bettinger's flank.

Bettinger swung his paw at Wade and missed, then stood partially on his hind legs, claws extended, and scratched at Wade.

Wade swung away, leaping out of the path of Bettinger's claws, and circled him, tail swishing.

A crash in the distance caused both cats to look in the direction of the noise. The ATV was no longer moving, but the engine was still rumbling.

Wade pivoted to face Bettinger before his focus returned to the fight. Wade jumped at Bettinger's back, tearing at his spine with his massive canine teeth and powerful jaws. The jaguar's preferred target was the skull for larger animals—the quickest way to bring down their prey. This would have to suffice.

Bettinger attempted to shake Wade off, trying to get out from under the attacking cat, but Wade was relentless, sinking his claws deep into the other cat's flesh like oversized fishhooks. He had to end this now. To get to Maya.

Bettinger collapsed on his belly, and Wade struck the fatal blow: one growl, a bite into the back of the neck, and a hiss as a final adieu. He waited as Bettinger shifted from his cat form into his human one.

They'd have to return for his body later. Wade took off, following the sounds of another ATV still in pursuit of a cat, and heard more gunfire. He roared for Maya.

No responding roar from Maya. His heart stuttered as he raced in the direction of the moving vehicle. Then she roared back.

Thank God she was still all right. He ran through the trees, sure she'd stick to them to be shielded from the hunter in the vehicle.

The rain was still pouring down. Streaks of sharp, white light striking the ground in the distance alternated with voluminous sheets that blanketed the whole sky for a second or two like a light switch turned on and then off.

Resounding booms shook the earth.

He saw movement, heard a low growl, and stopped, glancing to his left. A female jaguar was sitting in a tree. Not Maya. He hoped the cat would stay there until this was all over. He again ran off to where he'd heard gunfire and saw an ATV smashed into a tree, the engine rumbling, but no sign of the hunter. Wade was surprised the hunter hadn't suffered serious injuries, considering how bad the wreck looked. At least Wade was glad the hunter was now on foot. They didn't want to kill the human hunters, though. Well, they would have liked to just because they were trying to kill the cats. But they couldn't without causing problems for the jaguars.

Wade heard a low growl and saw George standing some distance from Maya. She was growling at George, not knowing he was on their side. Wade nudged George in greeting to show Maya he was friend, not foe, and then ran to join her. They quickly nuzzled each other, rubbing their bodies together, sharing their scent—two big, wet cats.

Maya was panting and purring, and he wanted desperately to get her to safety.

The second ATV had stopped somewhere nearby, tires spinning angrily, engine revving loudly, but the vehicle wasn't moving from it's current location. Wade and George exchanged looks. Then Wade growled and the two took off to disable the machine and the driver. Another hunter was on foot out there somewhere after he'd crashed his ATV into the tree, and was still a possible danger to them. Unless he was running as fast as he could back to the safety of the ranch.

Half hidden in the trees, Wade and David saw the hunter's vehicle was stuck in mud. The hunter was behind the vehicle, attempting to pile dead sticks underneath the tires to get traction. His rifle wasn't on him.

George moved in from the north and Wade from the south as if they were a couple of wolves on a hunt instead of cats. The hunter must have seen George out of the corner of his eye because he ran for the ATV. Too late. *Never* run from a cat.

George and Wade were on him in a heartbeat. The hunter was screaming and crying out, terrified.

Maya watched as Wade took care of the hunter. She heard heavy breathing nearby and the sound of boots squishing through the mud as the other hunter sneaked closer to his prey. The hunter who had crashed his vehicle while he was chasing her. His forehead was bloodied, the rain mixing with the blood still pouring out of a head wound.

Wade and George were concentrating on the man

Wade had pinned down when the other hunter raised his rifle, not seeing Maya. She was certain he thought to rescue the other hunter and kill a couple of jaguars while he was at it.

She leaped, thinking only of saving the other jaguars and not knowing if she'd be shot.

She slammed into the hunter, and his gun went off, the explosion so close that it was deafening to her sensitive ears. A startled cry escaped his throat; a hiss and a growl came from hers. A burning sensation at the tip of her ear made her growl, and her ears were stilling ringing as she pinned him down in the mud.

Wade swiped at the hunter he'd pinned to disable him. The hunter cried out, then was silent. Not dead. Just knocked out. Stunning their prey into inaction was just as useful as killing it with a fatal blow.

A bolt of lightning struck a nearby tree, snapping it in half, and then a second lightning strike hit another tree only a foot away.

Crack! The first pine keeled over with a snap, the top landing with a thud as it broke from its base and fell to the ground. Crack! The second pine toppled, flames erupting at the break in the massive trunk, heat filling the water-laden air, and the vibration from the two strikes making the ground and air tremble. Maya leaped out of the second tree's path, but the hunter was not so lucky.

The man was pinned under the massive trunk, his breathing labored, his face pained. Broken ribs?

She hoped.

Maya padded over to check him out. His flushed face turned ghostly pale. She should have growled at him, put the fear of the wild jaguar into him. Instead she pawed at him, claws retracted, making sure he was going to live. His eyes were so wide that his Adam's apple was moving up and down. He couldn't have been any more frightened. Then she licked his face and smiled so that he got to see all her big, sharp teeth. She smelled the odor of human urine.

Thunder continued to rumble throughout the area, though the rain was quieting from the torrential downpour to a steady patter.

Across a grassy plain she saw lights on in a ranch house. She was thinking about the steaks Bettinger and Gunther had cooked on the grill last night, and then she heard chaos.

—◦◦◦—

Wade hurried to join Maya, licking her face and urging her away from the injured hunter.

Shouts outside then inside the ranch house made Wade believe the cavalry had arrived.

They had to leave. They couldn't be found out here in their jaguar forms.

They headed for the lake with George. Wade hated having to leave the other female jaguar behind, but someone would soon recapture her and then they could reunite her with the zoo.

When they reached the lake, Maya growled. Facedown in the water, the clothed man still floated.

Wade checked the man for vital signs, but he was dead. Maya was still growling at the man as Wade led her to the portion of the fence that ran across the lake. She quickly began swimming out, ready to leave this place. Wade and George followed her.

Once they had surfaced on the other side and made their way to shore, they heard the shouting of men combing the area, looking for them. Everett, Huntley, and even Martin had come to join the search, as well as others that Wade didn't recognize.

He shifted and said to Maya and George, "The car is up the road. It's George's. Go with him, and I'll be there in a minute."

She looked at the other cat. He bowed his head.

She was really going to be pissed at George when she learned of his part in bringing her here.

"Go. I'll be right there."

She nodded, and she and George raced off to the vehicle.

Wade cupped his hands and shouted, "Martin! We're by the lake, all accounted for and heading for the car."

Men began running in his direction like a stampede of wild horses. Everett saw him first and hurried to take off his raincoat, then frowned. "Not sure I can toss it over that high fence."

He tried three times, but with the rain and wind, it was useless.

"I'll shift and return to the car in a moment," Wade said. "The female jaguar is sitting in a tree about three hundred yards north of the lake. Be careful. And Bettinger is about a hundred yards west of here. The two hunters aren't feeling very well. One's pinned beneath a tree with a head wound from crashing his ATV. The other might have a rip-roaring headache. And a dead man's floating in the lake. Not sure who that is."

Martin ran up to join them. "That's the buyer. Gunther Jaemison. He's got Jim Bettinger's smell all over him. It appears that Bettinger drowned him. Why don't you go back to the vehicle and get dressed before the police and reporters arrive? We'll talk more later."

"Call Connor and tell him Maya's safe, will you?"

"Will do."

Wade shifted and ran toward the car. But headlights were moving in his direction, and he hesitated before he ran across the dirt road, intending to conceal himself in the trees and brush. Then he recognized the rumble of the engine. George's car. The driver honked twice. It was George.

The car stopped and Maya got out. She was wearing only a shirt—his shirt—and was getting soaked as she motioned to Wade. "Hurry up, Wade."

Sirens sounded in the distance.

Wade raced to join her, rubbed up against her, then jumped into the backseat of the car. She climbed in with him and closed the door.

Wade shifted and said, "Drive, George. Head back to your hotel so we can grab our car."

Wade dressed in his boxers and jeans and shoes and socks. He ran his hand over his shirt where it was plastered to Maya's breasts, looking damned inviting, and leaned over to kiss her mouth, his hands sliding over her breasts. He groaned with need.

"I want to date only you," she said against his mouth, breathless, the words rushed.

"I wouldn't have it any other way," he murmured against her ear.

She looked up at him, her arms around his neck as he continued to massage her breasts with his hands, loving the wet, sexy feel of her. "I missed you, too." She gave him a thorough tongue kissing, then said, "Everett asked me to dance with him the next time we go to the club. And Huntley, too."

"Family is the exception. The only exception," Wade conceded, though he would agree to anything as long as she was safe with him.

She took a deep breath as if she was ready to discuss what had just happened. "Is… Bettinger really dead?"

"Yeah, he is."

She curled up in Wade's arms like a needy cat. "He killed Gunther, the buyer," she said. "The other jaguar's all right, isn't she?"

"Safe in a tree. The others might have a time getting her down, but they'll take good care of her."

"Good."

Wade stroked her wet hair and held her close. He still couldn't believe she was here, safe and in his arms.

"What the hell…?" George said, slamming on the brakes, the car sliding to a halt on the wet road.

Chapter 28

WADE AND MAYA TURNED TO SEE WHAT GEORGE was viewing, although the rain was hitting the windshield so hard that it was difficult to see what was going on. A dripping-wet naked woman was walking toward the car, dark hair hanging over her shoulders, her eyes amber and staring straight at the car. When George didn't move, Wade kissed Maya and released her. "Be right back," he promised.

He quickly got out of the car and hurried toward the woman, smelling her cat scent. She was a shifter. The jaguar he'd seen in the tree on Gunther's property?

Hell, she hadn't been the zoo cat.

"Are you okay?" he asked, making sure she was un-injured as he placed his arm around her shoulders to comfort her, afraid she might be in shock because of all that had happened to her.

"Yes, thank you. I… didn't want to wait for the men to find me and make it harder for them to explain me if the humans learned I was the female jaguar."

"I understand." He opened the front passenger door for her and had her sit there. "Give her your shirt, George," he said when George just gaped at her. Wade shook his head, reminding himself that not all shifters were hero material.

"Yeah, of course. Sure." George fumbled to remove his shirt, his cheeks turning crimson.

Wade got a call from Martin as he climbed back
into the car and Maya slid into his arms again, settling
against him like she was his, and he was hers. His heart
stuttered with the notion. She finally had decided she
wouldn't look elsewhere for a shifter mate.

He lifted the phone to his ear as he rubbed Maya's
arm, holding her close and sharing his body heat.

"We can't locate the jaguar," Martin said. "Where did
you say you saw her last?"

Wade smiled and put the phone on speaker as he
looked at the woman sitting in the front seat of George's
car and wearing his T-shirt. "She just joined us. She's
a shifter."

"My name is Caryn Breming. From Houston. I was
running as a jaguar in the woods near here when a
human hunter saw me and shot me with a tranquilizer
dart. He sold me to Gunther. I've been in that cat run
ever since then. I couldn't let them know the truth, not
when Gunther was always around. I didn't know that
the rest of you were shifters, too. Thanks for rescuing
me," she said.

"Got all that?" Wade asked Martin.

"Hell, yeah."

"What about Candy?" Wade asked his boss.

"Police collected her and several hunters at the ranch
house. The two hunters that tried to kill the jaguars have
been arrested. One of them appears to have several broken ribs due to the tree falling on him and a concussion
and a pretty bad gash in his head from the ATV crashing
into the tree. Pays to wear a helmet. The other one is
more open to speculation. My guess? One of the jaguars
hit him pretty hard."

"Served him right," Wade said.

Caryn gave Wade a thumbs-up.

"Gunther's body was fished out of the lake. We've already taken care of Bettinger's body to avoid anyone seeing him. Good job," Martin said.

"Even if you had to come here yourself?" Wade asked.

"On one of the biggest problem cases we've had in years? My being here means I can take all the credit."

Wade smiled. One thing they always said about the director of the Special Forces unit was that he gave credit to the men and women who deserved it.

"I've informed the police detective that Maya had been kidnapped by Gunther. We'll have to come up with a viable cover story for that, and she'll need to talk to him. David also said you needed some time off. It's granted."

"Thanks, boss." Wade rubbed his hand over Maya's arm as she snuggled against him. He knew just what he'd do with that time off. "I've got to make a call to Thompson. Talk to you later," he told Martin.

At a run as he headed for George's car, David waved to them. He was about to open the front passenger door when he saw the woman sitting in the front seat. He quickly pulled open the door to the back. "Sorry, Wade," he said to his brother as he climbed in. "Hate to have to ride back here with you… considering you probably wanted a little privacy."

"No problem," Wade said.

David eyed the new woman in the front seat. "I'm David Patterson."

She gave him a small smile. "Caryn Breming."

"George Tucker," George said, as if he was so

tongue-tied around the woman that he was having a time saying anything. But with another shifter sounding interested, he jumped right in. "How come I've never seen *you* around?"

"I never do the club scene," Caryn said, "if you frequent those kinds of places."

"Me either," David said. "Not all the time. Hardly ever. Four times now, actually. But two of the times I was just on a job."

She smiled and nodded at David.

Score one point for David, Wade thought, amused.

"Are you wild?" George asked. He knew that David was because he was in the Service.

"Not me. I've never been to the jungle. No interest." Caryn glanced at George to see his take on it.

"Me either," George said.

Score one point for George. She cast a look over the seat back at David to hear his response.

He folded his arms and gave a half smile. "Wild all the way."

Wade was trying his damnedest not to laugh. He had to give his brother points for being an original.

Caryn smiled back at David as if she was intrigued.

Score a point for David? Maybe?

Maya said to David, "And here you called *me* a wild cat."

"Yeah, you are, Maya. But I'd rather be in the jungle with you protecting my back than not."

"Um, what happens after I drop you off at your car?" George asked Wade, sounding as though he wanted to get the topic off wild cats.

"Caryn needs a ride home," Wade said, then punched

in a number on his phone. "So we need to decide how she gets home." The call he was trying to make went through, and Wade said, "Thompson, how are you doing?

Thompson said, his voice strained, "Hell, they got Maya."

"We got her back. She's okay. How about you?"

"Headache the size of Alaska. My wife will be here any minute now. I'm okay, but they wanted to keep me overnight for observation."

"Good."

More silence. Wade looked at David and raised his brows. Wade had to know if Thompson had seen Maya shift, but he couldn't very well just come out and ask him.

Thompson cleared his throat. "Is Maya with you?"

"Right here."

"Can I talk to her?"

"Sure." Wade handed the phone to her.

"Maya?" Thompson said.

"Are you okay? I was afraid after the truck crashed and you didn't move that you were dead."

"I'm fine. I have a hard head, or so my wife always tells me. I'm sorry I didn't protect you better."

"Ha! The crash knocked you out. You couldn't have done anything differently."

"Your secret's safe with me," Thompson said.

"Thanks, Thompson. You don't know how important that is. I think Wade was planning to mention to you that the female jaguar wasn't from your zoo."

Thompson didn't say anything for a moment, and Wade was afraid he'd ask to see the jaguar to prove to himself the cat wasn't her.

"It… wasn't?" he finally asked, cautiously.

"No. Believe me when I say she wasn't."

"Okay, I do." Thompson sighed. "I have to find her."

"People who Wade and I know are looking for her as we speak. They won't let you down, Thompson."

Thompson paused. "I believe you. Will I see you again?"

Maya smiled up at Wade as she told Thompson, "Maybe at the club sometime. We could dance."

"I'd like that. My wife just arrived, and she's taking me home. The last time I got knocked out when I was searching for clues about a wolf, she wouldn't let me go anywhere for days." Thompson paused. "Wolves. Hell." Another long pause. "Werewolves," he said under his breath.

Maya laughed. "No way."

Thompson said good-bye to Maya, then spoke to Wade, thanking him for his continued help in trying to locate the Oregon Zoo jaguar.

After he hung up, Wade kissed Maya's forehead, loving her but not sure what he should do about the fact she had shifted in front of a human. He should report this to Martin. They couldn't allow a human to know what they were. Yet he couldn't do it. He sincerely believed that Thompson was one of the good guys. And he didn't want Maya to be in trouble, either. Besides, if Thompson started telling the world that werewolves and jaguar shifters were real, he'd be laughed out of existence.

"You won't say a word," Maya whispered against Wade's ear as if she could read his thoughts. "You don't want to be in the doghouse."

Wade chuckled and squeezed her in a hugging

embrace. "No, I don't." He was thinking of getting one of those suites at the classy hotel where George and Candy had taken a room.

Maya had other plans.

Before they reached the hotel where the Pattersons' car was packed, George said, "I'm sorry for… my involvement in this, Maya. I didn't have all the facts when I helped Jim Bettinger. I… know… Martin has to review the case, but maybe you can put in a good word for me?" He looked terrified and hopeful at the same time.

As angry as she was that George had helped hand her over to Bettinger, she had to admit that he'd risked his life to help Wade protect her from the hunters. She nodded. Maybe next time he'd know better.

Before dropping Caryn off at her home, Maya vowed to get together with her for lunch in Houston sometime, while Caryn said she'd come out to see their nursery. Then, after making arrangements to secure Maya's car and dropping David off at the hotel where he and Wade were staying, Wade drove Maya back to the Anderson Garden Nursery. She couldn't wait to see her brother and Kat.

When they finally arrived home, Kat and Connor greeted her, and Maya felt overjoyed to see them. Though she'd had a swim in the lake and been thoroughly rained on during the storm and was still wearing only Wade's shirt, she wanted to take a hot shower and slip into bed with him.

What she didn't expect was to see a strawberry-blond-haired woman crossing the living-room floor, ready to greet her, blue eyes smiling. "I'm Tammy," she said, "your other cousin." And then she pulled Maya into a hug as if they were the best of friends and always had been.

"What are you doing here?" Maya asked, loving her already. "I'm so glad you came, but no one said anything about it."

"You know men. My brothers were too intent on rescuing you. Minor details like my being here wouldn't have been important enough to share with you. I'm trying to get a lead on Thompson's missing zoo jaguar, but I wanted to come down and meet you all, too, since you're my only known cousins."

Tammy glanced at Wade. "I take it you're the man of the hour?"

"If you mean I helped free Maya, I'd say she was doing a great job on her own," Wade said, shaking Tammy's hand. "I'm only one of the men who came to rescue her."

"I understand you are practically family now. Don't be shy." Tammy pulled him into a hug, and Maya had to really curb the urge to hiss. The only reason she didn't was that Wade looked nearly as uncomfortable with the woman hugging him as Maya felt.

When Tammy released him, Wade swept Maya up in his arms, and she gave a small cry of surprise. "You think too much," he whispered against her ear. "We'll see you all later. I think we might be flying out to Belize *real* soon."

"Um, we're going to go out for lunch and a double feature with Tammy and dinner after that," Kat said as she grabbed Connor's arm and headed for the door.

Connor looked surprised, but then getting the point, he nodded. "See you later."

"And maybe check out that shifter club," Kat teased.

"Not on your life," Connor said.

Tammy smiled, waved, and followed them out of the house.

Maya couldn't have loved Kat more for the suggestion. She breathed in Wade's musky, sexy cat smell. He wanted her as much as she wanted him. Wade was one happy male jaguar shifter.

When he entered her bedroom, he shut the door with his hip. "You don't know how badly I wanted to join you here the first night I stayed in your home."

"Yeah, I do. If my cousins and your brother hadn't been here…"

He laughed. "Yeah. I knew you wanted me in here." His mouth curved up, his eyes heating with fire.

"Whirlpool bath first," she said.

He stalked with her into her bathroom, set her down on the floor, then considered the whirlpool tub, and smiled.

"What took you so long to come for me?" she asked, leaning over the bathtub to turn on the faucets.

He took hold of her hips and pressed his growing arousal against her ass. She wriggled a little against his groin and smiled when he groaned. *That would teach him to play with fire*.

"If I waited long enough," he said, slipping his hands under the shirt and cupping her breasts, "I knew you'd *really* appreciate the rescue."

She moaned with delight. "I thought you were a hot-shot Golden Claw," she said, turning around as the water filled the tub, her hands sliding up his bare chest over rock-hard abs, her nails softly raking his skin. "And would have come sooner."

He slid his hands up her shirt—well, technically *his* shirt—again to fill his large hands with her breasts and rubbed his thumbs over the taut and sensitive nipples. "I *am* a hot-shot Golden Claw." He kissed her mouth, his tongue tangling with hers as he tightened his grip on her breasts.

She wrapped her arms around his neck, smiling, just waiting to hear what he would say next. His eyes were sparkling with good humor.

"Some wild cats are just a lot harder to get a handle on."

His voice had grown husky and his eyes had darkened with lust. She rubbed up against him, sliding a leg over his hip and caressing the back of his thigh with the heel of her foot. He took advantage of her posture to slip his hand between her legs and insert two fingers deep inside her. "But I'm getting a handle on it," he whispered against her mouth as her lips parted on a sigh, and she felt she was dissolving in a puddle.

With their mouths fused and their breathing labored, she was ready to skip the bath and take him to her bed. But he quickly remedied that and stopped the water from filling the tub.

"It'll take too long," he said brusquely. When she looked up into his gorgeous blue-green eyes, he smiled. "I can't wait."

Then he flipped on the water in the glassed-in shower stall, carried her into it, clothes and all, and shut the door before he began kissing her all over again.

She was trying not to laugh, thinking he must have some kind of fetish for feeling her up when she was wearing clothes in a shower, when she was soaking wet with the fabric clinging to her like a slippery second skin.

The first time had been when she was wearing her nightie on the cottage deck, and he'd pulled her into the shower with him. And now again, his hands were stroking her breasts through the wet shirt, his smile saying how much he enjoyed being with her like this.

She smiled back, loving the hot Special Forces cat and all he meant to her. She grabbed a bottle of body wash, poured some of it out, and began soaping his chest, his muscular arms, and his jeans, focusing primarily on the rigid arousal begging to be freed.

He groaned as she stroked him through his jeans, and he began to struggle to unbuckle his belt. She wasn't giving up and continued to run her hand over his swollen cock.

He fumbled with his zipper like a man being exquisitely tortured. *That'd teach him to wear his pants in the shower if he was going to get* her *all worked up*.

He jerked his pants off and tossed them on the shower floor.

She slipped her hand inside the opening of his wet boxers clinging to his erection and felt his hard flesh jump at her touch. He leaned down and kissed her again, his mouth claiming hers as he slid his hand between her legs and began to stroke her hard and fast, making her melt under the warm water. His stroking was drawing her to the zenith of pleasure, her eyes closing as she absorbed the sensual onslaught.

She gave a strangled cry of pleasure as he took her over the top, released her, and then pulled off the sopping wet boxers that had molded to the most delectable parts of him.

In one smooth movement, he lifted her, centered

himself, and impaled her eager body. She straddled him, his steel-hard erection embedded inside her. With her back against the smooth porcelain wall, he rocked into her, thrusting deeper, harder, faster. His sexy male cat smell and the vanilla body wash mixed in a tantalizingly delicious fragrance.

She combed her fingers through his wet hair as her legs wrapped tightly about his lean hips. He kissed her again, his tongue plundering her. Ready for him, she sucked on his tongue hard, arching against him. And he lost the battle.

Groaning her name in a wickedly lust-drenched voice as he climaxed, he leaned his forehead against hers and laughed.

She furrowed her brows at him.

"You're still wearing my shirt," he said, grinning.

"And whose fault is that?" she asked as she slid down his length and rested her feet on the shower floor.

"As long as you don't wear my pants." He started unbuttoning the shirt and dropped it on the shower floor to rest with the other garments. Then he rinsed off and turned off the water. "What's next on the schedule?" He grabbed a towel and began drying her hair.

"You have to ask?" she said, cupping him.

He grinned down at her. He might think he was one hot Special Forces Golden Claw, but she had some pretty nifty moves of her own.

The bed was next. The lake after that. Maya had to smile at Wade's request. He had wanted her to wear a black lace bra and panties like she'd worn in the Amazon River. Then it was back home to the whirlpool bath to clean up. And then to bed again.

Later that night, lying against Wade's naked chest on the soft mattress, she thought she heard Kat and Connor sneaking in through the front door and making a quiet retreat to their bedroom. She wasn't sure. Jaguars and their shifter cousins could be as quiet as shadows.

She snuggled against Wade and wondered again about her dad and if he was or wasn't her father. And where Thompson's jaguar had gone off to. She wanted to ask Wade what he thought. She wanted to have resolution.

"Wade?" she said softly.

"Yeah?" He sounded like one worn-out cat.

"I love you."

He smiled at her, then wrapped his arms around her tightly, kissing her on the forehead. "Good, because there is no doubt in my mind that you're the only one for me."

She kissed his chest and looked up at him. "Want to prove it to me? Again?"

"Insatiable," he murmured, rolling her onto her back.

She was. She hadn't realized it… not until she met the cat of her dreams.

USA Today Bestselling Author

A SEAL in Wolf's Clothing

by Terry Spear

—◦—

Her instincts tell her he's dangerous...

While her overprotective brother's away, Meara Greymere's planning to play—and it wouldn't hurt to find herself a mate in the process. The last thing she needs is one of his SEAL buddies spoiling her fun, even if the guy is the hottest one she's ever seen...

His powers of persuasion are impossible to resist...

Finn Emerson is a battle-hardened Navy SEAL and alpha wolf. He's a little overqualified for baby-sitting, but feisty Meara is attracting trouble like a magnet...

As the only responsible alpha male in the vicinity, Finn is going to have to protect this intriguing woman from a horde of questionable men, and definitely from himself...

—◦—

Praise for Terry Spear:

"High-powered romance that satisfies on every level." —*Long and Short Reviews*

For more Terry Spear, visit:

www.sourcebooks.com

Tall, Dark, and Vampire

by Sara Humphreys

She always knew Fate was cruel...

The last person Olivia expected to turn up at her club was her one true love. It would normally be great to see him, *except he's been dead for centuries.* Olivia really thought she had moved on with her immortal life, but as soon as she sees Doug Paxton, she knows she'd rather die than lose him again. And that's a real problem...

But this is beyond the pale...

Doug is a no-nonsense cop by day, but his nights are tormented by dreams of a gorgeous redhead who's so much a part of him, she seems to be in his blood. When he meets Olivia face-to-face, long-buried memories begin to surface. She might be the answer to his prayers...or she might be the death of him.

Praise for Untamed:

"The characters are well-developed, the twists and turns of the plot are well-crafted, and the situations are alternately funny, action-packed, and sensual."—*Fresh Fiction*

"An excellent paranormal romance with awesome world-building and strong leads."—*The Romance Reviews*

For more Sara Humphreys, visit:

www.sourcebooks.com

Undone

by Sara Humphreys

She's far from human…

With her secret race of shapeshifters embroiled in civil war, all Marianna Coltari wants is to stay far from controversy. Even so, when her overprotective brother insists on hiring his human friend Pete as her bodyguard, Marianna is furious.

Does she dare to love one?

Like most retired cops, Pete Castro resents his new job as a bodyguard. It's even worse because he'll be babysitting a party girl like Marianna. But that's before he meets her for the first time and discovers his instincts on red alert. Would he kill to protect her?

"Humphreys's skillful storytelling is so intriguing, you'll have a hard time putting this book down."—*RT Book Reviews* Top Pick of the Month, 4.5 Stars

"Searing lovemaking, interesting world-building— lions and tigers and bears, oh my!"—*Booklist*

For more Sara Humphreys, visit:

www.sourcebooks.com

Flirting Under a Full Moon

by Ashlyn Chase

—✧—

Never Cry Werewolf

Brandee has been dumped in every way possible, but by text is the last straw. That's it—she's officially done with men. Unfortunately, she's just been told her "soul mate" is the drool-worthy hottie all her friends call One-Night Nick.

Nick has been searching for true love for one hundred years. After all, werewolves mate for life, and he does not want to mess this up. As soon as he kisses Brandee, he knows she's the one. But how will he convince a woman who knows nothing of paranormals that she's about to be bound to a werewolf forever?

—✧—

"Hot sex scenes and a breezy tone with a nice, happily-ever-after ending makes Chase's story a fun read."—*Booklist*

"It made me laugh, crafted a mystery that had me guessing, and the romance was sweet, steamy, and paranormal."—*The Romance Reviews*

For more Ashlyn Chase, visit:

www.sourcebooks.com

About the Author

USA Today bestselling and award-winning author of paranormal romance and medieval romantic suspense, Terry Spear also writes true stories for adult and young adult audiences. She's a retired lieutenant colonel in the U.S. Army Reserves and has an MBA from Monmouth University. She also creates award-winning personalized teddy bears, Wilde & Woolly Bears, that have found homes all over the world. When she's not writing or making bears, she's teaching online writing courses or gardening. Her family has roots in the Highlands of Scotland where her love of all things Scottish came into being. Originally from California, she's lived in eight states and now resides in the heart of Texas. She is the author of the Heart of the Wolf series and the Heart of the Jaguar series, plus numerous other paranormal romance and historical romance novels.